As Barb walked past the teakwood chest, she stopped stock-still. Without thinking, she flung up the lid.

Just as she'd thought, the chest still held a stack of winter blankets. She was relieved to see only blankets, although last night there hadn't seemed to be quite so many. As she lowered the lid, her hand halted midair. Almost imperceptibly, the thick yellow blanket on top appeared to rise, as if alive and breathing.

The lid of the chest flew up. The blanket was unfurled and flung in her face. She felt hands pulling it over her head and pressing the thick, woolen fabric hard against her cheeks. An arm of steel encircled her waist in a vise-like grip, holding the blanket in place. Strong fingers gripped her nose, cutting off air, and what felt like the heel of a hand ground against her lips. The scratchy, springy wool filled her mouth.

Dear God, she thought, *he's trying to smother me . . .*

* * *

Praise for Dee Stuart's *BLOOD TIES*:

For Helen,
One of my very favorite
bridge partners!
Fondly,
Dee

DEADLY
LEGACY

Dee Stuart

ZEBRA BOOKS
KENSINGTON PUBLISHING CORP.

ZEBRA BOOKS are published by

Kensington Publishing Corp.
850 Third Avenue
New York, NY 10022

First Printing: May, 1996
10 9 8 7 6 5 4 3 2 1

Printed in the United States of America

With special thanks to my friend Pansy Chan Caso for her assistance in the preparation of this manuscript.

My apologies to the Hong Kong Zoological and Botanical Gardens for creating a fictitious crocodile pool to fulfill the needs of this story.

One

Ho Kar Wei clenched his teeth and gave the tourist standing hopefully before him an abrupt nod. He wished he had not told the woman to go to Dong Po MacGregor's Antiquities. Here was the luck of a lifetime tossed in his lap and he had almost missed it. He wished he had not had to report for work immediately after his plane had landed in Hong Kong. Now he would have to act quickly.

He was desperate to get away. But there seemed no letup in the endless parade of people filing through passport control. Though it was a cool, brisk September day, his brow was beaded with perspiration, and his heart pounded like the jackhammers of the workmen nearby.

An hour later, so distraught that he could no longer keep his mind on his job, Ho Kar Wei left his post and hurried to the office of his superior. Clapping one hand to his brow, he said, "I must excuse myself—a virus—a stomach virus. I fear I'm going to be ill."

His superior scowled. "You may leave for ten minutes, no more."

He dared not call from his place of work, dared

not risk being overheard. Wishing he could remember where he had seen a public telephone, he dashed out onto Queen's Royal, teeming with people, cars, taxis, buses and trams. He wanted to run down the crowded street, but people were packed together as tight as sardines in a can, moving at a maddeningly slow pace. Ho shoved them aside, jabbing them with his elbows.

Almost five minutes had flown by before he saw a dim sum cafe. He lunged inside, found a phone atop a tall desk, and a directory on a shelf below. With shaking hands, he leafed through the pages till he found the number he sought. As he dialed, he murmured a fervent prayer to his ancestors that the line would not be busy. Luck was with him. A high, wheezy voice answered.

"My friend," said Ho Kar Wei in his most ingratiating tones, "I have something I want you check for me."

A bored voice on the other end of the line replied, "Not another one."

"This is big, big, big. Even you will be impressed."

"I've heard that before." The voice sounded skeptical.

His hands began to sweat. "Just look it up, that's all I ask."

He had to. He just had to! Ho Kar Wei murmured another prayer to his great great grandfather.

"Tell me about it," the man wheezed.

Ho's voice trembled with excitement. "On the plane, after visit sister in San Francisco, I sit by American woman. Before land in Hong Kong all fill out landing card. The woman need pen. Not find in handbag. Too much things. Put things on tray table: billfold, passport, hairbrush, lipsticks—" he paused, then in breathless tones added, "and small mutton fat horse."

"Go on, go on."

"Woman see me look at horse. She say, 'You like horse?' I say, 'Yes. Is cost many dollars?' She not know. Came from late husband's ancestor. She bring to show friend in Hong Kong." He did not think it necessary to tell the man he had looked at the woman's landing card to see where she was staying. "Now I must know is horse on list."

"Hold on," the man said.

Moments later, he returned to the phone. "It's not on the list."

Ho Kar Wei drew in his breath between his teeth, making a sucking noise. The gods were smiling down upon him. That it had not been reported as a stolen artifact made it of even greater value. But caution was called for. He must not sound too anxious. "Do you find this item of interest?"

"I must see the merchandise," said the man, ever cagey.

"I will bring it to you."

"When?" the man snapped, sounding more eager than usual.

"Soon. Before the Festival of the Moon."

Elated, Ho Kar Wei slammed down the receiver. As he plowed through the mass of people on his way back to work, he thought, *All I must do is acquire the horse. Since I alone know where it is to be found, that will not present a difficulty.* Pleased with his own cleverness, he smiled to himself. Tomorrow he would take the morning off.

TWO

As soon as she entered the parquet foyer in Lily LeMaitre's high-rise Hong Kong flat, Barbara McKee, D.V.M., knew something was wrong. Frowning, she stared at an arrangement of three white lotus blossoms in a low, green jade bowl on the rosewood table. Lily had placed it precisely where she wanted it, at a slight angle, enhanced by its reflection in the mirrored wall. Now it faced the door head-on.

An uneasy feeling swept through Barbara. Some-one had moved the bowl. And the small glass, brass-bound curio box that always sat to the left of the bowl had been pushed to the back of the table. Lily's magazines, *Asia-week, Antiques, Financial World,* and the *Asian Wall Street Journal,* normally spread in a neat fan formation, were all askew. "Don't be silly," she told herself, shrugging aside her apprehension. Rosa, the little Filipina maid, must have been here—or maybe a neighbor had dropped by. No doubt Lily would have some per-fectly rational explanation for these departures from her orderly lifestyle. Barb set her black leather shoulder bag and her packages on the foyer table, then turned, grasped the brass doorknob and closed the door.

In a loud, cheerful voice she called, "Lily? Lily, I'm home."

Silence pressed around her. Again she called, "Lily? Anyone here?" She glanced at her thin gold wristwatch. Six-thirty. American Fidelity where Lily worked closed at five. Even though she often worked late, she should be home by now. Probably some confused, distraught customer was holding up the parade. Barb smiled to herself, envisioning Lily steamed at being delayed today, of all days, when she was on fire to go home to visit with her house guest. But that was life in the loan department. She would give Lily a break and start dinner. But first she had to get out of these shoes.

Unlike Lily, shopping till she dropped was not Barb's favorite thing, and her feet were killing her. She never should have worn heels. She kicked them off and, standing on one foot then the other, rubbed her aching feet. Abruptly, she paused. She thought she heard a faint sound, a sharp snap, or crack. She cocked her head, listening. Could it have been a door in the outer corridor slammed shut by a neighboring flat dweller? Or a floorboard creaking? The silence thickened, seemed to engulf her. She felt the tiny hairs on the back of her neck prickle. Deep within her, some primal instinct stirred. She sensed a presence, as if someone had been here and, like some mysterious forest animal, crackled the underbrush as he passed.

Sternly, she muttered, "Don't be ridiculous."

Into her mind rose a warning whisper. In the past

her total lack of fear had plunged her into trouble. Years ago, when she had raced horses at the State Fair, a rival jockey had edged his mount close to her side. In low, menacing tones, he'd said, "You scratch that nag today, or I'll make you wish you'd stayed home."

Through clenched teeth, Barb had snapped, "No way."

Two-thirds of the way around the track, she had dug in her heels, let Mariah flat out, and within seconds had left her rival swallowing dust. But all that was past. Now she had control of her life, or almost.

Still, the uneasy feeling persisted. She glanced nervously to her right, down the shadowy hall that led to the bedrooms. She heard nothing. Swinging left, she rounded the corner of the foyer and stepped into the living room. She stood unmoving, arms folded, hands clasped about her elbows as if fending off a sudden chill. For a long moment she remained motionless, listening for any shred of sound. An unearthly silence pervaded the flat.

"Get a grip!" she told herself. "You've never been afraid of anything in your entire life. Why now?" She paused, remembering. Actually, she had never been afraid of anything she could see, or any situation she could face head-on. But here in this alien land, dealing with the unseen, the unknown, she felt alone, lost in a green darkness in the depths of a forest.

She sensed danger as surely as she could sense when a sick, injured or frightened animal was about to sink its teeth into her arm.

Her gaze fastened on the colorful, hand-painted porcelain lamp on the table beside the lounge chair. A soft light shone through the beige silk shade. *Odd,* she thought. Why was the lamp lighted in this bright, airy flat? Her gaze shifted to the floor-to-ceiling draperies that blended with the pale, ivory-colored walls. Odder still, the draperies were wide open. Lily was a tiger on wheels about keeping them closed during the day so the sunlight beaming through the sliding glass doors wouldn't fade the carpet. Barb was certain they had been closed when she had left the flat this morning. Had someone entered the darkened flat, switched on the lamp to light the room, then opened the draperies? She stiffened, struck by a chilling thought. Why had she assumed that whoever had been here had gone? Was someone even now hiding on the small terrace, pressed against the wall to one side of the glass doors? A shiver ran through her.

Yesterday evening, soon after she had arrived, Lily had led her onto the terrace to view Victoria Harbour. There Barb gazed out over a vast fringe of glass and concrete skyscrapers, past towering blocks of high-rise flats, like the one where Lily lived here on the steep slope of Victoria Peak. As though mesmerized, Barb stood dazzled by the spectacular sight of great ocean liners, container ships, customs cutters, fishing junks, ferries, tugs, and fan-sailed sampans swarming through the silver-green waters.

Across the mile-wide straight rose the steel and glass buildings of the bustling Kowloon Peninsula and the New Territories. Beyond the New Territories, on the far side of the border like a slumbering behemoth, crouched the solemn, gray mountains of Red Communist China. As she stood looking out over the waist-high parapet from the fourteenth floor, she had felt suddenly light-headed. Her hands grew damp, her knees felt weak and her stomach rose to her throat. She had turned and stumbled inside.

Now, just thinking about the dizzying height made her queasy. No way would she go out on that terrace. She stood as though transfixed, reluctant to go near the doors. From here she could see the sun, a white disk hung in a brilliant gold sky. She closed her eyes, shutting out the breathtaking scene.

For several agonizing moments she stood unmoving. Finally, in a loud, stern voice, she told herself, "Don't think about it, just go!"

With an effort of will, she marched across the room. If anyone had taken refuge on the terrace, she would simply lock the doors. The interloper would be trapped outside until she could get help. Swiftly she thrust out both hands, tugged at the latch, then let out a relieved breath. The door was locked. No one could be hiding on the terrace.

She turned from the sliding glass doors and halted midstride as the sole of her stockinged foot pressed down on something lumpy. She looked down and saw a tangle of fringe on the edge of the carpet. The ancient Isfahan, a floral pattern in shades of blue, green and beige, was a rare find that Lily had bought on a trip to Iran. Barb's straight brows drew together in a frown. Another anomaly. Lily couldn't bear untidy fringe. Every morning before she left for work, she knelt down and combed out the fine white strands, and again at night before she went to bed. Now, Barb saw that the thickly fringed edge of the carpet at the far end of the living room was tangled in several places as well. If she'd had any doubts before, she had none now. Someone had cased Lily's flat.

Like an animal sensing danger, all Barb's senses were alerted, her breathing shallow and uneven. Her gaze darted beyond the white leather couch to the black, inlaid-ivory coromandel screen in the corner. Was someone hiding behind the screen? From an end table she swept a fierce-looking blue china dragon and hefted it in her hands. Not as heavy as she hoped, but it would do. Her fingers tightened about its open mouth. In commanding tones that could bring the most defiant dog to heel, she said, "Whoever is behind that screen, come out, now!"

She took a deep breath and held it. Nothing moved. Without warning, a loud *bong, bong, bong, bong* erupted into the silence. Barb jumped, then gave a shaky laugh as the resonant chimes of a Westminster clock on a teakwood shelf struck seven. Carefully, she set the dragon back on the end table, strode to the coromandel screen, grasped the end panel and peered around the edge. Hidden behind the screen stood a folding table and four chairs. Feeling suddenly foolish, she let out a relieved breath.

Now that she thought about it, a burglar would surely have taken off before the end of the day when people came home from work and burrowed into their flats. But if someone *had* searched the flat, what was the lure? Had anything been stolen?

Instantly, she turned to the shelves that held Lily's collection of Swarovski figures, jades and netsukes. Intently she scanned the sparkling crystal, the translucent jade figures, and the painted ivory netsukes. The netsukes were tiny carved mandarin characters, some in comic, others in scandalously erotic poses. They all appeared to be there, but she couldn't be certain none were missing. Lily loved every tiny character as she would a beloved relative, and allowed no one else to touch them. Lily would know instantly if any were gone.

Aware that she was squinting at the figures in the fading daylight, Barb switched on the lamps that lighted the display. A fine sheen of dust lay on the shelves. To the right of two of the figures there appeared a clear crescent. Someone had moved the figurines. Strange, she thought, that they had been moved, but it appeared none had been stolen.

What else did Lily have that would tempt a burglar? Her curious gaze swept past the TV, past the Chippendale writing desk, across the shining parquet floor to the dining room. There stood a rosewood table and four Ming dynasty chairs with low, rounded-rail, key-hole backs and plump, persimmon brocade seat cushions. Nothing appeared out of place. Barb crossed to the dining room and eyed a buffet that dominated one wall. She let out a relieved breath. Lily's Ming china tea set still sat in royal splendor atop the buffet.

That nothing appeared to be missing made her more uneasy than if something had been stolen.

Why had the place been searched? For clearly, someone had searched it.

Cautiously, she tiptoed into the bright, white-tiled kitchen. *Nothing here worth stealing,* she thought. The little figure of Tsao Kwan, the kitchen god, grinned at her from a shelf over the counter. Toaster, teakettle, glass apothecary jars were all in place. Her gaze lingered on the broom closet. Though she was sure the intruder had gone, she was taking no chances. She slid a carving-knife from a wooden wall rack. For once she was grateful for necropsy class in vet school. If there was one thing she had learned doing post mortems, it was how to carve.

Knife poised to strike, she stood back of the broom closet door, then flung it open. From inside the closet came a sudden clatter. She flattened her spine against the wall, and let out a choked scream as a broom and dry mop crashed to the floor. Shaking her head in disgust at her witless reaction over nothing more lethal than a mop and a broom, she picked them up and stuck them back in the closet.

Dusk had begun to filter in through the windows, and as she ambled through the rooms, strange shapes and shadows triggered her imagination. Was that hulking shape at the end of the hallway an intruder poised to leap out at her?

"Stop being ridiculous," she chided herself. "See if anything is missing from the bedrooms."

Quickly, she flicked on the light switch in the foyer and hurried down the hall to the bedrooms.

At Lily's doorway, she stopped short. Someone could be hiding in Lily's closet waiting till the coast was clear to slip down the hall to the foyer and out the door. Her heart beat in her throat. No way could she check out this room without knowing if someone was hiding in the closet. In a voice meant to be sharp and commanding, but came out as a feeble croak, she said, "If anyone is in this closet, come out now or I'll lock the door and call the police."

Nothing happened. It occurred to her then that the intruder might not speak English, might not understand a word she said. Her fingers tightened around the knife handle. Quickly she stepped behind the closet door and yanked it open. Holding her breath, she waited for what seemed several interminable minutes. No one appeared. Feeling foolish, she reassured herself that no thief would hang around the flat this long and slammed the door shut.

The faint, sweet fragrance of the jasmine scent her friend had worn this morning lingered on the air like an echo. Barb slid past Lily's white lacquered bed and bureau and paused before the mirrored dressing table. A fascinating array of perfume bottles of all shapes and sizes, some centuries old, graced the surface. Barb's eyes narrowed. She had learned first-hand, rooming with Lily during her first week at Midwestern University, that when Lily closed a drawer, she slammed it home. Now none of the drawers were quite flush with the surface. Had the interloper been searching for jewelry?

She pulled out the top drawer. Necklaces and earrings, bracelets and rings of jade, ruby and diamonds sparkled up at her. As far as she could see, no jewelry was missing. Was nothing worth taking? Barb grinned to herself. How indignant Lily would be that none of her jewels were worth stealing.

She turned toward the dresser. There stood a collection of photographs that Lily fondly called her rogue's gallery: a photo of Lily's parents shortly before their tragic deaths seven years ago; one of their white-pillared old home place; pictures of family and friends, long gone; several of Lily and Barb in college at picnics and parties; a sorority costume party with Lily swathed in diaphanous white veils over a flesh-colored bodysuit, arms outflung, as Venus rising from the sea. Barb, as Medusa, sported a nest of writhing snakes. Here was another of the two of them after Lily's graduation from Midwestern U.

With a feeling of nostalgia, Barb picked up the photo and studied it closely. Lily, hazel-eyed, with a dimpled grin and shoulder-length, curly blond hair, in stark contrast to today's bangs and ruler-edge cut, clutched her degree in Oriental art. Her own long, dark chestnut mane in a single braid over her left shoulder was now worn in a short classic cut for a fast wash and dry. She set the photo down next to another of herself in her gray cap and gown after graduation from vet school. How solemn she looked, as though weighed down with the responsibility of the oath she had taken, the seriousness of her calling. They had shaken their heads at the capricious hand of fate. Lily, after receiving her parents' accident insurance payment, was devastatingly wealthy, but mourned the lack of a family. Barb, rich in family, but dirt-poor, had worked her way through college and vet school.

Smiling to herself, she gazed at a photo of her own family: Mom, Dad, her brother Hank, his wife

Amy and their daughter Anna Lee, all of whom had become Lily's family as well.

She checked the bureau drawers; then confident that nothing was missing, she moved from Lily's bedroom across the hall into the guest bedroom where she had slept last night. Clean white walls were hung with watercolor paintings of Victoria Harbour, the mist-wreathed mountains of Guilin and the floating fishing village at Aberdeen. Her gaze swept over the rattan furnishings: a bed, nightstand, a low, three-drawer dresser and mirror and a fan-shaped bamboo chair. Surely there was nothing here anyone would want.

Nevertheless, she went straight to the closet. Clenching the carving knife in her right hand, she stood behind the door and wrenched it open. A wave of relief flowed through her when no one emerged.

She stepped around the door and took stock. Her light-weight, all-weather beige coat, navy linen jacket, forest green suit, red cardigan, slacks, and a two-piece aqua Peter Popovitch dress were all hanging in place. She reached inside and pulled all of her clothes forward.

Odd, she thought, that all the empty hangers had been shoved to the far end of the closet where Lily had stashed her summer clothes. As she glanced at Lily's summer things, she stopped short. Here hung two pairs of slacks, one black, one gray, much too long to be Lily's.

She lifted them from the wooden rod and looked them up and down. Her brows rose, her eyes widened in wonderment. They were men's slacks. A slight shock ran through her. Why would a man's slacks be hanging in Lily's closet? Had the cleaner sent them along with Lily's cleaning by mistake? If so, Lily surely would have noticed. Her lips curved in a small smile. Could they belong to Lily's "someone special"?

She hung the slacks on the rod with Lily's clothes and turned her attention to her empty suitcase, now gaping open, and her blue nylon fanny pack which lay on the floor. All three pockets had been unzipped.

As she picked up the fanny pack, it struck her that after all she did have something of great value. Her passport—which was zipped securely in an inside pocket of her big, black leather shoulder bag. Shaking her head, she allowed herself a wry grin. Someone must have gone away more than a little disappointed in the haul.

She eyed the heavily carved teakwood chest under the picture window, and immediately dismissed it. Born with a curiosity that rivaled a cat's, last night she had peeked and knew it held winter blankets. She only felt slightly guilty, for after all, wasn't Lily the same as a sister to her?

She halted before the dresser. Her eyes narrowed. The drawers were slightly out of line, as if someone had been in too much of a hurry to close them all the way. Here, a thief would find slim pickings, for she traveled light, with a few mix-and-match tops and wash-and-wear underwear. It would be easy to see if anything was gone. She set the carving knife on the dresser and yanked open the top drawer. She let out a gasp. Comb, brush, makeup, notebooks, pens, maps, guidebooks, and flashlight were all strewn about the drawers. She pulled open the next one. Her underwear was as scrambled as sale merchandise on a bargain table. In the third drawer, tops, shorts, and red plastic poncho lay in a jumble. Nothing appeared to be missing.

As she walked past the teakwood chest, she stopped stock-still. If at that moment, she had carried out her intention and gone on into the kitchen to start dinner, everything might have been different. But she hadn't. Without thinking, she flung up the lid.

Just as she'd thought, the chest still held a stack of winter blankets. She was relieved to see only blankets, although last night there had not seemed to be quite so many. As she lowered the lid, her hand halted midair. Almost imperceptibly, the thick yellow blanket on top appeared to rise, as if alive and breathing. Barb started, screamed, dropped the lid and threw up her hands in a gesture of self-defense.

The same moment, the lid of the chest flew up. The blanket was unfurled and flung in her face. She felt hands pulling it over her head and pressing the thick, woolen fabric hard against her cheeks. An arm of steel encircled her waist in a viselike grip, holding the blanket in place. Strong fingers gripped her nose, cutting off air, and what felt like the heel of a hand ground against her lips. The scratchy, springy wool filled her mouth.

Oh, God, she thought, *this creep is trying to smother me!*

Gagging, choking, gasping for air, she wrenched

her head from side to side. Blinded, arms wedged against her chest by the thick folds of the blanket, she was forced backward against a wall. If only she could reach the knife. She aimed a vicious kick at her assailant, missed, lost her balance and fell on the far side of the bed, striking the floor with a thud. A sharp pain shot through her left hip.

Furiously, she fought free of the blanket, and flinging it aside, leaped to her feet. Pain knifed through her hip as she raced around the bed and out the door into the hallway. At the end of the dimly lighted hall she saw a figure, crouched low, running. A blue-clad arm reached out, whisked open the door. She caught only a glimpse of a straw coolie hat, a long, black queue hanging down a blue-clad back, and the back of a blue-clad leg as the intruder slipped out through the doorway.

"Wait!" she shouted. "Come back here!" She tried to run toward the door, but with each step a stabbing pain slowed her down. The door slammed shut. She wrenched it open and limped into the corridor. At the end of the corridor, the brass elevator doors slid slowly, silently closed.

Three

Barb limped back inside the flat, slammed the door, locked it, and gasping for breath, leaned her back against it. She folded her arms across her chest and gripped her elbows, trying to still her shaking. She felt cold all over, as if fright had frozen the blood in her veins. Her heart pounded in her ears. Frantically, she thought, *I have to* do *something.* Nine-one-one. She would call 911. Would 911 work in Hong Kong? Not likely. She would call Lily, and Lily would call the police.

Her hip throbbing with every step, she hobbled into the kitchen and grabbed up the white wall phone. Beside the phone hung a list of numbers. She zeroed in on Lily's office number. Her hands began to sweat. With trembling fingers, she stabbed the buttons. Now, staring at the phone list, she saw that "help" was 999.

In heavily accented English, a high, singsong female voice that rolled *l*'s into *r*'s, answered, "American Fidelity Bank."

In urgent tones Barb asked, "Do you speak English?"

"*Hai.* Yes, yes."

"Lily LeMaitre, please, I must speak with Lily LeMaitre."

"Bank closed now. I stay late for work. Miss Le-Maitre not here. Gone home please."

Barb's fingers tightened around the receiver. "When? How long ago did she leave?"

"Gone, long time."

Oh, lord, Barb thought, had something happened to Lily? Unconsciously, she reverted to her old pattern, looking after Lily.

"How long?" she shouted, as if by shouting, the girl would understand her anxiety. "Tell me, how long?"

"Twenty-fi' minutes. One, two, three, four, fi'! *M'goy, joy geen.* Goodbye, please."

"Wait . . ." She heard a click, then silence.

It was hopeless. It would be futile to try to learn anything further. Barb dropped the receiver on the hook. If Lily had left twenty-five minutes ago, she should have been home long since. The terrible vision of Lily run down by a tram, a car, a bus flashed into her mind. Quickly she put it down.

Normally, Barb took an optimistic view of things. Now she told herself sharply, "Stop imagining the worst! Lily has to be all right, she *has* to!" Nevertheless, she would wait only ten more minutes, and if Lily hadn't come home, she would call 999.

As she turned away from the phone a surge of pain coursed through her left hip. Here was one thing she could do something about. She yanked open a drawer, took out a large plastic sack, opened the next drawer, found a turkish towel and set them both on the white countertop. From the fridge, she slid out a tray of ice cubes and emptied it into the plastic sack. Wrapping the towel around the sack, she fashioned it into a pack, then limped into the living room and eased down onto the couch. She loosened the waistband on her skirt and slid her skirt and briefs down to view the damage. An angry red patch spread over her skin below her hipbone. She touched it, and winced at the pressure of her own fingers. She lay on her right side and, gritting her teeth, draped the ice pack over her left hip. Resting her head against the arm of the couch, she closed her eyes and tried not to think about what could have happened to Lily.

Through thinned lips, she blew out a long, frustrated stream of air. Furious at the invasion of Lily's apartment, she was more furious with herself for letting the intruder get away. As soon as she realized someone had invaded the flat, she should have called for help. Why did she persist in thinking she could handle everything herself? Why hadn't she called the police? The instant she saw the blanket move, she should have slammed the lid down on the teakwood chest. Why hadn't she acted faster? She started at the sound of a key turning in the lock.

Unmindful of the pain in her bruised hip, she jumped up from the couch and, adjusting her clothes, ran into the foyer and nearly collided with Lily as she burst through the door. Far from looking as though she'd been run down by a bus, Lily, in a royal blue suede suit and creamy silk blouse, looked as fresh as a page from *Dress For Success*.

Laughing, Lily said, "Hold it. You're not running any races today. Save yourself for chasing dogs."

Barb wasn't laughing. Her face was flushed, and her dark eyes were filled with concern.

"Thank God you're home. I was worried about you."

Smiling, Lily tossed her purse on the foyer table. "No catastrophe, except for Mrs. Druce-Thomas. As usual, she wanted to borrow money because she'd overdrawn her account. Naturally, she swore the bank had made an error. I went over every last one of her checks for the past three months and didn't leave the bank until after six." Lily sighed and, continuing to talk non-stop, strolled into the living room and sank down onto a jade-colored armchair, legs stretched out before her.

"The traffic was horrendous, wall to wall. But you shouldn't have worried. How much trouble can I get into on a bus?"

"It's not only your safety I was worried about."

"So why are you so up in the air?"

Barb perched stiffly on the seat of the chair across from her and regarded her anxiously.

"I was worried because something weird happened here and—"

Lily laughed. "Life in Hong Kong is a whole different ball game from life in the Midwest, but you'll learn to love it. In fact, you may never want to go home, you'll be so—"

"Listen, Lily, be quiet a minute, and let me tell you." As Barb told her what happened, Lily's face turned pale, and her delicate features grew tense and strained. When she explained how someone had leaped up from the teakwood chest and tried to smother her with a blanket, Lily sat bolt upright, her greenish golden eyes filled with alarm.

"My God, you could have been killed by that maniac. Are you all right? Did you hurt yourself when you fell?"

Barb shook her head. "A bruised hip. No problem. The problem is, someone entered your flat while we were gone. That someone came here looking for something. If he hasn't found it, he could be looking for you, to force you to tell him where it is. What do you own that would be worth stealing?"

Lily's gaze flew to the shelves that held her collection of figurines. "I started that netsuke collection years ago, and by now some of them are worth a mint." She jumped up, crossed the room and slowly, carefully, scrutinized each shelf.

Barb limped after her and stood at her elbow peering anxiously over her shoulder. "Anything missing?"

In tones of mingled astonishment and relief, Lily said, "Nothing. All present and accounted for." She turned to face Barb. "You think this—this creep went through the entire place?"

"Right."

Lily bolted from the living room, down the hallway into her bedroom. Barb, following after her, watched nervously as Lily jerked open the dressing table drawers and sorted through her jewelry. To their astonishment, nothing had been taken. Barb pulled open a drawer in the nightstand. All she found was a half-empty package of Camel cigarettes. Odd, Lily didn't smoke, never had. *Humm,* Barb thought, *the "someone special," perhaps?* She turned her questioning gaze on Lily.

But Lily was rummaging through the bureau drawers, muttering, "Looks as though a tornado has passed through, but at least nothing's gone."

Barb shoved the pack back in the drawer and closed it. Lily whipped open the closet door and let out a shocked wail.

"Oh, no!"

Barb remembered she had flung open Lily's closet door, stood behind it and demanded the intruder come out, then slammed it shut. She had not looked inside. Now, peering past her, Barb shuddered. Lily invariably hung her clothes neatly on the rack, sorted by color and use: blouses, skirts, slacks, dresses, coats and suits, each in its proper place. The closet was a shambles. It looked as if someone had grabbed up bunches of clothes and tossed them aside. Her shoes, always lined up on the floor, her handbags on a tier of shelves, and hats on an overhead shelf, lay scattered among the clothes. Every handbag gaped open.

With a defeated sigh, Lily poked through the jumble. "Well, someone really did a piece of work here, but nothing seems to be missing."

"What about your passport?"

"In the bank, locked in a drawer of my desk."

Barb stepped inside the closet, knelt down and began to pick up Lily's hats and set them back on the shelf. With grim satisfaction, she said, "Whatever this—this thug was looking for, he obviously didn't find it."

Lily, leaning against the doorframe, looked devastated. "I hate it that somebody's been rooting through all my things. It's as if they know everything about me. I feel stripped naked, violated." She shook her head from side to side, then put her face in her hands. "It's horrible."

Gazing at Lily, so defenseless, Barb felt anger boiling up inside her. She got to her feet, clasped Lily's shoulder and gave her a little shake. "Come on, Lil, pull yourself together. You need to report this to the police."

Lily looked up, tears glistening in her eyes. In incredulous tones she asked, "How could anyone get in here? I mean, you'd have to be a human fly. Are you sure you locked the door when you left?"

Barb shot her a level look. "Absolutely."

"Sorry. I just can't imagine . . . I'll, I'll call the police."

After she left the room, Barb continued to put Lily's clothes back on the rod, trying to hang them in the same meticulous order.

Lily's obsession with neatness and order was nothing new. The first morning they had roomed together at Midwestern U., Barb had watched flabbergasted as Lily made up her bed with square hospital corners and sheets so tight you could bounce a dime off them. She had arranged her comb, brush and mirror, the photos on her bureau, just so, and her desk was clear of everything except her green student lamp, clock radio and calendar. Barb, taken aback, had wondered, *What in the world have I gotten myself into?* Had she made a mistake allowing the college to assign her a roommate even though they had both expressed an interest in Oriental art?

To Barb's everlasting relief, Lily never tried to reform her, to change her own casual lifestyle, her habit of draping her clothes over her desk chair, armchair and bed, or piling her desk and bureau high with notebooks, books and papers, packs of cookies and candy. By tacit agreement, they lived as if an invisible line had been drawn down the middle of the room, each in control of her own territory, and had become the best of friends.

Barb returned to the living room just as Lily marched in from the kitchen with a reassuring smile on her lips.

"We're in luck. The police give foreigners in trouble high priority, and residents here in the midlevels evidently warrant special consideration. They'll send someone around as soon as possible, within the hour for sure."

Arms hugging her sides, Lily paced the floor, striding to the sliding glass doors and back again.

Barb sat on the couch, surreptitiously rubbing her bruised hip. "I hope they'll try for fingerprints, but if the intruder is smart, there won't be any."

Lily halted before Barb and threw out her hands in frustration. "Why me? With twenty-seven floors of flats to choose from, why mine?"

Looking up at her, Barb allowed herself a wry grin. "Maybe they're part of some drug cartel, searching the flats systematically, working their way up."

Lily let out a snort and resumed her pacing. "This is the last place on the island they're apt to find drugs, and flat number four on the fourteenth floor is the last one likely to be searched. The Chinese are incredibly superstitious. The number four is bad luck. That's the reason I was able to rent this flat. No one else would touch it. I can't imagine any Chinese searching it unless he had a damn good reason." She halted before the glass doors and stared out over the busy harbor.

Barb ran a hand through her hair, thinking aloud. "Maybe there was to be some kind of deal and this thug was on the wrong floor. Because the first floor isn't on the ground floor, but on what we call the second floor, he may have meant to be on the floor below this one, and . . ."

Lily turned to look at her and gave a hopeless shake of her head. "My friend, you've been watching too much TV. The floor numbers show up on lighted buttons in the elevator."

"Lily, think about it. If a superstitious Chinese wouldn't rob your flat, somebody who wasn't superstitious, a non-Asian, wouldn't think twice about it, so the intruder must not be Chinese."

Lily laughed. "So you've narrowed our intruder down to only two percent of our six million population." She fell silent, staring gloomily into the distance.

The fast-falling darkness cast a pall over the pastel-tinted sky and invaded the living room. Barb switched on the porcelain lamp which shed a pool of light on the carpet. She leaned forward, then straightened quickly. Her hip was giving her fits.

"Lil, concentrate. Who knows what treasures you

have hidden away here? How about the 'someone special' you want me to meet?"

Lily wheeled to face her. Indignation blazed from her eyes. "Andre? You're out of your mind! I'd trust Andre Durand with my life. In fact, I'd call him right now, but he's off to Paris, at a chefs' convention. Won't be back till Monday. Besides, there's really nothing he can do about this—this break-in."

Realizing she was treading on dangerous ground, Barb quickly backed off. "Who else do you know here in Winslow Gardens who's visited your flat?"

"Well, there's Pete Chang, the t'ai chi instructor, lives here. We see each other occasionally, but he's only been in my flat a few times . . ."

"Does he have a key?"

"Of course not."

"Who does have a key?"

"Only Andre and Rosa the cleaning girl, and the doorman, and the superintendent. If they were going to rob me, they'd have done it long before now."

"Well, *some*body else must have a key. The place wasn't actually broken into."

"Maybe this creep has some kind of skeleton key, a one key fits all." Lily gave her a sidelong glance that Barb always thought of as "the fishy eye."

"Who else do you know who lives here?"

Lily gazed upward as if the roster of residents were written on the ceiling. "There's Mei Ling. She sings soprano in the local Cantonese opera. I forgot, she has a key as well. We play mah-jongg with two of her friends, and take turns meeting in our homes. We've only played here three or four times."

"Who else? What about your Hong Kong friends who don't live here in the tower?"

Lily crossed to the Chippendale writing desk. She took a blue silk brocade-covered address book from a drawer, then sat down beside Barb on the couch. One by one they went over Lily's friends and acquaintances in Hong Kong. Half an hour later Lily slapped the book shut and tossed it aside.

"That's it. The people I know just don't ransack or rob each other's flats."

"Then it's got to be someone who robs at random—unless someone is watching this tower of flats and hits prosperous-looking residents—like you in your full-length mink."

Lily folded her arms across her chest and regarded Barb with frank curiosity. "How would this robber know where I live?"

"Easy. Any thief, or his sidekick, could follow you onto the elevator and watch where you go when you get off."

Lily shook her head. "The doorman would have seen him and stopped him in his tracks."

"Not if he looked—presentable—and pretended to be the guest of a resident."

Lily looked stunned. "Stop! You're making my skin crawl. Besides, nothing was stolen."

Barb brushed a lock of dark hair back from her forehead. "Could be he didn't find what he wanted. Just considering all the possibilities."

"Hey, you're not diagnosing an animal; this is me, your best of friends, remember?"

"I'm trying to be helpful."

Lily sat down beside Barb on the couch and

gazed at her with troubled eyes. "Barb, I can't tell you how sorry I am that this had to happen when you were here. I wanted everything to be so wonderful for you. I wanted to show you Hong Kong. To take you to the market you wanted to see. To give you a chance to look into acupuncture. Wanted you to meet my wonderful Andre. Most of all, I wanted to try to give you a new lease on life after all you've been through with Hal. You've been so damn brave, so steadfast, these past two years; then to watch him die in such agony, I know how vulnerable and upset you must be."

Barb's eyes filled with pain, and a deep sigh escaped her. Dear Hal—Doctor Hal Halstead, associate professor of anatomy at State. From her first day in his classroom, he seemed to be speaking directly to her. She couldn't drag her eyes away from him. Hal, twenty years her senior, a shock of dark hair threaded with silver, dark bushy brows over warm brown eyes, a broad smile that graced the kindest, gentlest face she had ever seen. Completely at ease with himself, he had a calm, quiet way about him—the sort of man that students sought out to unburden their souls. For both of them it had been love at first sight. They had married during her last year of vet school.

Sorrowfully, Barb said, "He put up such a terrific battle, it seemed so unfair for him to lose the war."

Lily's face mirrored compassion. "It was unfair for you as well."

The heart-wrenching memory of Hal's wasted body, the countless chemotherapy treatments, flashed through Barb's mind.

"I had to be grateful that he no longer had to suffer. At the end, he hardly knew me. Though he's only been gone six months, it seems like a year." She forced a smile. "Don't worry about me, Lily. I'm doing fine."

Lily reached over and gave her hand a squeeze. "I'm sure. But you've always been so great to me, saved my life, really."

"Not really. I was just there when you were going through a tough time."

Ruefully, Lily said, "This was my chance to do something for you, blown sky high."

"But you are," Barb insisted. "You have no idea—"

She was interrupted by the ringing of the door chimes announcing the arrival of two khaki-clad officers of the Hong Kong Police. One, a robust Chinese lieutenant wearing wire-rimmed glasses and a sympathetic expression; the other, a tall, efficient-looking sergeant with a ruddy complexion and a small black mustache. Barb felt greatly reassured when she saw on their shoulders a small red stripe which meant they spoke English.

After writing down all the details of what Lily kept calling "the break-in," and examining the door, the lieutenant said politely, "I regret to say, ladies, we find no evidence of a break-in."

"But the only people who have keys are my friend, my cleaning girl, and my neighbor, whom I would trust with my life. I can't believe the doorman or janitor would . . ." Her voice trailed off.

The lieutenant gave her an understanding glance.

"Nor can we. It is possible that the intruder opened the door with a credit card."

His companion's serious expression turned grave. In perfect Oxford English, he added, "I would suggest you have a deadbolt installed on your door, for if the intruder has not found what he sought, he may return."

Barb, glancing at Lily, rolled her eyes heavenward.

The robust officer sighed. "Next time we catch, maybe."

They strode through the flat, examining each room in a competent, professional manner, eyeing the disorder in Lily's closet and the jumbled contents of Barb's rattan dresser with obvious sympathy and disgust.

To Barb's satisfaction, they shook black powder on the shining surfaces of the tabletops and shelves in an attempt to lift fingerprints. After urging Barb and Lily to call them immediately any time of day or night if there were any further trouble, they left.

Closing the door after them, Lily said, I feel much better. They acted so concerned, and so efficient; they made me feel as if they would catch the culprit at any moment."

"Speaking of the culprit," Barb said, "my hip is protesting. Where's the BenGay?"

"BenGay is out, Tiger Balm is in."

Barb did a double take. "Tiger who?"

"Balm. Heals everything but wounded hearts. It's in the bathroom, in the medicine chest. I'll get it."

Barb, already on her feet, thrust out a hand in protest. "Sit still. After all, I'm not an invalid."

She went down the hall to the bathroom and pulled open the mirrored cabinet door. Her glance swept over the glass shelves, past a razor, toothbrush, a can of menthol shaving cream, and a bottle of men's shaving lotion—Lagerfeld. She held it up to her nose and breathed in a whiff of the pungent, spicy scent. Her brows rose in surprise. *Humm,* she thought. *Someone has good taste.*

When she had finished rubbing the ointment on her hip, she found Lily stirring around in the kitchen.

Together, they got dinner on the table and tucked away sweet and sour pork, fried rice and snow peas, along with almond cookies and green tea. Despite having been fortified by food, they were still uneasy when bedtime rolled around. Lily insisted on dragging one of the heavy Ming dynasty chairs into the foyer, where they wedged the round, curved back tightly under the doorknob.

With a final shove, Barb said, "I don't think this will keep anyone out who really wants to get in."

"Well, if it doesn't keep anyone out, surely the sound of the chair falling will wake us, so we can at least defend ourselves."

Barb smiled to herself, thinking that Lily defending herself would be rather like a mouse defying a lion, but she held her tongue.

In her room, Barb donned a red flannel sleep shirt, opened a window and slid into bed. The stringent odor of Tiger Balm tainted the crisp night air. Lying in bed in the darkness, Barb felt suddenly disoriented, thrust amid alien corn. Though it was well past midnight, the streets of Hong Kong were as bright as high noon. Neon lights tinged the darkness with a pastel pink, green and yellow glow. The island churned with excitement. Did the place never sleep? She couldn't shake the eerie feeling that there was a lot going on beneath the surface here in Glitz City.

Not for one minute did she believe that the break-in had been some random act. Lily had lived here for more than four years without incident. Barb's intuition, coming on strong, told her it was no coincidence that the day after she'd arrived the flat was searched. Was there some connection? Was it her passport the intruder wanted? Had she made a mistake coming to Hong Kong? Of course not. It was so terrific of Lily to send her a plane ticket, she could never disappoint her by refusing to come to see her. In fact, Lily's invitation had come at a most opportune time in her own life. Moreover, she was dying to meet Lily's "someone special," someone Lily might well marry.

Her mind drifted to thoughts of home, of her debt-ridden animal hospital and the astronomical monthly rental, and the staff to be paid. Determinedly, she pushed the thoughts far back in her mind. It was silly of course, but she missed Berin. Though her big black furry Rottweiler was a throwback, unrecognized by the AKC, and had the temperament of a pussycat, she scared the bejeez out of anyone who didn't know her, particularly burglars who leaped out of teakwood chests. No less lethal were Crystal and Alice, the best watchcats in the western world. She missed them all.

As she drifted off to sleep she conjured up a vision of Steve Lindsey, D.V.M., astride his Harley, head thrown back, thick, dark hair curling over the collar of his leather jacket, zooming up to her clinic, swinging off the bike and loping inside, smiling the dimpled smile that could charm the coat off a fox. Though she would never admit it, she missed Steve most of all.

Four

The sound of bells woke her from a restless, terror-filled sleep with frightening images of Orientals chasing her, knives flashing over their heads, as she raced through dark, narrow alleys that had no end. Men were shouting in a dialect she couldn't understand, their voices accusing, demanding she knew not what. Slowly she surfaced through layers of sleep, trying to identify the sound. Church bells? Bicycle bells? Tram bells? No, louder, closer. Faintly she heard Lily, calling her name.

Her bedroom door burst open, and Lily's tousled blond head appeared. "Barb, wake up. Steve's on the phone. Hurry."

She sat bolt upright. "Uh-oh, something's wrong, or he wouldn't be calling me in the middle of the night." An entire scenario of emergencies flashed through her mind. Had Doc Roeder, who was filling in for her, konked out? Had the kennel boy who walked the dogs lost one? Had there been a robbery, or the worst nightmare of all, a fire? Quickly she slid out of bed.

"What time is it, anyway?"

Lily laughed. "You overslept. It's practically the middle of the morning, ten after seven. Roll out.

I'll tell Steve you're on your way." She left, the *slap-slap* of her thongs echoing down the hallway.

Thank God! Steve hadn't called in the middle of the night after all, for seven in the morning here in Hong Kong was six P.M. back home. Shivering against the chill that swept through the wide glass window, she flung on a red terry cloth robe and scuffs.

As she ran down the hallway, narrowly missing the legs of the mandarin chair braced under the doorknob, suddenly she missed Steve so much, she wished like crazy he were here to kiss her hip and make it well.

As she barged into the kitchen, Lily thrust the receiver into her hand. Barb dropped down onto a black lacquered chair at the glass-topped table. Lily poured a mug of steaming coffee, set it down in front of her and left.

Though she felt nervous, apprehensive, she managed to keep her voice calm. "Steve, what's happening?"

The sound of his voice, so close it could have been in the same room, sent a small thrill of happiness through her.

"Doctor McKee, Doc Lindsey, reporting in. How in the world are you?"

"I'm fine as frog's hair." She took a deep breath, bracing herself for bad news. "But you're doing the reporting in. How are things at the ark?"

"Great. Roeder has everything under control. Jake, the parvo dog, has miraculously improved; Mrs. Smythe brought Oreo in to be delivered of her offspring, in a pair of pink satin p.j.'s; the white

Angora has feline leukemia; the tests came back on Buttons and you were right, he has Cushings; and so far, the kennel boy hasn't lost any dogs on their walks in the back forty."

She blew out a relieved breath and in low, exaggeratedly patient tones said, "Steve, why are you calling me at seven A.M.? I thought there was some dire emergency."

His cheerful tone turned serious. "There is. I couldn't get along one more minute without hearing your calm, sweet voice assuring me that everything is wonderful and life is beautiful."

His words flowed through her like warm honey. Grinning, she said gently, "You're crazy. You really are." She took a gulp of the hot, fragrant coffee.

With mock severity, he said, "You ungrateful woman. You should be glad I waited till seven Hong Kong time to call you. I never dreamed you'd still be lazing abed! What you need is someone to roust you out, someone who has your best interests at heart, someone who cares enough to get you to work on time, someone who will be forever at your side."

"Humm," said Barb thoughtfully, "I wonder who that might be?"

In lofty, loving tones, Steve said, "I'd think that would be obvious, precious darling."

"Right! It's got to be Berin."

With mock outrage, Steve bellowed, "Berin! That mangy, flea-bitten, AKC reject!"

"Watch it, Lindsey. You're speaking of the dog I love. One 'Kill!' command from me, and you're history."

"The only thing that hound would kill is time."

Barb laughed with the pure joy of hearing his familiar banter. "Let's not get personal here. Tell me how things are going at Lindsey's Pet Vet."

"Great, just great, business is booming, but not to worry, I'll still cover for you Wednesday afternoons and Saturdays. But your clients miss you like blazes, and so do I. In fact, I tried to call you yesterday, but no one answered; and last night I couldn't get through. What have you and Lily been up to?"

Smiling at his open display of curiosity, she said, "I spent the day shopping, and listen, Steve, that book you gave me *Born to Shop* was not for this chicken. I did pick up a few things, a Gucci purse, a couple lengths of wonderful ivory silk fabric, a gift for you . . ."

"What, what?"

"It's a surprise."

"I can hardly wait. Anything else happening?"

She took another sip of coffee, and her tone turned serious. "Actually, it's what's *not* happening. Someone went through Lily's flat from one end to the other, but the weird thing is, nothing is missing."

"Good lord. Did you catch the—the sneak-thief, or whoever?"

"No. I let him get away."

"Hold it. Just hold it! *You* were *there* while this criminal searched the apartment?"

"I guess so."

His voice rose to a high, nervous pitch. "Whaddya mean, you *guess* so?"

"I thought he'd gone, but when I went into my bedroom, he jumped me. Leaped straight out of a blanket chest."

"Oh, my God, Barb. Did he hurt you?"

"No, I told you, I'm fine, really."

"Then you *let* him get away? That's not at all like you, to let a criminal off the hook."

"He ran faster than I did. I couldn't catch him."

His tone turned loud and decisive, "Well that does it. It's not safe for two females alone over there. I'm coming over—"

Barb laughed. "You talk as if I'm just around the corner.

"You're only a plane ride from Frisco. I mean it, Barb, I'm going to hang up, pack a bag, fly to Frisco and then sit in the airport till I can get a flight out."

"Steve, that's not necessary, really."

"I know you won't come home, you're so determined to visit Lily, so if Mohammed won't come to the mountain, the mountain will go to Mohammed."

"Don't you have that backward?"

"Never mind. I'm flying to Hong Kong, today."

"Steve, no! These two weeks were to be your cool down time, remember?"

"Forget that. It's not working."

"I've only been gone two days! Give it a chance. Besides with Roeder filling in for me, who would cover for you?"

"Easy, I'll send all my clients to Roeder at your clinic."

"Look, Steve, I promised Lily we'd have these two weeks together, that it would be like old times when we were in college, sisters under the skin. So, much as we both love you, stay home. No one wants to steal me, or they would have carried me off yesterday. I'm not in any danger, believe me."

There was a long silence. She envisioned his mouth stretched in a grim, determined slash, bracketed by laugh lines. She smiled to herself. He'd tried this tactic before, keeping silent till she felt compelled to speak. She would then capitulate, and wind up with both feet in her mouth. This time she was determined to wait him out. She kept silent.

At last he said, "Okay, but we'll keep in touch, and if anything else happens, call me immediately."

"I will, I will." Eager to drop an argument she might easily lose, she said, "Have to go."

"Wait! Have you shown Lily the jade?"

"Not yet. I'll show it to her now. Don't worry. Gotta go. Bye, Steve."

Softly, he said, "Love you, Doc."

"Love you, too." She hung up.

Thoughtfully she sat sipping her coffee. She heard Lily drag the heavy Ming chair across the wooden floor and open the door. Where could she be going at this hour? Then she remembered that Lily didn't feel her day had begun until she had browsed through the *South China Morning Post.*

"Lily," she called, "I'm off the phone. Come on back to the kitchen and be my guest."

Lily, yawning, wearing a white satin, embroidered happy coat, strolled into the kitchen, holding the paper before her, scanning the headlines. She dropped the paper on the table, poured herself a cup of coffee and sat down across the table from Barb.

"What's new with Steve?"

"He said he's flying to Hong Kong, within the hour—to save us from our invisible intruder."

"Wonderful!"

"I told him not to come."

"Why?"

"I don't want to encourage him. You won't believe what he did just before I left."

"Try me."

"Actually, it was your letter asking me to come to Hong Kong that got him going."

Lily rested her elbows on the glass tabletop and clasped her hands under her chin. "Tell—from the beginning."

"Well, it was on a Friday, end of the week, end of a horrendous day. We'd already had a full schedule, plus two walk-ins. It must have been well after six, way past closing. Karen was counting the day's receipts, ready to go to the bank. I heard the bell chime over the front door and thought Karen had left. But no, she traipsed back to the treatment room, and told me we had another walk-in."

Lily nodded. "Here we go. I know you can never turn anybody away."

"I asked her what the problem was.

" 'This guy says to tell you it's an old dog, and this is an emergency.'

"I said, 'What is it?'

"Karen had a funny look on her face. 'He said to tell you it's a Heinz 57, fifty-seven unidentifiable ancestors.'

"I meant, what's the emergency?

" 'He thinks it's a heart attack.'

"Did you weigh him?

" 'No, he refused. Says he weighs one-sixty.'

"Sounds like a bull mastiff.

" He said to tell you Doc Roeder sent him.'

"By this time, Karen looked as if she were going to burst out laughing. She knows Steve and I have this friendly competition going, and I figured she thought I was one up on him since he was as good as admitting he couldn't handle the case.

"I told her to put him in an exam room. I washed up, opened the door and walked in. You could have knocked me over with one puff. There on the table, under one of my green surgery sheets, is this inert body." Barb's eyes rolled heavenward.

Lily gasped. "The dog had died on the table?"

"No way. The weird thing about this dog was that it was six feet long. The sheet was hanging over the end of the table, almost to the floor."

Lily giggled. "Long tail?"

Barb's brows flew up. "I wish. I picked up a corner of the sheet and flung it back over the body. And what did I see? Long legs. I told Karen, 'Looks like we have an out-of-control growth here. Let's wheel him into the surgery.' With that there was a blood-curdling yelp and the sheet flew off."

Lily burst out laughing. "A bull mastiff?"

"Steve. He yelped, 'Take it easy, Doc. Don't you realize that I practically have to make an appointment to see you?'

"Poker faced, I said, 'So what's the big emergency?'

" 'I told you.' He clapped a hand over his chest. 'It's my heart. Ever since you told me you were tripping off to Hong Kong, it's been fibrillating like crazy. I think I'm having a heart attack.'

"I turned away so he wouldn't see me laughing and told him, 'I have a cure for that—a big shot in the hip will—'

" 'No, no. I've tried everything. Nothing works. Now drastic measures are called for.' "

Barb folded her arms across her chest and looked at him with exaggerated patience.

"What measures?"

"Marry me! I love you, Doctor Barbara. I will love you forever and always, and—"

Incredulous, her voice rose. *"Marry* you!"

"Marry me." He sat up, swung his legs around to the side of the table and flung his arms about Barb's waist pulling her close to him. He looked up into her face with such longing and desire that her heart seemed to swell to bursting.

She placed her hands on his shoulders. Softly she said, *"Marry* you? Steve, why now? I don't understand . . ."

"Which word in that sentence did you not understand?"

She shook her head from side to side. "None."

His dark eyes, filled with pleading, gazed deeply into hers. "People do still get married you know. The custom is here to stay."

"Steve, I can't marry you, I can't marry anyone . . ."

"I thought you felt the same about me as I do about you."

"I—I do love you, Steve, but it's too soon. Much

too soon. I'm just not ready for another commitment."

Steve curved a hand around the back of her head and drew her face down to his. Gently, he kissed her. "I understand, believe me. Hal was a terrific guy. He went all out to help your start your clinic. But with Hal gone, you're left to pay off a small business loan that seems like the national debt. It won't go away. I want to look after you, care for you. Hal would hardly object to that. In fact, if I don't miss my guess, he'd heartily approve."

She stepped back from the table and threw out her hands in a plea for understanding. "Look, Steve, I've spent years studying to be a vet, and now I need a chance to prove I can make it on my own."

In a low voice filled with emotion, he said, "Barb, darling, please don't tell me you're married to this practice. It won't wash. We can combine our practices and we'll have it made. Don't you see? We'll have the best of both worlds."

She wished he would lighten up. Gently, she said, "But what would we talk about?"

He got to his feet and, arms encircling her waist, drew her close to his chest. "Animals. Our clients. What else?"

Earnestly, she said, "That's just it. We'd be totally submerged in our practices. We'd be the dullest people in the world. Besides, when I get home at night I need something to take my mind off my four-footed friends. I want to relax."

"Is that why you give your clients your home number and tell them if they have any problems to call you? I can hear them now, 'Oh, Doctor Barbara, my dog is chewing his stitches, is that all right?' "

She scowled up at him. "They only call if there's a real emergency."

"How many times have you gone to the clinic in the middle of the night, and twice on Saturdays and Sundays, to check on a sick patient?"

Barb shrugged. "It comes with the territory."

"Countless times."

"I don't mind. I *want* them to get well."

"Sure, but if we were married, there'd be two of us to carry on. If you'd had a rough day, I'd take over."

"That's sweet of you, Steve." She eased his arms from around her waist and held his hands in hers. Softly she said, "Listen, my love. You've been in practice almost six years. You're well established. I've had my own practice for exactly thirteen months and twenty-three days. I don't have it made by far. I have to know that I can make it on my own. I don't want to lean on you, on anybody. Don't you see?"

Disappointment suffused his features, and his eyes looked bleak. "I understand, I honestly do, but oh, Dr. Barbara, this old dog needs you so. I do want you so, my love. For the rest of my life and yours, together. How will I get along without you at my side all the while you're proving you can make it on your own?"

Barb laughed softly. "I'll still be here; I haven't died, after all. I'll fly off to Hong Kong, and you'll see that the world will continue to turn without Dr. Barbara at your side. You'll be surprised how easy it is."

"Oh, it's possible, my love, I grant you that, but it won't be easy."

Tears clogged her throat, but it wouldn't be fair to put him on hold, to give him false hope. "I'm sorry, Steve, but that's the way of it."

Now, seated at the table across from Lily, she saw tears brimming in her friend's greenish golden eyes.

Softly, Lily said, "And that's still the way of it?"

Barb nodded. "That's it."

"That's the saddest thing I ever heard—and the dumbest."

Barb reached across the table and patted her hand. "Because *you're* in love, you want the whole world to be in love with you. I'm just not ready to walk down the aisle."

Lily nodded as if she understood, but pity shone in the depths of her eyes.

Eager to change the subject, Barb rose from the table. "Hold on a minute, Steve wants me to show you something."

She went to the bedroom and returned carrying her black leather shoulder bag and set it on the table. She delved in the depths and pulled out a small, clear bubble-plastic-wrapped package. Slowly she unwound the wrapping. In the palm of her hand, carved from a lustrous reddish brown and white jade, lay a small sleeping figure.

Lily's eyes widened in an incredulous stare. Her mouth fell open, and for a moment she seemed unable to speak. When at last she recovered her voice, she shrieked, "Oh, my God, where did you ever find that horse?"

Five

Lily, perched on the edge of her chair at the glass-topped table, turned the small figure over and over in the golden morning sunlight. With slender fingers she stroked the cool, smooth stone, examining the recumbent horse intently.

"The colors are so unusual, this milky, translucent white with the reddish overtones. And the carving looks so primitive, yet it's really finer than any abstract sculptures I've seen on the market today." A long, appreciative sigh escaped her. "It's unique, exquisite, I love it."

Surprised by Lily's enthusiasm for the small horse, Barb threw out her hands in a generous gesture. "In that case, it's yours."

"No way. It could be quite valuable. I wouldn't dream of accepting such a gift."

"Please, it's my pleasure."

Lily looked up at her, her eyes bright with excitement. "I'll bet this was one of your flea market finds."

Laughing, Barb said, "No, not this time. Would you believe Grandma's attic?"

Lily's eyes widened in an incredulous stare.

"You're asking me to believe you found this in your grandma's attic, in a farmhouse in Iowa?"

"Not really. The truth is, it was in Hal's grandma's attic. He loved it. When we became engaged, he gave it to me because he knew I would love it, too. Last year after he died, I put it away with his other things." Her eyes misted, and she swallowed unbidden tears. "Reminders of Hal were too painful."

"I understand," said Lily gently. "Now tell me what in the world the horse was doing in his grandma's attic."

"Hal told me that sometime around 1931 or '32, his great grandfather, a geologist, was sent to China by his company to search for possible oil deposits. At the time, the Chinese were excavating sites to lay railroad lines, and they would often cut through ancient Chinese tombs. Some of the workers were robbing the tombs and selling whatever they could find. In those days you were allowed to buy artifacts and take them out of the country.

"His great grandfather brought back a trunkful of souvenirs for his great grandma: bronze cooking pots, beautiful silk kimonos, china, cloisonne bracelets, jade rings and a few curios, chopsticks, small dishes, carved ivory letter openers and so on.

"The souvenirs trickled down to their children— his grandparents—and aunts and uncles. They were happy to have the brass cooking pots and china dishes, but the only one who wanted the curios was his grandfather. After he died, his father inherited them. But his mom, who believed in a place for everything and everything in its place, complained that they cluttered up the house. She stored them in a box in the attic of the old home place."

Lily, wide-eyed, asked, "And Hal never knew they were there?"

Barb grinned. "Not till his parents decided to sell their farm and move to town. When they cleaned out the attic, they found his great grandfather's box of treasures from the Orient. Ivory letter openers, delicately carved fans, cloissone pins, a scroll or two. This little horse was among them. Because Hal was a vet, and had gone to China as an exchange teacher for a year, his dad thought he might like to have it and sent it to him. Then, when I knew I was going to Hong Kong, I dug it out of the attic."

"And brought it with you to show to me?"

"Right. Steve and I are having a—" she paused, grinning—"a discussion over whether or not it's real jade. I think it is, but he doesn't think so, because it isn't green. Actually, Steve suggested I bring it along to show to you. He thought, since you majored in Oriental art, you'd know whether it's real jade."

With a doubtful shake of her head, Lily set the horse down on the table. "Even though I majored in Oriental art, I was more into paintings and scrolls. We only touched on carvings. But I do know a stone doesn't have to be green to be jade."

"Do you know if this horse is real jade?"

"All I know is, the word 'jade' covers a multitude of sins. There ain't no such animal as 'real' jade. There's jadeite and there's nephrite, both of which are called jade. Nephrite is old jade or white jade, but impurities in the stone give it many colors: a yellowish, spinach green, and what they call mutton fat jade, which is what this horse looks like, an entire rainbow of colors.

"Jadeite, or kingfisher, is the bright green color that's so popular, but it, too, can be red, blue, a dark greenish black, pink, beige and so on. Jadeite comes from Burma, and Burma dealers and collectors claim it's the only true jade and the source of imperial jade."

"Then the horse could be carved of any kind of stone."

"Right. Dyed jade, new jade, red jade are all passed off as 'jade.' On the other hand, it could be honest jade, so I hope you guarded it well."

Barb grinned. "You bet! Your influence, to leave nothing to chance. Kept it in my purse from my door to your door."

Lily nodded, and poured a second cup of coffee. "Good move."

"Oh, I did take it out once, when I was filling out the landing card on the tray table before we landed in Hong Kong. A Chinese man sitting next to me saw it and asked if I had any idea of its value. When I told him I hadn't the foggiest, he suggested I take it to an antique dealer and have it appraised."

"Right. Best to have it appraised. Did he tell you which dealer to take it to?"

"Yes, I wrote down the name and address. Something like Dong Po Antiques on Hollywood Road."

Lily shrugged. "Never heard of him, but chances are, if a Hong Kong resident recommended him, he must be reliable." She glanced at her watch. "Heavens, it's almost nine." She pushed back her chair and stood up. "I'd better head out to work."

Barb rose, too. "And I'm off to the antique dealer's."

"Be sure to lock up as you leave," Lily warned.

Barb glanced at her in surprise. "Do you think I didn't lock up yesterday?"

"Of course not. It's just my usual 'better safe than sorry' hang-up kicking in." She started toward the door.

Barb placed a hand on her arm, halting her mid-stride.

"Wait, Lily, we need to talk about this. Maybe it was my passport the thief was after, and maybe it wasn't. But obviously he hadn't finished searching for whatever it was, or he would have been long gone. There's a good chance he'll try again."

"Right. I'll call the manager and ask him to have a dead bolt installed. And I'll ask for a burglar alarm as well."

Barb smiled. "Good thinking. So onward and up-ward!"

With the small jade horse tucked inside her purse and a map of the city in hand, Barb set off at a brisk walk downhill from Lily's Winslow Gardens tower toward Hollywood Road. A cool breeze ruf-fled her hair and stirred the leaves on dense stands of bamboo, sycamore and locust trees that bordered the walk. Farther along, she skirted block-long, mat-covered bamboo scaffolding erected around a site where an old building had been leveled and a new high-rise was climbing skyward. Weaving her way down sidewalks among people hurrying on their way, faces impassive, she was struck with how well dressed they were. Most of the men wore gray or black business suits, or dark slacks with white shirts, or sport shirts and jackets. Many women wore blouses and skirts or slacks. Others sported colorful mini-skirts and skin-tight tops. All looked clean and neat. She saw no one wearing sloppy or ragged clothing, so popular back home.

By the time she reached Hollywood Road, the sun had hidden behind a mottled sky, and the colorful neon signs, now unlighted, left the streets looking dingy. Strolling past shops and restaurants, it occurred to her that she was probably on a fool's errand even bothering to have the carving appraised, but Steve was so sure it was worth its weight in gold that he'd be disappointed if she didn't follow through on her promise to check it out.

She paused before an ancient temple dominated by a red-and-green-tiled roof that curved upward at the corners and was adorned with a frieze of porcelain figures. A white signboard identified the structure as Man Mo Temple, now closed for repairs. The doors stood open. Curious, Barb ambled across the yard and stepped over the high threshold.

Inside, a wide painted screen blocked her way. She tiptoed around it, then stood still, silent. She opened her guide book and leafed through the pages. Yes, here it was, Man Mo Temple, built in 1842. She read aloud:

"This is one of Hong Kong's most important temples, and is dedicated to the god of literature and the god of war."

Strange, she thought, the two gods were hardly compatible.

As her eyes adjusted to the gloom, she beheld a massive gold Buddha mounted on a dais, flanked on each side by an altar. Her gaze shifted to two huge, waist-high copper pots adorned with dragon heads, filled with sand, mounted on stands. Stuck into the sand were a dozen or more lighted red sticks which appeared to be incense. These must be the joss sticks she'd read about, so named because they were placed before gods, or joss, to bring their bearers good luck.

Tall columns upheld the roof from which were suspended giant, red, cone-shaped coils exuding incense. The pungent odor filled her nose and throat. A mystical atmosphere pervaded the temple. A sudden chill coursed through her.

Though she saw no one, suddenly, she sensed a presence. She felt the hair prickle on the back of her neck, and she was sure that any moment someone would come striding out and tell her to be on her way. Yet she stood captivated, unable to move. She felt transported, a thousand or more years, back into antiquity, strangely, unexpectedly in tune with this alien culture.

Impulsively, she delved deep inside her purse, and dug out several coins. They made a loud, clinking sound as she dropped them into a small brass dish that stood on a table nearby.

It was then she saw him. Or rather the glowing tip of a cigarette in a long, ivory holder, held by a hand with long, thin fingers on one of which glittered a diamond ring. The owner was concealed behind one of the thick columns to the right of the central altar, less than twenty feet from where she stood. She stifled a gasp.

Slowly, she backed away, then spun around toward the entrance. As she reached the doorway, she cast a furtive glance over her shoulder. The figure had stepped from behind the column, but all she could see in the dim light was a man of medium height, dressed in black. She paused, expecting him to step forward and either greet her or demand to know what she was doing here. Her face flamed with embarrassment. She felt she owed him an explanation or an apology for invading his sacred temple, when it was obviously closed.

He came no farther, but stood unnaturally still, watching her, as a cat watches a bird. Why had he not identified himself? Perhaps that would have been considered rude, to approach a woman alone. In any case, standing here trying to figure out what was going on was futile. As he continued to watch her, with his long, silent stare, she suddenly felt threatened. She turned and fled around the screen, through the doorway, into the crowded street.

The clouds had thinned, and fingers of sunlight poked through the holes in the mottled cloud cover, making Barb squint against the brightness. At the corner she paused. On her left, a narrow stairway with shallow stone steps led upward. She glanced at the map. This was Ladder Street. It was lined on both sides with vendors who hawked their wares under a patchwork of awnings and tin roofing that stretched from side to side overhead. On her right, Ladder Street continued downhill and gave onto Cat Street.

Intrigued, she ambled down Cat Street. Here all sorts of household goods, books, jewelry, watches, electrical appliances, silk shirts and shopworn clothes were laid out on rickety tables or in pasteboard boxes on the ground. Hawkers called out to her. One short, pudgy man stepped forward and, thrusting a silk shirt close to her face, shouted, "Good price, you buy."

Barb shook her head and murmured one of the quick Cantonese phrases with which Lily had armed her, *"Mm yew,* don't want any," and hurried on.

She was disappointed to discover that bargains were few, and the only treasure she found was a great book about bats by Brock Fenton. At the end of the block, she turned around and retraced her steps to Hollywood Road. She paused before the Yue Po Chai Antique Company, a shop with wide windows where countless porcelain vases, cache pots and Fu dogs were displayed. Other items spilled out over the sidewalk. Overhead, a wide crimson and gold marquee was adorned with Chinese characters and lanterns. Tourists with fanny packs and cameras slung over their shoulders paused to browse. Now Barb saw that the shop number was 132. Soon she should come to the number she had written down on her map. Ambling past a parade of antique shops with windows crammed with laughing Buddhas, swords, clothing, jeans, leather jackets, jewelry and bric-a-brac, she paused before Dong Po MacGregor's Antiquities. Frowning, she stared at the name. Dong Po was the right name, and this was the right number, but who was MacGregor?

She gave a little shrug and stepped inside among a welter of artifacts: blue-and-white Ming porcelain vases, cloisonne, bronze vessels of all sizes and shapes, laughing Buddhas, furniture of teak and rosewood, sculpted stone Fu dogs, antique paintings and objets d'art of jade and ivory.

She glanced about her. A damp, musty smell pervaded the shop, and the place seemed deserted. She turned and started to walk out when a voice with a burr, and a pitch that made her think of the skirl of bagpipes, piped, "Good morning. You English?"

Barb turned to face the owner of the voice. Though of stocky build, he stood a head taller than she. A scarlet plaid hunter's cap rested on a crop of thick sand-colored hair, the matching beard streaked with gray. The tip of his rather long nose was suspiciously red. He wore a black suit coat over a yellow plaid sport shirt, and brown slacks.

Inwardly, Barb thought, *A dyed-in-the-wool Scotsman.* She managed a smile. "American."

A sour expression crossed his face. "Bad joss."

Undaunted, mindful of Lily's warning that Chinese put the family name first, Barb said, "I'd like to speak with Mr. Dong, please."

The shopkeeper's direct gaze held her at arm's length. "Mr. Dong is not here."

"Oh, when you do expect him back?"

Without blinking an eye, he replied, "Never."

"Never?" echoed Barb, nonplussed.

"Mr. Dong is deceased."

"Oh, I'm sorry . . ."

He folded his arms across his chest and in haughty tones said, "You needn't be; he died five years ago. I'm Duncan MacGregor."

Though put off by his abrupt manner, Barb was determined not to show it. Pleasantly, she asked, "And are you the owner of this shop?"

He gave a curt nod. Everybody knows Dong's shop, so I kept the name. If you wish to *buy* something, I'll quote you a price."

Barb forced a polite smile. "Thank you. Actually, I'm here because someone sent me for an appraisal of a very old sculpture that I've recently inherited."

Looking bored, the man compressed his lips, as if to suppress a sigh. "Everybody who inherits something old thinks that because it's old it must be worth a fortune."

Barb could feel her temperature rise. "I'm sure that's true, but won't you at least look at it?"

Duncan MacGregor shrugged. "Suit yourself, if you think it's worth making another trip back here."

"Oh, but I have it with me." She sat down on the dusty seat of a heavily carved teakwood chair, and holding her purse on her lap, opened it and withdrew the bubble-wrapped horse. His hand shot out, as if to grab it, but Barb held it out of reach while she carefully rescued it from its bubble nest. Cupping the horse in both hands as if it were a sacred vessel, she offered it to Duncan MacGregor.

For a long moment he gazed down at it as if it were a live scorpion about to lash out with a poisonous sting. Barb fixed her gaze on the black pompon atop the man's red plaid hunter's cap. Somewhere a cuckoo clock chimed the hour, shattering the silence. Reluctantly, it seemed to Barb, he picked up the horse in one hand and strolled toward the pale golden square of daylight that crept inside the door of the shop. She jumped to her feet and followed him. Sunlight gleaming down on the small horse seemed to light it from within, so that it glowed with a fine luster.

To her own surprise, she found herself holding her breath, waiting to hear the man's appraisal. He continued to hold the horse in one hand, then glanced down at her, cocked his head, and crooking the forefinger of his free hand, stroked his beard in the manner of one considering how best to break the news. A row of wrinkles creased his forehead. His raised eyebrows slanted downward, reminding her of pictures she'd seen of Mephistopheles. His pale brown eyes regarded her from under hooded lids, giving him a sinister expression.

Barb's chin rose. "Well?"

He set the horse down on an embroidered, beige silk pillow cover atop a counter. Regarding her with what she felt was a calculating stare, he gave a weary sigh.

"It's not true jade, I'm afraid, but it's a decent little carving. I can give you," he paused, as if to force himself to quote the highest possible price, then burst out, "eight hundred Hong Kong dollars."

"Eight hundred!" Barb echoed, incredulous. Quickly, she reached in the side pocket of her shoulder bag and pulled out a currency converter.

"That's one hundred American dollars," said Duncan MacGregor, as if he'd promised her the moon.

It was actually more than she had expected. But Mr. MacGregor, evidently mistaking her shocked echo of his offer, said testily, "You won't find anyone who will offer you more than eight hundred, Hong Kong."

Barb gave a vigorous shake of her head. "Actually, it's a family heirloom. I don't really want to sell it."

Duncan MacGregor appeared shocked. He threw out his hands in an exasperated gesture. "Then why do you waste my valuable time and expertise asking me to give you an appraisal?"

Embarrassed, Barb felt hot color stain her cheeks. "Sorry, but I had no idea you'd offer to buy it."

For a moment he was silent. She saw one cheek bulge out as he explored the inside of his mouth with the tip of his tongue. She wished she could fathom what was going through his mind. She reached out and took up the horse. As she rewrapped it and tucked it away in her purse, the significance of his silence bore in on her.

Quickly, she said, "I'll be glad to pay the cost of the appraisal."

His greedy gaze locked with hers. "Ten Hong Kong dollars."

As she fished the money out of her purse, he said, "You can leave me your name, phone number and address here in Hong Kong. If I happen to run across someone who'd be willing to pay a tad more for the carving, I'll ring you up."

"No, as I've said, I really don't care to sell it."

He shoved a pad of yellowed paper and the stub

of a pencil across the counter toward her. "Jot it down anyway, you may change your mind."

Annoyed that he wouldn't let it drop, to shut him up, she picked up the pencil, scribbled on the pad and hastily left the shop. She had written her name and phone number. There was no need for him to know her address.

That evening before dinner, over glasses of Chinese beer and crisp fried noodles, Barb regaled Lily with the details of her trip down Hollywood Road and the stranger in the temple with his menacing manner.

Lily shrugged off the watcher in the temple. "Probably a priest who wanted to make sure you didn't make off with any sacred treasures."

But when Barb finished recounting her meeting with Duncan MacGregor, Lily burst out, "Ridiculous. I don't blame you for not wanting to sell it. Aside from being a family heirloom, it's an exquisite carving in itself."

"I think so. In fact, the more I handle it, the more I love it."

Lily gazed at her sympathetically. "Sorry it wasn't worth an arm and a leg."

Barb laughed. "Bite your tongue. Even I wouldn't take an arm and a leg for it."

Lily got to her feet. "Enough of this suspense. We'll see what the bird has to say."

Barb narrowed her eyes at Lily. "The *bird?*"

"The bird. Tonight you're going to have another unique, unforgettable experience."

"I can hardly wait. When are we going?"

"Now."

Barb sighed inwardly. Why was she having to pull this information out of Lily like a dentist pulling teeth? *"Where* are we going?"

"We're going nightclubbing."

Now Barb understood why she wasn't forthcoming. Barb hated nightclubbing. She gave a doubtful shake of her head. "Nightclubbing isn't my thing."

"You haven't lived till you've seen this one. It's the Temple Street Night Market, also known as the Poor Man's Nightclub, open every night, on the Kowloon side. There's another one on the Hong Kong side near the Macau Ferry Terminal. I hope this is the market you wrote me about, the one you were dying to see. And by the way, how come you're so eager to see it?"

A shadow crossed Barb's face, and a nostalgic expression came into her eyes. "During the year Hal spent in Hong Kong as an exchange teacher, he went to an old fortune-teller in a street market. Hal helped him learn to speak English; he helped Hal learn Cantonese. They became good friends, and the old man told Hal's fortune time and again. The thing was, the old man's prediction was right on the money. Told Hal he'd marry late in life." Barb's expression turned solemn. "It was later than either of us ever dreamed."

"Who was the fortune-teller?"

"I can't remember. It was a funny name, like Pooh. But that was ten years ago. He's probably long gone."

"We'll do our best to find him. So grab your

jacket and purse and we'll move on out—on the MTR."

"You'll have to translate that one."

"Mass Transit Railway, also known as the subway."

They rode the subway to the Yau Ma Tei station. As soon as they strolled down Temple Street, Barb was swept by a strong premonition that the evening would be all Lily had promised and more.

Six

The Poor Man's Nightclub was as far from what Barb had imagined as a landing on the moon. She stood dumbstruck, surveying the dazzling scene before her.

With an expansive gesture, Lily said, "At six o'clock, Temple Street is closed off, lights are strung up and vendors rush in and set up their stands and tables. By eight o'clock the place is transformed."

Under the glare of countless clear glass light bulbs that made the area bright as day, Barb surveyed what appeared to be a full-scale carnival. Her lips curved in a wide grin. "Let's jump in."

"Watch out for pickpockets," Lily warned. "Go!"

Along the sides of the area stood small cafes with tables and chairs. At least a hundred stands bore signs that advertised different Cantonese food specialties. There were rows of stalls and tables where *shmateh,* Chinese rag dealers, hawked jeans, sportswear, shoes and practically every other type of clothing available. Others sold costume jewelry and baubles. Sundries merchants offered combs, brushes, cosmetics and toothpaste.

They ambled down one of the aisles and paused before an old man seated on a chair. Around him children of all ages had gathered, looking up at him with rapt expressions on their faces.

"What's happening?" Barb asked.

Lily listened for a moment, then smiled. "The old man is a storyteller. He's telling the kids an old Chinese fable about a mischievous monkey."

They wandered on through a mishmash of dancers, jugglers, musicians and Chinese gypsy queens, while around them surged a babble of high-pitched chatters and the rise and fall of the voices of impassioned bargainers. Small boys darted about. A little girl, wearing a fluffy, pink party dress with a wide, pink ribbon tied around her head ending in a big bow, licked a frozen ice cream bar. They stopped at stall after stall to watch vendors whip up steaming noodles, dumplings and appetizing concoctions of meats, seafood and vegetables.

People pushed and shoved their way through the throng to watch costumed girls performing graceful dances. Barb looked around in time to catch a glimpse of a small figure in old Mao blue jacket and pants several yards behind them. The figure quickly looked away. As she gazed farther back, it struck her that she seemed to be followed by any number of figures in Mao blue. Firmly, she told herself, "You're imagining things." Determinedly, she turned her attention to several agile acrobats who were tumbling about in an impressive gymnastics show. Later, Barb and Lily stopped before a troupe of theatrical players performing a Chinese opera.

Barb watched entranced, totally at sea as to what was going on. Frowning, staring intently at the pantomime taking place before her eyes, she murmured, "It looks as if the girl is opening a chicken coop and feeding the chickens."

Lily laughed. "You've got it! This is *The Jade Bracelet,* one of the Chinese people's favorite operas. It's a story about a young couple who fall in love at first sight, but are too shy to say so. The girl, who raises chickens for a living, finds a bracelet the man has left for her as a token of his love. A good-hearted neighbor asks the girl for a handkerchief and gives it to the man to show the girl's love for him. So love wins out. It's really an old folktale."

But to Barb's Western ears, the high-pitched voices and the music had the same effect as a fingernail raking a blackboard.

"The music is a little—uh—hard to follow. The flute is okay, but the violin has a few strings missing."

Lily laughed. "That's an *er hu, er* means two. A fiddle, and two strings are all the player needs. See the woman center stage, with black hair wearing the pearl-studded headdress? That's Mei Ling, a friend and neighbor at Winslow Gardens, and also one of my mah-jongg playing friends. You'll have a chance to meet her later on. Meanwhile, let's see what the bird can tell us."

"Bird? What bird?"

"You'll see." She grabbed Barb's elbow and propelled her through the crowd, not pausing until they came upon several men seated behind tables on which stood round, red bamboo cages containing small birds. Other caged birds hung on nearby stands.

"This is the fortune-tellers' enclave."

They stopped to watch a bearded Asian man wearing a black robe and gloves set up a folding table on the dimly lighted aisle. On the wall behind the table he taped mystical-looking sketches of a face and a palm. He then lighted a gas lamp that hissed and gave off a ghostly glare which made the scene even more eerie. A middle-aged blond woman wearing a beige slack suit and a black fanny pack, obviously a tourist, approached the seer. Each took a seat at the table. She extended her palms toward him, and soon they were locked in earnest discussion.

Mr. Cosmos, in the next booth, wore a dark blue robe adorned with astrological signs. His neighbor sported an orange robe and a shaved head. By nine P.M. a dozen or more fortune-tellers, who ranged in age from fifty to seventy, had set up shop. Almost all had at least one client.

Lily said, "Most of these are palm or face readers. Let's go for the bird."

Barb laughed. "I think you're giving me the bird."

"Not at all. Birds are very popular pets. The old gentlemen take them for walks in the park and place the cages in trees to show them off and listen to them sing. They also take them into tea houses where they compete ruthlessly over whose pet has the healthier set of pipes. There are even songbird restaurants, and every morning at breakfast time old

men bring their caged swallows to let them sing
their tiny hearts out. Never underestimate the power
of a bird."

They walked on until they came to a white banner
that read, "Y. K. Poon, Fortune-Teller. Readings
$50HK."

"Poon!" Barb cried, elated. "That's it! Y. K. Poon
is the old man who told Hal's fortune."

Lily appeared skeptical. "Are you sure about
this?"

"Positive."

"I mean, are you sure you want him to tell your
fortune? He might tell you more than you want to
know."

Barb gave her a reassuring smile. "Don't worry.
I can handle it."

A crowd had formed around Poon's table. On the
table stood several round, red bamboo cages that
housed several small birds. Mr. Poon wore a black
tunic and baggy pants and a black billed cap from
which a fringe of white hair escaped and hung over
his large ears. Under bushy, white crescent brows,
his narrow, dark eyes were sunken in folds of skin
like those of an ancient turtle. Clear plastic glasses
perched on the bridge of his nose. A mustache
adorned his upper lip. From each end of his mustache grew long strands of white hair that merged
with a long-flowing white beard.

Lily nodded toward a young girl standing beside
a table on which a bird perched in an open cage.
Her features were set in a tense, hopeful expression.

"Evidently, she's just asked Mr. Poon a question,"
Lily murmured.

The girl watched intently as the bird hopped out of its cage and plucked a card from a deck of tarot-like cards.

"Mr. Poon will interpret the message on the card the bird picked up," Lily murmured.

As he read the card, Barb studied his face, lined as the bark of an ancient oak. Clearly, he had traveled a long road in this world. Now he spoke softly to the young girl, and a radiant smile lighted her face. Her hand flew up, covering her mouth, and she walked away with a jaunty, happy air.

Barb's eyes met the old man's gaze. He smiled at her, his cheeks wreathed in wrinkles. "Java rice bird tells the future," he said softly.

Returning his smile, Barb said, "Do you remember meeting an American named Hal Halstead?"

Old Poon's thin brows rose, his smile widened. "Yes, yes, a fine young veterinarian. We became good friends during the year he was here in Hong Kong. He never tired of hearing tales of ancient China, and in return, he helped me to speak English."

Softly Barb said, "You read his fortune, predicted he would marry late in life."

A guarded expression came into Poon's eyes.

"And so he did, in his forties. I am the wife of Dr. Halstead."

Y. K. Poon gave a slight bow. "I am honored to meet the wife of Dr. Halstead."

Barb's voice faltered. "The—the late Dr. Halstead. Your prediction was all too true."

Poon's dark eyes opened wide betraying shock followed by swift compassion. There was a short silence during which he appeared to be pulling himself together. When he spoke, his voice was filled with sympathy. "I deeply regret Dr. Halstead's passing." He placed his hands together, palms flattened, fingertips under his chin, as if in prayer. "May he find happiness in the world of his ancestors."

Over a sudden lump in her throat, Barb murmured, "Thank you." In choked tones, she went on. "And now I would like you to read my future."

Lily shot a concerned glance at Barb. "Are you sure you're ready for this?"

Barb shook her head. Somehow Poon's sympathy and compassion at hearing of Hal's death had unnerved her. "You go first. Be my guest."

Barb dug in her purse, found some Hong Kong dollars and offered them to Mr. Poon. He shook his head. "Poon does not accept money to say fortunes. Nephew Woo Chow takes money."

A stocky young Chinese man with a crew cut and eyes that glittered like black jade, who had been standing in the shadows behind Mr. Poon, stepped forward and held out his hand. With a little half bow, he said in stilted English, "You pay fifty Hong Kong dollars, please."

Barb counted out the bills and handed them to Woo Chow. Standing beside Lily, she watched the bird pluck a card. The card showed a heart pierced by an arrow. Below the heart was printed a parable in Chinese. Gently, the old man took the card from the soothsaying bird's beak. Onlookers pressed closely around them. In soft, solemn Cantonese he read the card aloud.

A troubled expression suffused Lily's features.

"What is it?" Barb asked. "What did he say?"

Lily turned to Barb and in a tremulous voice translated: "You can't prevent birds of sorrow from flying over your head, but you can prevent them from building nests in your hair."

Barb felt a shiver tingle down her spine. Not for one minute did she believe birds could tell fortunes, but the fact was, Lily *had* suffered sorrow in her life and had done her best to overcome it. Filled with compassion, Barb met Lily's bleak, disappointed gaze. Softly, she said, "You've been there, done that. It's over."

"I know that, but the bird foretells the *future*, not the past. It's some kind of evil omen. I know it is!"

"Lily, come off it. You're becoming almost as superstitious as the Chinese. You don't believe in their prophesies."

Dismally, Lily said, "The trouble is, more often than not, they're right. Look what he told Hal."

Barb mustered the firm, confident tone she used with worried clients. "Marrying late in life could have meant any age from twenty to fifty, depending on your point of view. And that our marriage happened to take place near the end of his life was pure coincidence. Whatever may be, you can handle it." She couldn't resist adding, "And if you believe that bird, let me tell you about a bridge I'd like to sell you."

Lily giggled, her normal common sense restored.

"Sorry, I'm not into buying bridges. Now it's your turn. Let's see what news the bird has for you."

By now a small crowd had gathered, pressing close around them. Barb glanced around her uneasily. She leaned toward Lily and whispered, "These people are invading my space, and I have this eerie feeling we're being watched."

"That's because we *are* being watched. But they're just curious," Lily said. "They won't bite, or attack. They only want to see what the future holds for us *gwailos*."

"*Gwailos?*" asked Barb.

"Foreign devils. That's us," Lily said, eyes twinkling.

Barb's head swiveled past one shoulder then the other, her uneasy gaze sweeping the crowd of onlookers. On the edge of the crowd, in the shadowy darkness just beyond the aureole of light shed by a glass bulb overhead, she caught sight of a man smoking a cigarette in a long, ivory cigarette holder. On his hand sparkled a diamond ring. Heart hammering, she spun toward Lily, nudging her elbow.

"Lily," she gasped, "that man I told you about in the temple, he's here. I'm sure it's the same one."

"Where, where?" Lily raised up on tiptoe, her hazel eyes scanning the crowd.

Craning her head over her right shoulder, Barb said, "There, just beyond those two men in the beige jackets."

"I don't see any cigarette holders."

Barb thrust out a finger, pointing directly at him. "There!" She caught a glimpse of hollow cheeks and deepset eyes in a sallow face just before the man quickly turned his back and melted into the milling crowd. All she saw was the back of a round head with straight, black hair cut even across the back of his neck, and a black-clad back. Without preamble, Barb took off running and plunged through the crowd after him.

Lily shouted, "Barb, wait, come back here!"

Ignoring her shouts, Barb pushed forward, but as if conspiring against her, the mass of people swarming around her formed a solid wall of humanity, blocking her way. Within seconds the man had disappeared from sight. Damn. This was the second time she'd let her quarry get away. Slowly she forced her way through the crowd back to Lily, who was waiting for her at the fortune-teller's stall, a worried frown on her face.

At the sight of Barb, Lily called in a voice with mingled relief and joy, "Barb, thank God you're back. Are you out of your mind, running off after a strange man? You just don't do that in Hong Kong. Besides, this place is thick as fleas with purse snatchers and muggers who could run off with your purse before you could blink an eye."

Barb smiled and, thinking Lily always did tend to overreact, gave her a reassuring pat on the shoulder. "Sorry, but if only I'd caught up with him, I could have found out for sure whether he really was watching me, and if so, why."

"How? He probably doesn't speak English—wouldn't understand your accosting him—would call the law and have you carted away."

"But you speak Cantonese. You could interpret. I wanted you to come with me to nail him."

Lily gave a vigorous shake of her head that made her golden sweep of hair shimmer. "Not this chicken."

"You can't tell me it's sheer coincidence that I'd

meet two men the same day who smoke cigarettes in an ivory holder and sport a diamond ring."

"Get real, Barb. There must be millions of ivory cigarette holders in Hong Kong alone, and millions more diamond rings, and men who wear them. Hong Kong is probably the richest island in the world, seething with millionaires. Seeing two men sporting diamond rings on the same day doesn't mean you're being followed."

In tones that rang with conviction, Barb said, "Believe me. Some people know these things. I'm one of them."

Lily rolled her eyes heavenward. "Let's see what the bird says."

They turned back to Y. K. Poon's table. He looked at them with wondering eyes, a baffled expression on his face. Clearly he found the ways of the round-eyes inscrutable.

Once again the old fortune-teller's hard-eyed, crew cut nephew stepped forward and collected the fee from Barb. She stood before the table, hands clasped at her waist, with the air of one expecting good news. She watched closely as the tiny brown bird selected a card, and found she was holding her breath, waiting for a pronouncement that could affect her entire future.

Gently, reverently, the fortune-teller removed a card from the bird's beak. For a long, silent moment, he sat staring at the Chinese characters. At last he spoke.

"He who stores treasures up for himself, loses them; he who gives them away, finds them."

Mystified, taken aback, Barb turned to Lily. "What do you think that's supposed to mean?"

In solemn tones, Y. K. Poon said, "You possess a great treasure. Guard it well."

Privately, Barb thought his words could apply to the lives of many people. Many had something that could be regarded as a treasure: a good job, fine sons, a fine place to live, a piece of jade, good health. In her own life, great treasure could apply to her veterinary practice, which so far was taking off like gang busters; or to her good fortune in finding a man like Steve, who loved her; or her good fortune in having a great family. She returned her attention to Lily, who had been gushing forth in a long stream of Cantonese to Mr. Poon.

"What was that all about?"

"I told him about your horse, of course."

Surprised, Barb asked, "What did you tell him?"

"I told him you'd inherited a jade horse that was worth many Hong Kong dollars."

As though she'd been hit with a board, Barb howled, "Oh, no! You didn't!"

"I did. I thought he'd be interested, since he was a good friend of Hal's. Then he said it could be priceless, and you should guard it well."

"But it's not a great treasure. We know that."

"Right, but if he wants to make you feel good, what's the harm in going along? Besides, it wouldn't do to embarrass him by telling him in front of all these people that he's dead wrong. He would lose face. Very bad for business." She turned to Mr. Poon and spewed out another volley of Cantonese.

Barb eyed her malevolently. "Lily, bite your tongue."

With the injured air of one wrongly accused, Lily said, "But I'm taking no chances, no risk. I told him we're going to stash it away in a safe-deposit box first thing tomorrow morning."

For a long moment Barb was speechless. When she recovered her voice, she said in warning tones, "Lily dear, my best friend and loyal supporter, tomorrow is Sunday. The bank is closed."

"Well for heaven's sake, you don't think Mr. Poon would steal it, do you?"

"No, not at all. But rumors, true or false, fly . . ."

"Not to worry. Mr. Poon has no idea who I am, much less where we live."

Barb shot her a ten-pound look and jerked her head toward Mr. Poon. "Ask him to put the card back."

"Why, for heaven's sake?"

"Ask him to put it back," Barb insisted. "You'll see."

Lily shrugged and in rapid Cantonese, spoke to Mr. Poon.

With no change in expression the old man replaced the card in the deck.

Barb fished fifty more Hong Kong dollars from her shoulder bag and handed them to the obsequious assistant. "Now ask him to tell his bird to pick another card."

Again, Lily repeated her request. Again the man complied.

Unhesitatingly, unerringly, the little brown bird hopped across the table and picked a card from the pack. Slowly, the fortune-teller turned it over, looked at it, then held it out to Barb faceup.

Barb stared at the bird, then the fortune-teller, in disbelief. The bird had picked the same card as before. She might have thought the bird plucked the same card for all Mr. Poon's customers, but it had chosen a different one for the young girl, another for Lily, and still another for herself. It was uncanny.

The old man nodded as if to say, I told you so, then opening his eyes wide, spoke softly. Lily translated: "My little bird knows the future. Trust him."

She could trust the bird not to speak, but she never knew what would come tumbling from Lily's sweet, innocent lips. She grabbed Lily's elbow and dragged her away from the fortune-teller before she could reveal any more about their private lives.

It was almost midnight by the time they got home and went to bed. At once Barb fell into a deep, dreaming sleep, but her dreams were filled with visions of a dark, hollow-eyed man with sunken cheeks like a death's head, standing in the shadowy darkness beyond a circle of light shed by a clear glass bulb. A cigarette in a long, ivory-carved holder dangled from his lips. She strained her eyes, trying to see him clearly; but a cloud of smoke obscured her view, and the sinister face faded away. The odor of smoke crept into her nostrils. Abruptly, she awoke, her heart beating like a jackhammer. The odor of smoke vanished along with the nightmare. Still, she felt an overwhelming fear, without knowing why.

Seven

Snuggled under the covers in the cool Sunday morning dawn, Barb felt a firm hand grip her shoulder and shake her gently. A voice from faraway called, "Barb, Barb, wake up, hurry."

Barb groaned and snuggled deeper under the covers. After a seemingly endless night peopled with frightening, threatening faces, she had finally drifted off. Now she was in no hurry to wake up. In a voice fogged with sleep, she mumbled, "Is the flat on fire?"

"Not that I know of." Lily's tone was abysmally cheerful.

"Then what's the rush?"

"T'ai chi time."

Barb's eyes remained firmly closed. "Who?"

"T'ai chi ch'uan. We talked about it last night, remember? You promised you'd go with me."

"That was last night. And it's still night."

"It only looks like night because your eyes are closed. It's really half past dawn." Mercilessly, with no warning, she flicked on the bedside lamp. Barb winced.

Lily persisted. "You promised—said you wanted

to experience all the wonderful things Hong Kong
has to offer. Remember?"

Barb groaned.

Grinning, Lily gave her shoulder another shake.
"Well?"

Slowly, carefully, Barb opened her eyes and
gazed up into Lily's face. Lily wore the stubborn,
determined look of a mule that refused to move.

"I'm mulling it over. Did I really say that?"

"Did. As we both know, you have a memory like
an elephant."

"I think the elephant's memory is a myth, an old
husband's tale."

"I refuse to be sidetracked into a discussion of
elephant myths. If you want to experience one of
China's many gifts to the world, rise and shine."

Ten minutes later, Barb, wearing red sweats, and
Lily in a yellow tee shirt and shorts, alighted from
the mirrored elevator and hurried through the black
marble-tiled lobby. As they stepped through the
doorway into the gray morning, Barb felt damp air
hit her face like a wet towel.

The circular flower beds bordering the two white
glass-and-concrete columns of flats in Winslow
Gardens were shrouded in mist. Snow pine trees,
their many branches like upflung arms, stood like
hulking shapes in the background. Crimson cannas
faded to monochrome tones of gray. As they
rounded the pool Barb gave a start. Misty figures
rose before them, stretching, bending like statues
come to life. Fifteen or more people wearing tee
shirts and shorts or slacks were gathered in an open,
grassy space before a circular fountain. One man,

taller than most Chinese men Barb had seen, led the group in the morning exercises.

"Is that the guru?" Barb asked.

Lily's brow wrinkled in a mock scowl. "That's Peter Chang, also known as 'the master.' "

"Isn't that unusual, that his given name is English, but his family name is Chinese?"

"Not really. I'll explain later. It's time to go into action."

Intrigued, Barb watched Lily, along with the others, stand on one foot, curl her fingers into a fist and stretch out her right arm. Most of the participants moved with flowing, rhythmic, deliberate movements, as if shadow boxing.

"Put your weight on your back foot," Lily whispered.

Barb, determined to follow along, stumbled through the routine. Gradually the mist lifted. The rich, dark green pine trees and crimson cannas came into focus. Somewhere a bird called, and the hum of traffic on the Queen's Road far below drifted upward, signaling the frantic start of the day.

Lily cast a quick glance at Barb, who was floundering on one foot, arms flailing. Smiling encouragement, she said, "It's not as simple or easy as it looks."

Her words made Barb feel better, but not much. It seemed like an hour, but was actually less than half as long, as she struggled to follow the slow, controlled movements. When the class was finally dismissed, everyone except Peter Chang hurried away. With long, loping strides, he crossed the lawn toward Barb and Lily.

His warm, friendly gaze swept Barb from head to toe and back again. In a crisp British accent he said, "And who have we here? An emissary from America?"

As Lily introduced Barb, Peter made a deep bow from the waist, clasped her right hand in his and planted a light kiss on her wrist. "Charmed."

Immediately, his appearance struck Barb. He had the burnished skin and high, prominent cheekbones of an Oriental, but the lightest round blue eyes she had ever seen. His hair, parted on one side, was the thick, straight black silken pelt of an Asian, but he had the tall, sinewy physique of an Englishman.

Barb smiled, withdrawing her hand from his. "T'ai chi is more challenging than I'd ever imagined. I'd love to learn more, to become really proficient."

His smile broadened, and he looked deeply into her eyes. His voice was as soft as a caress. "That would take years, and I would like ever so much to teach you. And I'd like even more for you to teach me about America. What a fantastic country you Colonials have carved from that vast wilderness."

His comment gave her pause. Though she was sure he meant it as a compliment, the remark, a little off-key, struck a sour note in the pleasant medley of the morning. Lily's head had swiveled from one to the other as if watching a tennis match. Now she jumped into the silence.

"Listen, Pete, since you and Barb seem to have a lot to talk about, why don't you join us for brunch around ten-thirty."

His eyes never left Barb's face. "My pleasure." He gave Barb another deep bow, then loped off toward the white towers of Winslow Gardens.

Watching him out of sight, Barb cocked her head, casting a curious glance at Lily. "Is he a close friend of yours?"

A rush of color tinged Lily's face. "I hope so. He lives in the same tower I do. We used to see each other fairly often, and we've gone out on the town several times."

"Till Mr. Wonderful came along?"

"Right."

"Peter Chang," said Barb thoughtfully. "Has he taken an English first name the way so many Chinese do?"

"Actually, his dad was Chinese and his mom was British. She named him Peter when he was born. It just shows that times have changed drastically. In the olden days no British lady would marry an Oriental, and the Chinese were very much against marrying Occidentals. For some diehards, the stigma still exists, so Pete's neither fish nor fowl. He deeply resents it. Tries to please both nationalities.

"His dad was an exporter—fine furniture, works of art, sculpture, porcelains and so on. His mother, a London interior designer, was a former client, so they had a lot in common. They were both killed in an airline crash several years ago." She gave a sorrowful shake of her blond mane. "Their deaths nearly killed Pete. He inherited his dad's business, then somehow lost it. Now he spends his life trying to control his fate. Talk about superstitious!"

Barb's brows rose. "Evidently, he's looking for a wife."

"You've got that right. And from the way he was looking at you, like a drowning man clutching at a life raft, I think you're a prime target. He can come on pretty strong." Lily laughed, and her face flushed scarlet. "So, to take the heat off you, I'll ask Mei Ling to join us for brunch."

"Mei Ling. The opera star we saw perform last night?"

"That's Mei Ling. She's very outspoken, says whatever she thinks, things other people would like to say, but don't. You'll love her."

By ten-thirty the dim sum Lily had ordered from a nearby cafe had been delivered, and Pete was knocking at the door of their flat. Mei Ling, apparently following theatrical tradition, arrived ten minutes after "curtain" time. Barb smiled inwardly, for Mei Ling did not simply walk through the door, she made an entrance. A statuesque figure, she stood center stage at the end of the living room as if poised to sing, waiting for the undivided attention of her audience.

Barb regarded her in mild astonishment. She had expected to see a toned-down version of the colorful opera star of the Poor Man's Nightclub. Instead, her appearance was no less dramatic than it had been during her performance. Her glossy black hair, caught up in a large chignon on the back of her head, was adorned with an intricately carved ivory comb. Several fine strands had escaped the chignon and dangled about her ears. From her ears hung exquisite jade earrings in gold filigree settings. Her dark eyes gleamed with life and vigor under brows plucked as thin as crescent moons. A bracelet of jade stones encircled her wrist. She wore a gold satin mandarin jacket, richly embroidered with dragons, over black satin trousers.

Pete leaped to his feet and made a salutatory bow. "I'm happy to see you once again, Mei Ling."

Mei Ling eyed him sternly. "Are you still torturing people every morning at the crack of dawn?"

Pete smiled. "As many as possible. I wish you'd join us."

Pleasantly, dark eyes twinkling, Mei Ling said, "I can worship the t'ai chi master just as well from afar, my friend." With that she ensconced herself in a jade green lounge chair as if prepared to hold court.

After introducing Barb and Mei Ling, Lily wheeled in a tea cart bearing a white porcelain teapot, cups, bamboo baskets of steaming dim sum, white china plates, chopsticks and napkins. They helped themselves to the selection of small, dough-wrapped delicacies: pork and shrimp dumplings, steamed barbecued pork buns and deep-fried spring rolls.

"Dim sum, a delight of the heart," Pete said, looking at Barb, "like our lovely visitor from America."

"Thank you," Barb murmured and turned her attention to her fingers struggling to conquer her ungovernable chopsticks. The appetizing aroma of minced meat and vegetables made her mouth water. Now, if only she could convey the food to her mouth.

With the quirk of an eyebrow, Mei Ling said, "I suppose you've heard that at last Brit'ain is handing Hong Kong over to the Chinese."

Barb nodded. "I've read about it. Will the take-over mean many changes, do you think?" Adroitly she maneuvered the two sticks around one of the small dumplings that back home was called a pot sticker. Squeezing the chopsticks together, she managed to bring it to her mouth and take a bite. The food seemed to melt in her mouth.

Pete said, "We hardly dare talk about it." He cast a wary, speculative glance at Mei Ling. "You never know who will be who after the takeover. Today's best friend may be tomorrow's worst enemy."

Defensively, Mei Ling said, "The Chinese say there will be no changes for the next fifty years— that Hong Kong can continue to govern itself."

In lofty tones, Pete said, "What the Chinese Communists say and what they do are often two entirely different matters."

Mei Ling scowled. "Do you speak for yourself, Mr. Chang?"

"I'm only telling you the way it will be. And there will be jolly little future for the arts, you can bet on it."

Mei Ling looked him straight in the eye and, with what Barb felt was unnecessary force, said, *"I'm* not a gambler, Mr. Chang." Her implication that Pete Chang was an inveterate gambler was grievously clear.

His face reddened. Not unkindly, he replied, "Perhaps you would have good luck."

Barb, sipping the hot, fragrant green tea, felt

tension building in the room like wind filling the batwing sail on a Chinese junk. Quickly, she said, "Haven't the Chinese agreed that there will be one country, two systems?"

"Agreed," Pete said, "and so there may be economically, but politically is a horse of another color."

Barb, ever the peacemaker, said, "I wouldn't worry. Mainland China needs Hong Kong for the billions of dollars she generates in trade. She's not going to kill the goose that lays the golden egg."

Gently, Mei Ling said, *"You* wouldn't worry because *you* do not live in Hong Kong. Here, people worry. Many fine doctors, engineers, artists, are leaving the colony by the thousands to be gone before 1997, the Year of the Rat."

"The rats deserting the sinking ship," quipped Pete.

Mei Ling's smooth, porcelainlike brow puckered. "I do not call myself a rat simply because I plan a trip away from a country that will not support the arts. Several of us are raising funds to form an opera troupe to tour America."

Pete sat stiffly erect in his chair, clearly taken aback by Mei Ling's news. "I had no idea you were tripping out."

Mei Ling cocked her head, thin brows elevated. "Why should you?"

Ignoring her question, he said, "Whyever do you think Cantonese opera will play in America?"

Bristling, Mei Ling slammed down her teacup. "We are professional performers, easily equal, even superior to the acrobatic teams that fly all over the world."

Pete threw out his hands in an expansive gesture. "If you can trip off to America, then surely I could teach t'ai chi there." He turned to Barb, an eager, hopeful expression in his light blue eyes. "Is t'ai chi popular in your country?"

"Oh, yes, and interest is growing by leaps and bounds."

To Barb's surprise, his shoulders sagged, and he threw out his hands in a hopeless gesture. In resigned tones he said, "Immigration is the problem. It's apt to be a sticky wicket."

Something clicked in the back of Barb's mind, the way it did when she was totting up symptoms to diagnose an ailment in a sick animal. How would he know that immigration might be a problem, unless he'd already tried to leave the colony and failed?

"Speaking of immigration," said Mei Ling, "thousands of emigrés from Mainland China are still pouring into Hong Kong, even though it's against the law."

Lily said, "Somewhere I read that if you deposit two hundred thousand dollars in a Canadian bank and agree to leave it there for three years, Canada will grant you citizenship."

Pete gave a short laugh. "Indeed, is that all, then?"

Mei Ling, looking at Pete, said, "You could marry with an American." Her lips curved in a knowing grin, and her dark, uptilted eyes slid toward Barb.

Following Mei Ling's gaze, Pete regarded Barb for a long moment. She quickly looked away, unable to read his expression. Was that an invitation in his eyes, saying, *I'm willing if you are.* Or was it mere speculation as though wondering, would she or wouldn't she consider marrying him? Or had Mei Ling simply suggested a new idea that he was now mulling over?

Inwardly, Barb regrouped. Pete was no slouch, no doubt ranked high in the brains department. Had marriage to an American been in the back of his mind from the start, when he'd dated Lily, and now with new hope, was he kowtowing to her? Deciding she wouldn't touch that with a bamboo pole, she made no comment.

They had devoured all the dim sum, and now Barb rose to her feet, stacked the bamboo baskets, chopsticks and plates on the tea cart and wheeled it out to the kitchen. She returned in time to hear Pete say, "I guarantee you, on the stroke of midnight, June 30, 1997, we'll find ourselves securely under the boot heel of Communist China."

Lily burst out, "Pete, stop being so gloomy. Let's talk about something wonderful." She turned to Barb. "Barb, do show them your new treasure."

Barb shook her head. "Treasure, no. New, no, but I'd love to show it off." She went to her room and moments later returned with the horse and gently set it down on the coffee table.

An expression of admiration lighted Pete's face. With a small intake of breath, he said, "Jade," and reached a hand toward it. But Mei Ling's long, beringed, red-tipped fingers shot out and grasped the

small carving. She rose from her chair and crossed
to the sliding glass doors. The sunlight striking the
small horse gave it a luminescence that made it
glow from within.

"It's exquisite," said Mei Ling in reverent tones,
turning it this way and that.

Pleased, Barb said, "I see you're a jade worship-
per."

"Like everyone else in China," Pete said. "To us,
jade is more precious than rubies, diamonds or
gold."

Barb suppressed a start of surprise. He appeared
much more knowledgeable about stones than she
would have expected a t'ai chi instructor to be. But
Lily had said Pete's father had exported works of
art, sculpture. Had he dealt in jade? Or maybe most
Chinese people were knowledgeable about jade.

Lily rose from the couch and crossed to Mei Ling
at the window. Eagerly, she asked, "Do you think
it's real?"

Mei Ling's lips pursed in thought. "It looks like
true jade." She strode back to her chair, sat down
and held the horse cupped between her palms as if
she were holding the royal seal of China.

In sharp, impatient tones Pete asked, "May I see
it, please?" Mei Ling extended her hands, and with
a casual air, Pete picked up the recumbent horse,
balanced it on his outstretched hand and began to
stroke it. "It feels warm, almost as if it were alive."
Casually, he remarked, "It could be worth quite a
bit of money."

Lily said, "Barb's had it appraised. It's only worth
about eight hundred dollars, Hong Kong."

Mei Ling nodded. "Some carvers carve anything and call it jade."

Pete stroked the back of the little horse soothingly, as one would caress a beloved dog. Without looking at Barb, he asked, "Where did you have it appraised?"

"A shop called Dong Po somebody." She ran a hand through her hair, trying to think. "Dong Po MacGregor Antiquities, I think it is, on Hollywood Road. A Mr. MacGregor examined it."

"Never heard of him, but you can bet he appraised it on the low side rather than the high side. I once bought a laughing Buddha, bronze, about eight inches tall at one of those shops. It was signed, dated, Mid-Qing. The fellow was asking eighteen hundred U.S., but I beat him down to nine hundred dollars." His lips curved in a small, self-congratulatory smile. "A month later I saw the same Buddha in a high-priced shop on the Queen's Road. I ducked inside and asked to see it. It was the same mould, signed and dated. The price was ten thousand, eight hundred, not negotiable."

Barb eyed Pete speculatively, thinking that bargaining was one thing, but beating a poor shopkeeper down to half his asking price was nothing to brag about.

Lily's hazel eyes narrowed as if to summon memory. "Pete, I've never seen a laughing Buddha in your flat. Where do you keep it?"

For a fraction of a second he appeared confused, then recovering, said, "I, ah, lost it."

"You *lost* a laughing Buddha? How could you?"

He smiled and waved a hand in airy dismissal. "Don't ask."

Barb, too, wondered how anyone could *lose* an eight-inch-tall brass Buddha. Clearly, there was more to good-natured Pete Chang than met the eye.

Mei Ling gave Pete a look of reproof. In lofty tones, she said, "Mister Chang, we are not impressed with the Buddha that is no more." Her head swiveled to Barb. "I'm most impressed with your fine jade horse."

Lily gave a vigorous nod. "So was Y. K. Poon, the fortune-teller at the Poor Man's Nightclub. He thinks it may be priceless."

As though suddenly losing interest in the horse, Pete glanced at his watch, then stood up abruptly. "I must be on my way. Off to Happy Valley, ladies."

"Happy Valley?" Barb repeated. "Sounds fantastic."

"That depends on whether you're winning or losing," said Mei Ling. She glanced at Pete. "Is that not so?"

Ignoring her comment, Pete turned to Barb. "It's a racecourse. The horses run every Saturday and Sunday afternoon and Wednesday evenings. The proceeds go to charity, so you see, it's quite a worthwhile pastime." His lips curved in a boyish smile that Barb suspected had charmed many a bird from the trees. "I think you'd enjoy the races, and I'd enjoy them even more if you were with me."

Barb forced a smile. "Some other time, maybe."

Mei Ling rose to her feet. "I, too, must leave. I must rehearse for a performance this evening."

After they had gone, and Barb and Lily were sitting in the living room sipping cups of tea, Barb glanced over at Lily.

"How do you think Pete lost his laughing Buddha?"

"I think he 'lost' it paying off a gambling debt on one of his trips to Macau."

"Isn't gambling against the law?"

"It is in Hong Kong, except on the racetrack. But it's big business in Macau. And when you lose, you pay up, either out of your wallet or out of your hide. Someday Pete is going to push his luck too far."

"I hope not. He seems like such a neat person. Speaking of neat persons, when am I going to meet your Andre? He is *your* Andre, right?"

A radiant smile lighted Lily's face. "Absolutely. He'll be here tomorrow night. I wish he could spend more time with us; but he's master chef at La Parisienne, a high-dollar French restaurant at the Hong Kong Crown, and he's on duty afternoons and evenings."

Barb recognized the Hong Kong Crown as one of the city's newest five-star hotels.

"And—" Lily's voice took on an anticipatory tone—"tomorrow night he's taking the night off to cook us a gourmet dinner."

"The man cooks a real meal? How lucky can you get!"

"We both feel lucky we found each other, especially here among a ninety-eight percent Chinese population. When I moved to Hong Kong, I thought if I were lucky enough to find love, I'd probably marry an Asian." A sparkle came into her eyes. "It looks to me as if you've made a conquest. Pete couldn't take his eyes off you all morning."

Barb rolled her eyes heavenward. "He's a charmer, but Steve is all I can cope with at the moment."

"You're serious about him, then? I thought you two were just good friends. After all, you turned down his proposal."

Barb felt her heart turn over with a sudden rush of love for Steve. "We're good friends, the best of friends."

"But you don't want to spend the rest of your life with him, is that it?"

Barb gave a vigorous shake of her head. "Wrong. He's kind, loving, funny, gentle, a rock in time of trouble, all I could possibly want in a man with whom I'd spend the rest of my life."

A worried expression clouded Lily's eyes. "Barb, I don't mean to pry, but isn't your animal hospital doing well? You told Steve you weren't ready to get married because you needed to see if you could make it on your own, and well, I *thought* you told me it was going like gangbusters."

"I did, and it is. I guess I worry that too many cooks will spoil the broth."

Lily's brows flew up. *"You! Worry!* I'm the one who's obsessed with taking no risks."

Barb shook her head. "Actually, there's more to it than that. Things aren't quite what they seem."

"They seem great from where I sit."

Barb's brows drew together in a slight frown. "You're sitting in Hong Kong. Back home there's something else, something I haven't told you. You see, when I started the hospital a little more than a year ago, I borrowed fifty thousand dollars from the SBA, Small Business Administration. I had to redo the storefront space I'd leased, buy a bunch of equipment, hire a receptionist, well, there were all sorts of start-up costs.

She gave a small sigh. "The new business got off to a slow start, which was to be expected. Still, with Hal's teaching salary, I was able to pay the rent and make payments on the loan. Now, without Hal's income, I'm afraid I'm not going to be able to make the payments. It makes me crazy."

Lily leaned forward, and looked earnestly into Barb's face. "Barb, I have money I haven't even counted. Let me help you."

"No. Absolutely not. Borrowing from friends is the quickest way to lose them."

"It wouldn't be a loan, really, it would be an investment. You could pay me a dividend, like three cents on the dollar."

Barb laughed. "You might be lucky to get even that. And if the hospital goes down the drain, you and your investment would go with me."

"I'll take that chance."

"You!" Barb's lips curved in a wry grin. "You who take no risks, leave nothing to chance?"

"Right. Anyway, I don't consider your practice a risk."

"Another reason I can't marry Steve is that he wants to combine our practices."

Lily's eyes widened in astonishment. "There's your answer. You could move right into his clinic, and with two of you working, you could repay your loan—that would be perfect."

"But I'd still never know if I could make it on my own. You see, Lil, I'm a born risk taker. But if I go in with Steve, I worry that it will be a case of 'No dog can serve two masters.' "

"That's so unlike you."

"The thing is, I'd want to call the shots, and so would he."

"You're really saying you'd both want to be top dog."

"Not only that, probably the biggest problem is that it's much too soon after Hal's death." Sudden tears welled in her eyes. "I loved him with all my heart."

Gently, Lily said, "But your love for Steve is different from your love for Hal, and loving Steve doesn't mean you love Hal any less."

"I know. But I'm just not ready to leap into another marriage."

They continued to talk about whether she should marry Steve, when the sudden, jarring ring of the phone interrupted them.

Lily crossed to the white princess phone on the writing desk and lifted the receiver. As she listened, a scowl darkened her features. Crossly, she said, "Who is this?" She turned to face Barb. "Some man wants to speak to you, but he won't say who he is."

Rising to her feet, Barb said, "Maybe it's the appraiser. He said he'd call if he found anyone willing to pay more than eight hundred dollars for the horse."

Lily handed Barb the phone.

The voice was that of a stranger. In stilted English he said, "Your horse. I buy. One t'ousand Hong Kong dollar."

"Sorry, it's not for sale."

Louder, more insistent, he said, "I buy. How much?"

Firmly, Barb said, "I told you, the horse is not for sale."

The man's voice grew angry, threatening. "You sell me, *gwailo*. How much you wan'?"

"Nothing. The carving is priceless."

"Two, two t'ousand. I give you two t'ousand Hong Kong dollar."

"No. Not interested." She slammed down the receiver and, frowning, turned toward Lily. "That's odd. That was some man offering me one thousand HK for the horse. When I turned him down, he immediately upped it to two. Weird, don't you think?"

"Was it the appraiser?" Lily asked.

"No, and he couldn't have been one of the appraiser's referrals because he never said who he was, nothing—except that he'd pay two thousand, HK." Suspicion took root and grew. What if the horse was more valuable than she had thought?

Lily's brows flew upward. Two hundred fifty U.S. dollars! At least the horse is increasing in value."

"You'd think he was offering the world, he was so insistent that I sell it to him, and he refused to take no for an answer."

"I think you convinced him."

"But if he wasn't a referral, who was he? How

did he know I have the horse? How did he get your phone number?"

Lily shrugged. "I doubt he'll try again. I'd forget it."

Barb folded her arms across her chest and began pacing the floor. "I can't, Lily. I can't forget it."

Eight

On Monday morning Barb awoke with a start. A sense of anticipation swept through her. Today was special. A bonus, a spin-off from her visit to Lily. Today she'd delve into another of the gifts of the Orient: acupuncture. For more than a year she'd combed vet journals for news on the subject and had found almost nothing. She was dying to explore the mysteries of this technique and hoped she could use it to treat animals, to relieve pain and to cure various diseases.

Last night Lily had called a doctor friend who had told her about an acupuncturist who spoke English and gave demonstrations to visitors at his clinic on Mondays at nine.

Barb glanced at her watch. "Good lord, ten after eight." She jumped out of bed, ran to Lily's room and pounded on the door.

"Hey, Lil, up and at 'em. We've overslept. You'll be late for work and I'll be late for the demo."

Lily shouted back, "Worse, you've missed t'ai chi. Pete will be crushed."

Laughing, Barb said, "He'll just have to learn to deny himself."

Quickly she pulled on her clothes: a rust-colored

silk blouse, black-and-white-checked jacket, black slacks and loafers. Twenty minutes later she was on her way.

A sense of excitement gripped her as she strode down the walk on the steep sloping mountainside to the tram stop. Wouldn't it be terrific if she could relieve Marlene, the German shepherd, of the pain of hip displasia without giving her lifelong cortisone shots; and block out the pain of Sniffer's arthritis? Do surgery without anesthesia. A feeling of euphoria stole over her, and she breathed deeply of the fresh pine-scented air not yet polluted by clouds of exhaust fumes rising from the traffic in the city below. The sight of tall, luxurious pines, broad, leafy plane trees and colorful flower beds awash in golden sunlight as she passed by reinforced her optimism.

Once inside the clinic, an aide led her to a small room where a group of chatty American tourists had gathered to watch the demonstration. On the cream-colored walls hung big charts that depicted the human body, peppered with dots indicating where needles should be inserted. A short, slender Chinese man wearing gold-rimmed glasses and a white smock entered the room and introduced himself as Doctor Chiu. The tourists quieted and listened attentively as Doctor Chiu spoke in crisp, Oxford-accented English.

"Acupuncture was developed before 2500 B.C. in China and is now used in many other areas of the world. The techniques grew out of the theory of Yin and Yang. Yin represented by the earth and yang by the heavens keep the universe in balance.

The forces of yin and yang act in the human body as they do throughout the universe."

He paused and, brows lifted, peered over the rim of his glasses, searching the faces of his listeners as if to say, "Do you understand?" Several heads bobbed, and he went on.

"Disease and ill health are caused by an imbalance which obstructs the pathway of the vital life force, the *ch'i* in the body. Chinese medicine, through the placement of needles into any of hundreds of points over the body, affects the distribution of yin and yang. Acupuncture technique enables the *ch'i* to flow freely, brings the life force back into balance and restores the patient to good health."

When he had finished speaking, he asked for volunteers. For the first time in her life, Barb wished she weren't so blasted healthy, so she could offer herself up as a guinea pig. Several tourists eagerly volunteered some of their aches and pains for a demonstration of the treatment. A tall, stooped man with a shock of reddish hair and a wealth of cinnamon-colored freckles stepped forward. "I'd mighty like to get shut of this arthuritis [*sic*] that's giving me hell on wheels."

The doctor told him to remove his shirt and lie down on a table. He placed several needles in the patient's shoulder, then heated them by holding close two cigar-shaped bundles of smoldering herbs. A hush fell over the dingy room. A pungent smoke pervaded the air.

The patient, smiling at everyone, admitted that to his own surprise, he felt no pain, that the insertion of the needles felt like little more than pinpricks. When the red-haired tourist regained his feet, rolling his shoulders and smiling, another of his companions quickly volunteered. Barb watched with growing apprehension and doubt.

When everyone who asked had received treatment and gone, Barb stayed behind to speak with Doctor Chiu. After a long, friendly discussion regarding the use of acupuncture in veterinary medicine, in kindly tones, Doctor Chiu said, "May I suggest, if you have a client for whom you think acupuncture is indicated, you would do better to refer the case to a specialist, rather than spend years studying techniques you may use only two or three times each year."

Hiding her disappointment, Barb thanked Doctor Chiu and left.

Some of the shine had gone from the day. Dispiritedly she wended her way back to Lily's flat at Winslow Gardens. She turned the key in the lock, and as the heavy door swung open, she heard a strange sound, a hurried, rhythmic tapping. Quickly, she stepped inside the foyer, and glancing from side to side in the dusky morning light that seeped around the corner from the living room, she saw a shadowy form disappearing into the kitchen.

Sharply, she called out, "Who's there?"

A tall, regal figure suddenly loomed in the kitchen doorway. "Do not worry, Doctor Barbara. It is I, Mei Ling."

Barb stood staring at Mei Ling. Her questioning gaze swept down to Mei Ling's feet clad in high-heeled, thick-soled shoes, up the long black skirt, past the wild red, yellow, black and white figured blouse, to her glossy black hair. Today she wore it braided in a long plait secured by a huge yellow bow.

Barb wanted to ask what the hell she was doing in Lily's flat, but immediately thought better of it. It was possible that Mei Ling and Lily had some agreement that allowed her free access to the place. Belatedly, Barb recalled that Lily had told the police that Mei Ling had a key. Before she could question her, Mei Ling said quickly, "The rr-light in my flat is out—off—yes?"

"The electricity?"

It occurred to Barb that yesterday Mei Ling had spoken excellent English, yet today she was having trouble getting the words out. Why was she so nervous?"

"The electricity?"

"Y-yes," she stammered, "no rr-light."

Barb waited for her to go on.

Obviously ill at ease, Mei Ling said, "I must see—to sing my music."

Barb's curious gaze darted over Mei Ling's shoulder into the kitchen, seeking a libretto, sheet music, anything. "Where's your music?"

Mei Ling's hands made small circles in the air. "No music, I watch in mir' to see if I perform well." She nodded toward the mirror in the foyer.

Gently, Barb said, "But you were in the kitchen."

"Yes, yes, I want water." She placed a hand on her throat. "My voice, wants water."

Barb started walking toward the kitchen. "May I get it for you?"

"No, please." She pronounced it "prease," which Barb took as a further sign of her discomfort. "I finish now." She strode from the kitchen, slipped past Barb. Her footsteps beat a loud tattoo on the parquet floor as she hurried through the foyer.

Determined to find out why Mei Ling was here, Barb followed swiftly in her wake. "But you haven't finished practicing, have you?"

Over her shoulder, Mei Ling said, "Finished, finished, see you rater—later." She reached the door, flung it open, and without further words, ran out and closed it firmly behind her.

"Well if that's not the weirdest event of the day," Barb murmured to herself.

She turned, ran into the kitchen and glanced around her. As she'd thought. No water glass stood on the counter or in the sink. Could Mei Ling have washed the glass she'd used, then dried it and put it away? Maybe Mei Ling meant to say that she had just gone into the kitchen to get a glass of water and at that moment Barb had returned. She gave a small shrug. After all, Mei Ling was Lily's friend. She would give the woman the benefit of the doubt.

Shrugging off her jacket, she started down the hall to her bedroom. As she entered the room, she stopped short, stifling a gasp. Her new Gucci purse was lying on the seat of the white rattan armchair. She thought she'd left it on a shelf in her closet. She frowned, remembering. She *knew* she had, without a doubt.

She snatched up the purse and flipped it open. She slipped her fingers inside the side pocket where she kept a mirror and an extra lipstick, then inside the other side pocket where she'd tucked a notepad and pen. Both pockets were empty. She delved deeper inside the purse. Everything from the side pockets was bunched in the bottom of the purse. Nothing was missing. But then she had left nothing of value in her new purse. Her traveler's checks and Hong Kong dollars were in her shoulder bag.

Her mind seized on Mei Ling. Was Mei Ling a potential thief? Did she think Barb had changed a wad of traveler's checks into Hong Kong dollars and left some in her purse? Was this Mei Ling's way of collecting money for a Chinese opera troupe to tour the States? No, surely not. Barb wouldn't allow herself to think such thoughts of Lily's friend. But if not Mei Ling, who?

Suddenly she felt sick at heart. With an effort of will, she had put all thoughts of last Friday's intruder behind her, and now they came flooding back. A rush of anger surged through her. What was he after? she wondered. After his last search, he should have known she wouldn't leave her passport at home. Her passport identified her as a doctor. Maybe he was looking for drugs. Did some misguided fool think all Americans carried drugs with them? Possibly, but from what she had heard, they didn't need her to supply drugs. The thought crossed her mind that Mei Ling could be after the jade horse. She quickly dismissed it. No one would go to so much trouble to steal a carving worth one hundred dollars.

Angry, frustrated, she tossed her purse back up on the closet shelf, flung her jacket on a hanger, slammed the door, then stood staring out the picture window overlooking the harbor, trying to think what to do. There was no point in calling the police, that she knew. Should she call Lily at work? What good would that do? Standing here staring into space accomplished nothing.

She strode into the living room, crossed to the glass doors and yanked open the draperies. As sunshine streamed into the room, a flash of light caught her eye. She spun around and saw that a ray of sunlight was striking Lily's Swarovski crystal figurines. For a moment, she froze, staring at the figurines. Scowling, she murmured, "What's wrong with this picture?"

At the same moment she knew. They were all disarranged, all out of place. Had Rosa, the little Filipina maid, come today? Maybe, but even if she had, Lily never let her dust her collection. Further, the culprit couldn't be Rosa, for she had worked for Lily for more than three years and wouldn't dare risk losing her job. But Rosa could have sent a sub who wouldn't have known not to touch Lily's collection. Again, she toyed with the idea of calling Lily at work to set her mind at ease. But why get Lily in a snit? She would wait until she came home.

Nor could the culprit be Ah Fung, the maintenance man, for the man was a bundle of superstitions to whom the number four spelled disaster. Because Lily's flat was number four, on the fourteenth floor, he absolutely refused to enter the place unless Lily was here and the signs were right. Barb ran her hands through her hair as if to clear her mind. Who had Lily given a door key, other than Mei Ling? Mister Wonderful, the French chef? She

Dee Stuart

gave a hopeless shake of her head. Dear, naive Lily would trust a fox to watch a rabbit.

Thoughts of Lily's Mister Wonderful brought Steve to mind. Suddenly she needed to hear his voice, needed to hear his calm reassurance. She glanced at her watch. Eleven-thirty A.M. It would be ten-thirty P.M. back home. She picked up the white princess phone from the writing desk, snaked the cord over to the couch, then curled up in one corner and dialed Steve's number.

His deep, quiet voice flowing into her ear was as warm and smooth as honey. "Steve Lindsey here."

"Barb McKee here. What's happening?"

His tone turned loud, filled with good cheer. "Barb! Wonderful! I was just thinking about you."

Barb smiled. "First time today?"

"All the time, dumpling. I miss you like blazes, and especially after I close up the clinic, lonely time sets in."

Instead of her usual attempt to change the subject, or to convince him that being apart was a great idea, she said, "I miss you, too, Steve. Hong Kong has to be one of the most beautiful, exotic, exciting places in the world, and I love it; but I feel—oh—adrift. The truth is, without you, there's a big empty space in my life."

After a short silence in which Barb imagined Steve was mulling over her words, he said, "I'm glad to hear you miss me, darling, but it's so unlike you not to be springing onto your horse and riding off in all directions. What's going on over there?"

She hesitated. "You first."

"Well, we had two spays, filled with drama and excitement."

Instantly alarmed that one of her clients was in danger, she said, "What went wrong?"

"Nothing. I'm kidding. Dilsey forgot to refill the gas in surgery, but luckily for the patient, and for Dilsey, I checked before I started the spays. The spays were normal, routine, and they were the most exciting thing that's happened so far, except for a broken leg."

"Yours?"

"Nickie's—mini schnauser. Set the leg. Gave about a thousand shots. Diagnosed a heartworm, and a cushings, nothing mystifying. There is one little problem that I was going to put on hold till you got back, but the sooner you handle it, the better."

Here it comes, she thought, bracing herself, *a doggie disaster.* "Okay, let's hear it."

"Your X-ray machine konked out."

Barb felt as though her heart were sinking to her toes.

"We've been making do, carting patients that need X rays over to my clinic. I've had the guy out here to look at your machine, and there's no way he can fix it. A new one will set you back about twelve grand. Now don't worry, we'll keep on using my machine till you can replace yours."

Barb closed her eyes, as if to block out the devastating news. This expense, on top of the bank loan, with the hospital still struggling to attract new clients. She took a deep breath, trying to accept this news.

"Barb, are you still there?"

"Barely."

"Listen, sweetheart, it's not insurmountable. You can always snap up my offer and join in with me. I'd love to have you in my practice, you know that."

Her lips curved in a rueful smile. *My practice,* she thought. "My" was the key word.

Gently, she said, "Thanks, but no thanks. I've got to make it on my own. I just hope I can pay the rent next month."

"Look, I've got some money; I can lend you—"

"Steve, you're a lifesaver, and I love you for it; but try to understand. I still have to make it on my own."

"Okay. Have it your way. But look on the bright side. Maybe they'll let you charge the X-ray equipment on Visa or Master Charge. You know how you love those airline miles."

Even this happy thought failed to cheer her. "Is that it?"

Steve hesitated. "Not quite. But don't worry. We've taken care of it. It's all okay."

"What?" she almost shrieked. "What else?"

"Well, you probably didn't hear about it, but last week we had torrential rains here and all the creeks overflowed and . . ."

A choking sensation rose in her throat. "Don't tell me the hospital was flooded."

Silence hung heavy on the line.

"Steve?"

She heard a deep sigh. "I didn't want to tell you. Afraid it would spoil your holiday. We rented one of those vacs that suck up water and—and—" his words came out in a rush, "you'll only have to replace a few floor tiles."

A few tiles, she thought dispiritedly. After replacing the X-ray machine, what were a few tiles?

"Is that all?"

"That's it. Everything else is going swimmingly. No pun intended. How are things in the rice bowl?"

"Okay."

"Just okay?"

From his tone, Barb envisioned his dark brows lifting, a quizzical expression in his dark eyes.

"This morning I watched an acupuncture demonstration."

Steve hooted. "Do you believe a hyper chow or a Boston terrier will sit still while you jab it with needles?"

"It would work, Steve, I'm sure it would. There are fine electric needles you can use so the animal won't even feel it. Some techniques work if you find just the right pressure points. They would work with animals, but it isn't feasible for me to do it. It would take years of study to perfect them. The field is much more specialized than I realized. So I've decided to look further into homeopathic medicine."

Steve sounded baffled. "Why?"

"Oh, you know how some clients are. They're disillusioned with conventional medicine and demand an all-natural treatment."

"That's crazy. Scientists spend years and *beaucoup* bucks developing magic medicines to cure their animals, and they want herbs. Ridiculous."

"Not really. Homeopathic remedies boost the

body's defense mechanism against disease—activate the body's immune system. They're made from plants, minerals or animal products, and they're often very effective."

"Give me a for instance."

"Well, there's Addie, a yellow lab. She was in a car accident, slung from one side of the car to the other, suffered nerve damage and memory loss. Couldn't remember anything—how to bark, wag her tail, and could barely walk. I gave her a simple remedy made from chick-peas, and now she's nearly her old self again.

"Then there's Pablo the parrot, had all sorts of digestive problems till we put him on yogurt. And Fred, a black tomcat, had a mean skin condition, scratched and bit himself raw; we prescribed a remedy made from calcium sulfide, and he recovered after two visits."

"Okay, okay, I give. What else is new?"

"I had the horse appraised."

"And—?"

"It's worth about one hundred, U.S."

"Better than a stick in the eye," Steve said cheerfully.

"Right, but for me, it has sentimental value. It's a connection with Hal and his family. I like to think about his great grandad finding this little horse in China so long ago and bringing it back home, passing it down through the family. It gives me a sense of permanence and continuity. And the idea that it may have once belonged to an emperor is intriguing."

"Whoa, back up, lady. Earlier, before you flew

off to Hong Kong, you hoped it would be worth a few million, so in a few years you could chuck your rental space in the strip shopping center and build your own free-standing clinic."

Barb sighed. The dream seemed very far away. *"You* hoped it would be worth a few million. I had no reason to think the horse would be worth anything. The free-standing clinic idea was before the X-ray equipment broke down and the tiles floated away. Anyway, I'm not sure I want to sell the horse."

Enthusiastically, Steve said, "If you have to have a horse, that's the best kind."

Barb smiled to herself. He knew she loved horses. But Steve, a true biker, loved his Harley Davidson and was forever trying to talk her into letting him buy her a Harley Sportster so they could ride out on rallies together. Ignoring his comment, she said, "Another new thing: Yesterday Lily invited the t'ai chi coach and her neighbor the opera singer over for dim sum, also known as brunch."

"And . . . ?"

"They're both chomping at the bit to live in the U. S. of A."

"Isn't everyone?"

"But they're petrified of the Communist takeover and hell-bent on getting out."

"What about the t'ai chi coach? Is she Chinese, too?"

"Half-Chinese and half-Brit." Barb gave a light laugh. "Her name is Peter Chang."

"Oh? What's he look like?"

A mischievous glint came into her eyes. "Like

every girl's dream of happiness. Tall, tanned, muscular, jet black hair and eyes as clear and blue as the waters off Hawaii."

Steve's pleasant voice took on a sour note. "Sounds like an air-head."

"Far from it. According to Mei Ling, he's a gambling man, and most of the time comes off a winner. He likes to play the horses."

Steve's voice sharpened with disapproval. "Sounds dangerous."

"Oh, no. He couldn't be more charming."

Silence stretched from the other end of the line.

Barb jumped in. "There is something odd about Peter Chang, though. He says he wants to live in America, but he thinks immigration will be a problem. Maybe they don't give green cards to t'ai chi coaches."

There was another short silence. Then, with great conviction, Steve said, "I'd steer clear of him if I were you."

"Humm."

"Is that it for Hong Kong? No more intruders? You feel safe there?"

Hesitantly, she said, "I guess so."

His voice filled with concern. "Whaddya mean, you *guess* so? Is there something you're not telling me?"

She smiled to herself, envisioning protective, curly black hackles rising on the back of his neck. "Some strange man called and offered to buy the horse."

"And you turned him down?"

"I did. He offered one thou Hong Kong, and

when I said no, he immediately offered two thou HK. Made me suspicious."

"Anything else?"

"Well, it's probably nothing, but when I got home from acupuncture, Mei Ling was here and . . ."

"Mei Ling the Cantonese opera diva?"

"The same. Lily told me she had a key, so I suppose it was legit; but she said her electricity was off and she'd come down here to practice . . ." She let her voice trail off.

"Now tell me what you're not telling me."

"Mei Ling didn't have any music with her, and I think she went through my purse; and then I noticed that Lily's collection of figurines was all askew."

"Did you call the police?"

"Good heavens no. They would have been right over here, and I can't tell them I suspect one of Lily's best friends of—well, I don't even know what I suspect her of."

"What about Lily, did you call her? Maybe she could explain it."

"I'll tell her when she gets home, but I doubt she'd take kindly to my suggesting that her friend is a sneak-thief."

"Probably not. Could you chalk it up to curiosity? Maybe the diva wanted to see what the well-dressed American woman wears."

"Maybe. I hadn't thought of that."

"Nothing missing?"

"Not a thread. And it could be that Lily's maid was curious also—or a sub who didn't know not to touch Lily's collection came in to clean."

"Still, I'd keep an eye on Mei Ling."

"Do you think that whoever searched the place earlier was doing a rerun?"

"Not likely. In the first place, he—she wouldn't have known you'd be gone this morning. More importantly, since whatever he was looking for last time wasn't there, he has no reason to think it would be there this time. I think you've seen the last of him—or her."

She told him how Mei Ling had quickly snatched up the little jade horse, and how Peter Chang had held it in his hands, stroking it as if hating to let it go.

"They probably admire jade and were impressed with the horse."

She could feel her temperature rise. "Listen, Steve, it was more than that. I know it. I watched very carefully. You say I'm a good vet. Well, the reason is that I watch behavior, every detail, and that tells me what I need to know."

Good-naturedly, he said, "Yeah, yeah and you remember every detail, but I think you're tilting at windmills."

"You may be right. I hope so."

"Listen, dumpling, if anyone over there gives you trouble, any trouble at all, just call me and I'll be there."

She felt a rush of gratitude toward this man who was always there for her. Softly, she said, "I know you will, Steve, and I appreciate it; but Lily and I are having a blast."

They talked for several minutes more, until Barb

said, "Listen, Steve, this phone call is costing more than a free-standing clinic."

Earnestly, Steve said, "I know, but you're worth every penny."

By the time they hung up, Barb felt reassured and in control. Until Lily came home.

Nine

Barb waited till Lily had slipped off her beige jacket, sunk onto a jade green armchair and kicked off her shoes before she said, "Today when I got home from the acupuncture demo, Mei Ling was here."

Lily scowled. "I asked the manager to have a deadbolt put on the door, and he promised he would; but he said it would take a day or two. Meanwhile, anyone can walk right in. What was Mei Ling doing here?"

Barb kept her voice calm and even, devoid of suspicion.

"She said the electricity was off in her flat and she needed to see to practice her music."

Frowning, Lily cocked her head.

"All these flats are tied into the same power system. If the juice goes off in one, it goes off in all."

Barb's lips drew together in a moue. "So if it was off in Mei Ling's flat, it would have been off here, too."

Lily's brows rose, her tone defensive. "Do you think Mei Ling was lying?"

"I don't know what to think. Not only that, but I found my Gucci purse lying on the white wicker chair in my bedroom. I *know* I put it away on a shelf in the closet."

"Are you sure?"

"Positive. And—" her gaze shifted to the figures on the shelves—"your figurines have been moved."

Lily's head whipped around toward the glass shelves. "They look all right to me."

"I remember that all the taller carved mandarins stood on the back of the shelf. Now several have been moved toward the front. And your netsukes were arranged in pairs, facing each other. Now they all face forward."

Lily jumped up and strode to the shelves. "God, you have a memory like an—"

Barb threw out her hands in protest. "Please! Don't say it!"

Shaking her head, Lily stared at her collection. "You're right. But Mei Ling wouldn't have touched them, because she had no reason to. She's seen them all countless times."

Barb bit her lip, thinking, *Mei Ling could have been looking for a new addition to the collection,* and before she could stop herself, the words slipped out. "Could she have been looking for my jade horse?"

Lily spun around to face Barb. "Why should she? If she wanted to see it again, she knows all she has to do is ask."

"It crossed my mind that maybe she needs money . . ."

Lily gave an indignant shake of her head and in crisp tones said, "Mei Ling is no thief!" As if to reinforce her words, she crossed her arms across her chest and stared at Barb defiantly.

Quietly, Barb said, "Yesterday she told us she was collecting money to take an opera troupe on tour. Maybe she needs money to live here as well. People who are desperate sometimes do desperate things."

Lily slipped past Barb and returned to her seat on the armchair. "Mei Ling doesn't need money. She can afford to live here because she has a—a protector."

Barb crossed the room and sank down in the chair across from Lily. In calm tones, she asked, "Is that the same as a lover?"

"That and more. He supports Mei Ling in the manner to which she's become accustomed."

"Does he live with her?"

"Hardly. He's married, and holds a high-level job with the government."

Barb mulled over this news. "And where will his loyalties lie when Communist China takes over?"

Lily heaved a sigh. "I'm afraid, if he works with the Communist government, he'll have to go along with the party line, and Mei Ling's Cantonese opera might well be done away with. But even if it is, he'll still support her."

Barb started to say that if she were Mei Ling, she would be busy acquiring a nest egg in case her lover's loyalties changed, but the sound of a key turning in the door interrupted them.

Lily's hazel eyes sparkled with anticipation, and a happy smile lighted her face. "That has to be Andre."

She jumped up from her chair, ran to the door

and returned with her hand tucked in the crook of Andre's arm, gazing up at him with pure adoration.

As he smiled down into Lily's eyes, Barb surveyed him swiftly. Hair, black as night, parted and combed to one side; ruddy cheeks that bespoke a glow of good health; sculpted lips parted in a wide smile that revealed sparkling white teeth. His black turtleneck sweater worn over black slacks gave him a rakish air. Now he leaned forward and kissed the tip of Lily's ear. Totally composed, the man exuded a presence that completely filled the room.

Wow, Barb thought, *the guy is dynamite. "Swave and debonner," as we used to say back in our old college days. No wonder Lily is mad about him.*

At last Lily tore her gaze from Andre's and nodded toward Barb. "This is Barb, my one and only soul sister. Barb, Andre Durand."

He stepped forward and, looking straight into her eyes, clasped her hand in a warm, firm grip, bent his head and deposited a light kiss just below her wrist. In a charmingly accented voice as smooth as French silk, he said, *"Enchante, madame."*

With an effort Barb resisted snatching her hand from his grasp. She hadn't expected to be deluged with all this savoir faire. "My pleasure."

"Andre cooking dinner for us tonight is a busman's holiday, really, since Monday is his night off," Lily said. "And, he's brought us gifts as well." She dashed into the foyer and returned bearing a bouquet of white, yellow and rust chrysanthemums swathed in green tissue in one arm, and a box of candy in the other. As she handed Barb the candy, Andre gave her a broad smile, and said, "For you."

Barb felt a wave of mingled surprise and pleasure. "How thoughtful. Thanks so much."

"I hope you like French chocolates."

"I'm sure. Non-caloric?"

Andre laughed. "I make no promises." Though his dark eyes swept the length of her tall, trim figure, there was nothing sensuous in his gaze. "But you need not worry about calories."

He turned to Lily and gently lifted the flowers from her arms. "Let me take care of these for you."

He strode into the kitchen and returned with a tray of aperitifs in finely etched crystal glasses along with an assortment of small crackers. He set the tray down on the table between the jade chairs. "I want you to hear a Chinese melody, a favorite of Lily's and mine, 'Fishing Junks at Sunset.' "

He crossed to the CD player, selected a disk from the wooden case, slipped it in the slot and turned the player on.

All thought was driven from her mind as the music flowed around them, wonderfully sweet, haunting, and infinitely sad, that touched some responsive chord deep within her. She felt a sudden rush of longing, of missing Steve. Totally caught up in the music, neither Barb nor Lily protested when Andre insisted they sit in the living room and sip their aperitifs while he prepared dinner.

When the song ended, Barb asked lightly, "Did Andre learn to cook at his mama's knee?"

"No, he studied at the Cordon Bleu in Paris and later went to a famous chef's training school in Switzerland. He worked for several years in Paris, then last year, when the Hong Kong Crown opened, they hired him as master chef. But his dream of happiness is to open a restaurant of his own. He finds cooking tremendously creative, and he loves to try out new recipes to serve at La Parisienne."

Barb took a deep breath. "I smell wonderful things brewing in the kitchen."

Lily nodded knowingly. "You can bet he leaves the galloping gourmet standing at the starting gate. Does Steve like to cook?"

Barb grinned. "Steve needs detailed directions to boil water. Does Andre cook for you often?"

There was a long pause while Lily took another sip of her drink, picked up a cracker, took a bite and munched it thoughtfully. At last she said, "Only when he's off duty."

"Every Monday night?"

Lily nodded. "Normally, he goes to work at ten in the morning, comes home at one, then goes back at six and gets home about one or one-thirty in the morning."

"Has he by any chance mentioned the 'M' word?"

Lily gave a vigorous shake of her head. "Neither of us is ready for marriage right now."

Barb respected Lily's privacy too much to delve into the reasons they weren't ready for marriage. Instead, she asked, "How long has he lived here?"

"Actually, he moved in long before—before we fell in love. You see, Andre's grandfather and mine were distant cousins. So when he came to Hong Kong, he looked me up. Rents are so high here that no one can afford to live in a place like this on one salary. The only reason I can afford it is because the insurance company gave me a whopping settlement when my folks were killed and I inherited a sizeable chunk from their estate. I told Andre he was welcome to stay here till he found a place to live."

Barb's eyes opened wide. "And he never left?"

Lily shook her head, and a look of such happiness suffused her face that Barb didn't dare ask the questions swirling around in her mind: Was Andre truly in love with Lily? Or was the man an opportunist with an eye out for the main chance? Either way, she had no doubt that Andre Durand knew a gold mine when he found it.

Shortly, Andre summoned them to the dining room. Candlelight shed a soft, golden glow over the gleaming rosewood table and the colorful chrysanthemums Andre had arranged as a centerpiece. The dinner began with clear water crab, followed by a cold dish, slivers of chicken breast on noodles with a fiery sauce. Dipping into it, Barb exclaimed, "This sauce is perfection. What is it?"

Smiling, Andre said, "The dish is called *peng-peng-chi,* with a chili and sesame sauce."

This was followed by *kung-pao ta hsia,* palace guard big shrimp, accompanied by steamed rice, Chinese kale, baby ears of corn called jade sprouts, and a clear soup.

Though Andre politely included Barb in the conversation, throughout the meal his attention never strayed from Lily. His grace and charm never faltered. His speech, tinged with a soft French accent, was music to the ears. No wonder Lily hung on his every word. *Lily is blooming,* Barb thought to herself. *No pun intended.*

After dinner they adjourned to the living room, where Andre served small glasses of cognac. He sat on the couch at Lily's side with his right ankle crossed over his left knee. Though he appeared totally relaxed, Barb noticed that his right foot jerked up and down spasmodically. She also noticed that although he sipped his cognac continuously, he took only tiny sips and actually consumed very little. A man who likes to keep his wits about him, she decided, a man who likes to be in control.

They chatted amiably. Lily told how Andre had climbed the ladder of chefdom to five-star restaurants in Paris, and how a devoted clientele followed wherever he went. "And more than a few," she said proudly, "seek out the restaurant where he is chef whenever they visit Hong Kong."

Andre waved a hand in airy dismissal. "You give me too much credit."

Smiling, Lily placed a hand over his and gave it a squeeze. "At least no one has ever told you, *'Wu ku pu fen.'*" Turning to Barb, she said, "That means you can't tell wheat, sesame, barley, beans and rice from each other."

"Is that a cardinal sin?"

Solemnly, Andre said, "The worst sin of all. Anyone who cannot tell these grains apart, much less name them, is the ultimate blockhead."

Laughing, Barb said, "I hope you won't put me to the test." And in spite of herself, she felt her skepticism of Andre fade.

Lily and Andre both questioned Barb about her practice, and Lily asked eagerly for news of her family. Barb filled her in on her parents, her brother

Hank, and his wife Amy, and their daughter Anna Lee.

"That's it," said Barb smiling. "Now you know as much about them as I do."

For a moment everyone fell silent. Then, without preamble, Lily burst out, "Barb, you must show Andre your horse."

"A horse? That I must see," said Andre enthusiastically.

Lily snapped her fingers in a gesture of mild vexation.

"Oh, I forgot. You were going to put it in a safe-deposit box today."

"No problem. I went to the acupuncture demo; then I wanted to hurry back here to call Steve to tell him about it. Meanwhile Mei Ling showed up, so I forgot, too. Besides, it really isn't valuable enough to warrant stashing away in a box."

Barb fetched the horse and once again unwrapped it from the white bubble bedding and handed it to Andre.

For a long moment he looked at it in silence. His eyes narrowed as he scrutinized it more closely. Inexplicably, Barb had the eerie feeling that he was searching for something to say, other than what he was thinking.

At last, he said, "It is very beautiful. May I ask where you bought it?"

"Oh, I didn't buy it; it was given to me." She thought she saw a flicker of disappointment in his eyes that vanished so quickly she wasn't positive it had really been there. Had he hoped to buy one like it for himself?

Lily, unable to contain herself, said, "Barb's husband's great grandfather brought it back from China in the thirties, and it's been passed down through generations of his family."

Andre nodded, still staring down at the recumbent horse resting in the palm of his hand. "I see."

"Andre," Lily scolded lightly, "You could show a little more enthusiasm. Do you think it's a fake?"

"No, no. I only thought, that is, I think I recognize it."

"How could you?"

He gazed up at the ceiling as if to find the answer to her question written there. "I think, perhaps I've seen one in a museum in Paris. The French once conducted archeological missions in China in the early nineteen hundreds and brought back artifacts to France. Now, seeing what looked to be the identical carving took my breath away." He held the horse up before his eyes, turning it slowly on his palm, full circle. "I do admire it, profusely."

Abruptly, he set it down on the table, as if anxious to be rid of it, and became very busy pulling a pack of Camel cigarettes from his shirt pocket, shaking out a cigarette, fumbling in the pocket of his slacks, finding a lighter and lighting up.

She felt disappointed. If he thought he recognized it, why not tell her so? At the same time she had a gut feeling that he knew a great deal more about Chinese artifacts than he was telling. But why not share what he knew? And now, after his first lackluster reaction, came his surprising admission that he "admired it profusely." Was this a way to ingratiate himself with her? To win her good graces, to make a favorable impression for Lily's sake?

Crossly, she thought, *You bet I'm impressed. Andre Durand is too perfect. Too smooth. He makes all the right moves.* She stopped, backtracked. What was wrong with her? She should admire his enthusiasm, his ambition, his determination to get ahead, to own his own restaurant. Wasn't that her dream, too? To own her own free-standing clinic? Why was she downgrading Lily's lover? Was it simply the contrast between Andre with his Continental manner and her rough-and-ready, laid-back Steve that made her question his sincerity, made her wonder whether he loved Lily for herself or her income? Surely the devil made her think such thoughts. Firmly she put them from her mind.

Shortly after eleven Barb announced that she was going to bed. Smiling at Andre, she said, "I enjoyed meeting you, Andre, and good night all." As she made her way down the hall to her room, Lily followed her.

Hurriedly, she whispered, "Do you have any objection to Andre staying here?"

"Of course not." Barb flung an arm around her shoulders and gave her a quick hug. "I knocked off deciding what was best for you when we were in college, remember?"

Lily grinned. "That wasn't all bad. You were there for me when I needed you."

"And now you're here for me."

Once in bed, Barb heard Lily and Andre moving about the flat as they settled in for the night. The music on the CD ceased. The lock on the front door clicked into place. She heard hushed voices, then the sound of Lily's bedroom door softly closing.

Sleepless, keyed up after an evening of aperitifs, a gourmet dinner with wine, after-dinner cognac and the heady presence of Andre, she could feel the adrenaline coursing through her veins. Or was it the cognac? In the stillness, she lay on her back, reviewing the evening: her first astonished impression of Andre as he swept into the flat exuding charm, dinner prepared to perfection, Andre's interest in her clinic—and her jade horse. And then she remembered. She had left the horse lying on the coffee table in the living room.

Quietly she slipped from her bed and flung on her red terry housecoat. She eased her door open, cringing as the hinges gave a slight squeak. Barefoot, she tiptoed soundlessly down the hall, through the foyer into living room. The room was awash with a pale orange glow rising from the jungle of garish neon lights in the city below. Though the sleeping horse lay where she had left it, the clear bubble plastic was gone. Barb smiled to herself. Meticulous Lily strikes again! The paper was probably in the trash in the kitchen.

She picked up the horse and nestled it in her pocket, then padded into the kitchen and flipped on the light. Glasses, dishes and silver were stacked neatly on the counter. She crossed to the sink and pulled out the white plastic trash can from the cabinet below. Frowning, she gazed down at the contents. A corner of clear bubble plastic was sticking out from under a mess of shrimp and crab shells, leftovers from the scraped dinner plates, and coffee grounds. She shoved the trash can back under the sink. She would find another bed for the horse.

She felt a sudden thirst—all that seafood, she thought. She found a clean glass, filled it with water. Standing there, sipping the water, she thought about washing up the dishes. She hated to leave dirty dishes. So did Lily. Barb smiled to herself. Clearly, when Lily was faced with doing the dishes or hitting the sack with Andre, there was no contest. Barb's gaze flicked over the counter, the toaster, the coffee-pot, the mixer, the canisters containing flour, sugar, tea, coffee, and the big glass apothecary jars of rice and noodles. The kitchen didn't look all that bad. Her natural optimism won out. She'd feel much more like washing up in the morning. The problem was finding something in which to wrap the horse.

Quietly, she pulled open drawers and cupboards, looking for plastic bags or paper towels. Then struck with an idea, she lifted the lid from the big-gest apothecary jar and reached inside. With one hand she dug a well in the noodles. With the other, she grabbed the horse and, lowering it inside the jar, covered it over and replaced the lid. If anyone were searching for her horse, she hoped this was one place they would never think to look. She flicked off the light and padded back through the dining room, the foyer, and down the hall.

As she neared her room, she glanced at Lily's door. Her dark brows drew together in a frown. It appeared to be open a crack. Had Lily opened the door to let air circulate? It would have to be open wider than that to make any difference. At the door-way of her bedroom, she glanced over her shoulder and froze. From the corner of her eye, she saw Lily's door slowly, silently, close. She felt her skin crawl. Had Lily's door been ajar when she left her room to go to the kitchen? Had someone been standing there watching her, waiting to see if she returned with her horse in hand? She bolted into her room, closed the door and locked it.

Ten

Barb started at the sound of a loud, sharp crack. A gunshot. Or had a door slammed shut? Lily's door, blown closed? Or a door closed sharply by someone who didn't want to be seen? She opened her eyes. It was not pitch-black night, as she had thought. Sunlight billowed through the window. What looked like a toy plane flew straight across her line of vision. An indignant horn sounded, demanding the right of way in the busy harbor. The clink of china and silver echoed down the hall.

She slid out of bed, flung on her red terry robe and hurried into the kitchen. Lily, hands deep in soapsuds, stood at the sink washing up.

"Hey, I was going to do drudge duty after you left this morning." She nudged Lily's hip with her own. "Let me take over friend, or you'll be late for work."

Lily refused to budge. "Not to worry. Today's a national holiday and the bank is closed. No work for me."

"Good. If we hurry, we can make t'ai chi."

"Oh, I forgot to tell you. There was a notice downstairs in the lobby that t'ai chi classes have been temporarily postponed till further notice."

"Is Pete taking a vacation?"

Lily shrugged. "Probably won a few dollars and went to Macau to gamble big time, and lose them."

Barb grabbed a towel and a crystal glass. "What about Andre?"

"Gone. Big day at the feed bag."

So Andre must have slammed the door that had awakened her. She started to ask Lily who had been watching her through the crack in the doorway last night, then thought better of it.

If Lily had been watching, it was probably to reassure herself that everything was okay—no need to make a big deal of wandering around in the night. If it had been Andre, no way was Barb going to tattle on him.

Instead, she said, "Sorry he can't join us, but this means we'll have the entire day to sightsee. Right?" Barb grabbed another glass and polished it to a sheen.

"Wrong. Listen, Barb, I've been thinking about that old fortune-teller who told us your horse could be priceless. Well, I think we need another appraisal."

Barb laughed. "You've lived here too long. You really are becoming as superstitious as the Chinese."

"Maybe, but the old guy has been around a long time, seen a lot. He might know more than we think. *I* think it's worth another look." She shot Barb a sidelong glance. "Besides, as you so often say, it never hurts to have a second opinion."

Barb shook her head. "I can't argue with that. I give."

Privately, she told herself she had given in not because of the old fortune-teller's prediction, but because Andre had said he'd seen her jade horse in a museum in Paris. If he had seen an exact replica in a museum, the horse could be of some value, or no one would have thought it worth copying.

Lily slid the last plate in the rack, dumped the sudsy dishwater and dried her hands on a towel.

"One of the curators at Asia House, Museum of Chinese Antiquities, is a friend of mine. I'll give him a call—ask him to do lunch and take a look at it."

"Great. Be my guests."

While Lily called her friend, Barb rescued the horse from the noodle jar, dusted it off, and put it in her purse.

Shortly after noon, Barb and Lily alighted from the double-decker tram and amid a cacophony of bells and horns ambled uphill to Stanley Street. Surprisingly few people walked the dark, narrow street bordered by old, dilapidated buildings. Halfway down the block Lily stopped before a doorway that boasted new-looking double wooden doors with leaded glass windows and shiny brass trim.

Lily pulled one of the doors open. "Here we are. One of the oldest and best tea houses in Hong Kong."

They stepped inside a small foyer. Beyond the foyer in the dining room Barb glimpsed stained-glass panels on the walls, and dark wooden tables with straight-backed chairs. Wooden ceiling fans whirred softly overhead.

They were met by the harried, black-suited Chinese host who told them there were no tables left downstairs. Maybe they could be seated upstairs. He nodded toward a stairway on their left.

In fluent Cantonese Lily told him they were awaiting Professor Felix Fais and to please send him upstairs when he arrived.

A babble of dissonant voices greeted them as they climbed the stairs and stood waiting to be seated before an imposing gilt statue of Buddha in a wall niche. The host led them to a small wooden table with four wooden chairs. A white-coated waiter brought chopsticks wrapped in paper, a china spoon, plates, cups and glasses of water.

To Barb's astonishment, Lily immediately asked for a bowl of hot water. Moments later, the waiter set it down before her. Barb looked on aghast as Lily dipped her cup, chopsticks, spoon and china plate in the metal bowl of hot water then began to dry them on her napkin.

Smiling, Lily glanced up at her. "You needn't be so surprised. This is an old Chinese custom, to always wash your teacups and chopsticks with tea or hot water." She pushed the bowl toward Barb. "You?"

Barb said, "I'll take my chances. I figure I'm immune to just about everything by now. Tell me about your curator."

As she spoke, Lily's face brightened with enthusiasm. "He's a specialist in Oriental art, a collector of jade, a former professor at the university and extremely knowledgeable. I went to a few of his seminars when I first came to Hong Kong. He's

Chinese, but fluent in several languages, including English."

Having finished drying her dinnerware, she leaned to one side, peering over Barb's shoulder. "Here he is now." She gave a little wave.

Barb turned and saw a short, fat, bald man with a round face adorned with a thin mustache that trailed down each side of his mouth. His lips turned up at the corners in what appeared to be a perpetual smile. He wore a black and beige, diamond-patterned silk shirt that gaped open between buttons straining at the buttonholes.

When the waiter showed him to their table he lowered himself onto the chair beside Lily. Introductions over, he drew from his pocket a flat, gray-green stone which he rubbed between his fingers and thumb. Barb could scarcely keep from staring at the oddly shaped stone.

Evidently noting her interest in his talisman, Professor Fais smiled and said, "This fragment is half of an ancient axe head. Because it's broken, it's of no value, but I enjoy the satiny texture. There's a certain thrill, you see, that jade conveys when you handle it."

Lily broke in. "I've been giving Barb your credentials, and I've assured her you know all about jades."

His smile expanded, and his eyes narrowed to slits, reminding Barb of a laughing Buddha she'd seen at Dong Po MacGregor's Antiquities.

Barb smiled. "You specialize in jade, then?"

"It is the love of my life."

"In the States, we don't hold jade in as high esteem as you do in China."

"I'm not so sure," Professor Fais said pleasantly. "I have visited America and seen Mr. Gump's collection in California, and Oriental collections in the Fogg Art Museum in Cambridge, Massachusetts, the Nelson Gallery in Kansas City, and the Freer Gallery in Washington, D.C. They were most impressive. And now I believe I know all there is to know about jade." He resumed caressing his fingering piece.

Barb thought if he'd been trying to convince her that he knew honest jade when he saw it, he had succeeded.

An elderly waiter handed them large burgundy Leatherette menus with several pages of choices and accompanying color photographs. As Barb sat studying the pictures, the waiter tapped three or four items with his knuckles and spoke rapidly in Cantonese. Though she couldn't understand the words, she understood that this was what he thought she should order and this was what he would serve.

Lily and Professor Fais gave their orders, and before long the waiter wheeled a cart of dim sum in bamboo baskets to their table. He also brought a pot of black tea, which he poured into handleless cups. He lifted the lids from the bamboo baskets that contained steamed beef balls in watercress, rice wrapped in lotus leaves, steamed chicken buns, steamed barbecued pork buns, fried spring rolls, shrimp dumplings and other dim sum delicacies.

Barb, determined not to let the chopsticks get the better of her, clutched them between her fingers and thumb and attacked her dim sum. She managed to capture the little dumplings somewhat easier than before, but not much.

Throughout the meal Professor Fais couldn't have been more cordial. His obvious pleasure in meeting Lily's friend belied the myth of the inscrutable Chinese. He was as pleasant and outgoing as any man Barb had ever met.

As they lingered over cups of hot, fragrant tea, Barb began to wonder if they would ever get to the point of the luncheon. Lily had warned her that she must wait for the professor to broach the subject of the jade horse, that it would not be polite to appear too forward. With an effort of will, she held her tongue.

At last Professor Fais said, "You have a jade figure you wish to show me?"

"Yes, I have it here with me." She delved deep in her black leather purse and brought out the horse.

At the sight of the figure his head jerked back as though he had been struck a blow by an unseen hand. His face paled. The jade talisman slid from his fingers and fell with a clatter onto the tabletop.

Grasping the small horse with both hands, as if fearing he would drop it, he held it up to catch the feeble glow shed from a translucent ceiling light, then tilted his head back and gazed at it as if from a great distance. His dark eyes gleamed, and his plump fingers trembled as he turned it this way and that as if studying the form.

As his fingers caressed the surface, Lily whispered to Barb, "He's looking for flaws, fractures, or places where it may have been repaired."

Professor Fais glanced at Lily. "I'd have to see it in natural light to examine it properly. And of course there are tests to be made, to assure authenticity."

He looked again at the horse, then dipped the index finger of his right hand into his glass of water and gently rubbed the horse's rump, leaving a clear, satiny circle. His expression turned solemn, his voice grave.

"I cannot say for certain until I make proper tests, but this appears to be a sculpture from the Sung dynasty, A.D. 960 to 1279, possibly a burial jade preserved in a tomb."

"Is that good?" Barb asked. "Being so ancient— an antique jade?"

"Age is not a factor in determining value." His thin brows rose in question. "We do not treasure old diamonds more than new, do we?"

"No," Barb agreed, "I guess not."

"It is the shape and color that are important." He cradled the horse almost fondly in his left hand, stroking it as if it were a live pet.

"Why do the Chinese consider jade to be so special?" Barb asked.

"We believe that jade is a link between earth and heaven, a bridge from this life on earth to immortality. It has a place in all of our religions: Confucians, Taoists, Buddhists all accord it special powers. So it is known as the 'Stone of Heaven.' "

With a bright smile, Lily said, "The lines are so clean and simple, it could pass for a contemporary carving."

Professor Fais frowned slightly. "Another misconception. The word 'carving' implies a method of cutting or chipping away as a sculptor does with marble. Jade 'carvings' are actually drilled and ground, with the use of water and an abrasive such as Carborundum. Centuries ago, craftsmen cut jade with water, sand and a piece of string."

Lily asked, "Do you think the horse is real jade?"

"Ah, *real* jade." Still cradling the horse in his hands, he leaned back in his chair and squeezed his eyes shut, as if in deep concentration. "I cannot be completely sure." His lips spread in a broad smile.

"Many of today's artists are masters at carving look-alikes. And many objects are said to be jasper jade when they are actually jasper, or an opaque quartz. Or they are called colored jade, which is actually dyed jade; or pink jade which is dyed quartz. Mexican jade is dyed onyx and India jade is a green quartz. Or, sellers will say an object is Soochow jade when Soochow is merely the city where it was made."

Barb, listening with avid interest, set down her chopsticks and leaned toward the professor. "So it's very easy to mistake a fake for the real thing."

"Unfortunately, that is so. There are but two true jades. One is nephrite, a silicate of magnesium, that looks almost soapy. This is the older stone that is as ancient as the history of China, and known as antique jade. It is the hardest of the two, the world's toughest stone. The other is jadeite, an aluminum silicate. Jadeite is the most brilliant of the two stones."

"Lily told me they both come in all colors of the rainbow."

Professor Fais popped a shrimp dumpling into his mouth, but clearly unwilling to give up the podium, kept on talking and chewing.

"So they do, and they are named after animals, vegetables and minerals. There is chicken bone, kingfisher, bamboo, moss, melon, rose, and spinach jade as well as emerald, ivory, pearl and sapphire. Pure jade, of course, is white. It is the other minerals in the stone that give it its color."

"When was jadeite first discovered in China?" Barb asked.

"Jadeite, which comes from Burma, was not used in China until 1784. The strange thing is that as far as we know, no jadeite was ever found in China. It is thought to have been brought from Central Asia."

"Fascinating," Barb said. "Such a romantic, mystical stone."

"You may enjoy perusing a book on Chinese sculpture during the Han dynasty which was written by Edouard Chavannes in 1893. Also, between 1905 and 1915, he issued a three volume report on the French archeological mission in Northern China."

Something clicked in the back of Barb's mind. Andre had mentioned French archeological missions in China. Had one of his ancestors taken part in this expedition? Was this why he seemed so interested in Chinese sculpture?

"Yes," Barb said, "I'd like to read them, especially about the French archeological mission." She held out her hand toward Professor Fais. "May I have the horse, please?"

With obvious reluctance, he set the horse down on the table between them and leaned toward her.

"Miss LeMaitre mentioned that you would like an appraisal. All I can tell you is that if it is as I think it is, and I won't know absolutely until I subject it to a methylene iodide test, it would be worth about twenty-five thousand dollars United States currency."

Lily's eyes had the glazed look of a knight who's seen the holy grail. In a hushed, breathless voice she murmured, "Twenty-five thousand! I can't believe my own ears."

Barb stared at the roly-poly professor as if he'd told her the Red Sea had parted. Stunned, she couldn't speak beyond a whisper. *"Twenty-five thousand American dollars?"*

"Correct. Depending on who wants to acquire it. A dealer may pay much less. However, I'm certain we can offer you an acceptable price."

Barb did a double take. *"We?"*

Professor Fais gave her a long, level look. "My museum, of course."

"But I haven't decided to sell it."

He jerked his head toward Lily, glaring at her. His tone turned hard and hostile. "Wasn't that why you asked me for an appraisal, because your friend was planning to sell the sculpture?"

Lily looked distressed. "I'm afraid there's a misunderstanding." She paused, and when no one spoke, babbled on. "I wasn't positive she'd sell it, but I thought, that is, I was sure she'd sell it if she could get a decent price for it. Her dream of happiness is to build her own free-standing clinic instead of renting space and—"

"Lily!" Barb shook her head warningly. "Cool

it. We don't know for sure that it's real jade, and even if it should turn out to be worth *muy* bucks, we don't have a definite offer. So we can't make any decisions now. Even if it is worth that much I'm still not sure I want to sell it."

Professor Fais' face turned choleric red. His eyes bulged. Barb felt herself shrinking under his ill-concealed rage and resentment.

"Not want to sell it! This is outrageous, unconscionable! You *gwailos* have been stealing artifacts from our country for more than one hundred years, and now when you have an opportunity to return one to its rightful place, you speak of taking it home to America."

Barb felt her hackles stand at attention. Quietly, firmly, she said, "Professor Fais, it *is* my horse. My late husband's great grandfather bought and paid for it at the price asked at the time."

"Your late husband's great grandfather was no more than a tomb robber," he hissed. "A-a pirate!"

Barb bit back a furious reply and, in a voice that would cut jade, said, "He was an honorable man. You forget that in those days, years before your countrymen began to care about what happened to your antiquities, visitors were permitted to take artifacts out of your country."

Angrily, he leaned toward her, both hands knotted into fists on the edge of the table. "It is not as though we are not offering to pay you a fair price for the figure."

Coldly, she said, "Officially, you have made no offer."

Once again he glared at Lily, and rising to his

feet said, "I am sorry, Miss LeMaitre, but I do not think your friend and I have proper communication." He shoved his chair back, made a perfunctory bow, swept up his jade talisman and as swiftly as his bulk would allow, stormed from the room.

Miserably, Barb said, "I'm sorry as blazes, Lil, but his wild, out-of-sight appraisal threw me for a loop, and then, on top of that, his tentative offer to buy . . ."

Lily shrugged and threw out her hands in a helpless gesture.

"Forget it. The man's entire life revolves around jade. He's a collector himself. He thought he had the find of the century, so he overreacted. Not only is the horse a great piece of work, it would be a giant feather in his cap if he could acquire it for the museum's collection."

Ruefully, Barb said, "I wish he'd put it through his tests. Maybe it's worth nothing more than a curio, and then his museum wouldn't want it. Now the man won't even speak to me."

"He's noted for being more than a little stubborn. Give him a few days and he'll be back. He has to be darn sure it's worth the price, and you can bet your bottom dollar he won't be able to resist asking you to let him test it to see if it's the real McCoy."

Suddenly one of the hardest rocks in the world seemed very fragile. Carefully, gently, Barb picked up the horse and tucked it back inside her shoulder bag.

"Remember telling the fortune-teller we were going to put it in a safe-deposit box? I've decided that's not such a bad idea. How about we drop by the bank and stash it away?"

"Fine with me," Lily said, "but today is still a national holiday and the bank is still closed."

"Tomorrow, then, for sure."

"For sure."

All the way back to the flat they discussed the professor and his incredible reactions both to the carving itself and to his criticism of Barb's ethics, keeping it from its country of origin. But nothing could dim her elation over the value of the horse.

Once inside Lily's flat, Barb made a beeline for the phone and called Steve.

In a voice fogged with sleep, he shouted, "What, what? Oh, Barb, it's you! What's wrong? Tell me. Are you all right?"

"Of course I'm all right!"

"Then why are you calling me at one-thirty in the A.M.?"

"Have I got something to tell you! But I'll call back in the morning—"

"Wait! Hold it! Don't hang up! Lay it on me, Doc."

"You want to bet on a sure thing? Well, my little sleeping curio is worth twenty-five thousand American greenbacks."

"Oh, oh, oh!"

"Why are you howling like a wolf? Is that all you can say?"

"I'm trying to catch my breath."

"Hurry."

"All I can say is, it'll go a helluva long way toward paying off your debts and building your own free-standing hospital."

Barb felt herself tensing up. Her fingers tightened on the receiver. "Whoa. Hold it. I have a three-year lease on the storefront and owe everybody and his brother, plus the cost of the new X-ray machine. Can't you understand? I feel as if I'm drowning in debt. Twenty-five thou won't be a drop in the bucket. My dream of a free-standing clinic seems light years away."

In a sleep-fogged voice, he drawled, "I know that. But selling the horse would at least put you on an even keel, keep you from going under, bordering on panic."

In exaggeratedly patient tones, Barb said, "I am not bordering on panic. What you are failing to take into account is that my practice is growing, and growing fast. If you want to get anywhere, you have to take risks. I'm gambling on the future, hoping I'm a good enough vet to establish a solid list of clients. If so, they will keep me solvent. You talk as if I'm always going to be teetering on the brink of bankruptcy."

"I don't mean to, but statistics show that no vet makes money the first three years."

"I'll be happy to break even."

"Selling the horse would help."

Barb could almost feel a stubborn streak kicking in. "I'm not sure I want to sell it. Anyway, I'm not ready to make a decision."

Steve's tone turned crusty. "Are you out of your mind?"

Defensively, Barb said, "The horse has sentimental value."

In tones Barb knew Steve meant to be placating, but came off sounding patronizing, he said, "You have me for sentimental value."

More sharply than she intended, she said, "Why didn't I think of that?"

Softly, Steve said, "Barb, let's not argue. I'll always be there for you, you must know that."

"I do, I do know it, Steve."

"Good. And it's great news, stupendous that the horse is genuine jade. Let me know what you decide. I mean, if you decide to keep the animal."

"Speaking of animals?"

"Yes, well, today we had a doosie. This woman walks in with a border collie, bitten days ago by a neighbor's dog. We'll have to do surgery after the swelling goes down. I think we can save her."

"If anyone can, you can. Did you take pictures?"

"You bet, and gave some to the client in case the attack dog's owner refuses to pay."

"Good show, Steve. I'm going to hang up now. Let you get your beauty sleep."

"Listen, Barb, I'm serious. I'm not convinced that the break-in the other night is the end of this business. I don't go with the passport theory. There are much easier ways to swipe passports. I'm not convinced you and Lily are safe. What about her friend Andre? Is he on the spot?"

"Uh, well, some of the time. He has odd hours, working at the Parisienne. But Lily's asked the manager to put a dead bolt on the door and install a burglar alarm, so we'll be fine."

"All the same, I want you to be careful. Okay?"

"Yes, sir! Sir!"

"Love you, Barb."

"Love you, too, Doc. Nite, nite."

Unaccountably, after talking with Steve, she felt that all was right with her world. She could handle anything.

Eleven

Barb had just hung up the phone when Lily strolled into the living room with what appeared to be tickets in hand.

"Do you want to go to the opera tonight?"

"Do I want to go to the opera? Do I ever!"

Barb, seated before Lily's Chippendale writing desk, swiveled around in her chair.

"I love opera, have always loved opera."

Lily waved the tickets under Barb's nose. "Mei Ling dropped these in my box in the lobby—comps to the dinner theater where she sings. But this is nothing like the German, French and Italian operas you're used to seeing. So are you sure you want to go?"

"Are you sure she meant the tickets for you and me and not you and Andre?"

"Sure. She told me last Sunday she thought you might like to see a Cantonese opera performance and she'd drop the tickets in my mailbox. I'd forgotten about it until today. Besides, she knows Andre hates Cantonese opera. If only he'd take time to understand it, I think he'd like it, but he says he's too busy. It's unique, like no other opera you've ever seen. They bill it as a cultural experience, and it is."

"Sounds right up my alley. And since Mei Ling was nice enough to give us the tickets, it would be a shame not to use them." Privately, she thought it would be a relief to be gone from the flat tonight to escape any more menacing phone calls.

Lily smiled. "Right. Dinner's at six, the show at eight-thirty."

With nightfall, a brisk wind swept down from the north, and Barb pulled her blue blazer more closely around her and glanced at her watch. Quarter of six. The Dynasty Theatre Restaurant was ablaze with lights. The porte cochere, supported by tall crimson columns, sheltered the entrance lavishly decorated in crimson and gold. Mingling with the crowd of people flowing through arched doorways, Barb and Lily entered the elegant theater.

They mounted a shallow marble staircase and crossed the red-carpeted lobby into a huge, square room, bordered on three sides by a low balcony. At the far end stood a massive stage. Orange lanterns like giant pumpkins suspended from the ceiling shed a golden glow over the diners. A sea of white cloth-covered tables in blocks of eight arranged in crescent formation spread out before them. The host led them to a table for four, center front on the balcony.

Barb's attention was immediately drawn to the stage, where three young girls in flowing pastel gowns were playing a bamboo flute and three-string guitars. The music, in a minor key, high-pitched and dissonant, sounded strange and exotic, as beautiful in its own way as her favorites, Mozart and Beethoven. A small thrill of excitement tingled down her spine.

Once seated, the host invited them to visit the buffet table set up on the balcony. At the head of the table sat a giant-size, white papier-maché dragon's head, from whose mouth flowed a cascade of greens.

Lily and Barb picked up plates and moved slowly down the line of diners helping themselves from a colorful array of food that resembled photos in a gourmet magazine: hot casseroles, a selection of chicken, pork, and beef dishes; gleaming fish, heads intact, garnished with greens and lemon; bowls of rice, and vegetables of all description.

The end of the table held a display of cauliflower, miniature ears of corn, cherry tomatoes, water chestnuts and several exotic vegetables Barb could not name. A chef in a white jacket and tall hat stood, hands folded behind his back, smiling as he accepted compliments on his buffet.

Once seated across the table from Lily, Barb asked, "How did Mei Ling learn to sing Cantonese opera?"

"She studied for many years—started when she was in the middle of grade school, about age eleven, and continued lessons till she finished high school."

"Seems like a mighty long time to learn to sing."

"Not really. It's so much more than singing. The training is more rugged than you could ever imagine. The students need incredible self-discipline. They have to learn hundreds of precise body movements. In just the leg and foot movements there are staggering steps, slipping steps, up and downstairs steps, jumping, mincing, side-stepping and so on."

Barb swallowed a bite of what looked like seaweed Crisp and tangy, it was surprisingly good. "Do they do arms and hands, too?"

Lily nodded. "Many arm movements such as the long 'rippling water' sleeves. They also have to perfect more than fifty sleeve movements, such as the sleeve that hides what's being said, the sleeve that disguises the actor, the sleeve that greets, says farewell, used for dusting, weeping or shading the face. Hand movements are even more intricate. Every movement signifies something, shows some emotion or portrays some action. And it all has to be done gracefully, rhythmically. Mei Ling told me there's a list of twenty kinds of laughing and smiling facial expressions, all of which have to be performed to perfection."

"So Mei Ling is a polished actress."

"One of the best."

Was Mei Ling's scene the afternoon Barb surprised her in Lily's flat an act? Barb wondered. If so, why the masquerade? What was she hiding?

Barb speared a miniature ear of corn. "Somewhere I heard that men played the women's parts."

"There was a time, in the early eighteenth century, when women weren't allowed to appear on the stage with men. It wasn't until the People's Republic came into being in 1949 that this old tradition was changed."

Thoughtfully, Barb picked up clumps of rice with her chopsticks. Was Mei Ling as good at acting offstage as she was onstage? Apparently, she could convey any impression she wanted to. She appeared to be the dedicated opera star. Of course it would be a terrific career move to go on tour with a troupe. But when she came back to Hong Kong there would still be the new regime to deal with. Did Mei Ling have some private agenda? Could she be thinking of defecting to the U.S.?

Her thoughts were distracted by Lily asking, "Are you ready to hit the buffet for dessert?"

"Ready!"

They ambled down the line helping themselves to fried water chestnuts with a sweet coating, rice pudding, almond cakes, little dumplings with sweet bean paste, sweet buns and miniature mooncakes with lotus seed filling.

Barb started at the sound of a great burst of cymbals and drums. She glanced at her watch. Eight-thirty. Amid the fanfare the curtain parted, and a magnificently robed mandarin strode onto the stage.

"The emperor," Lily whispered across the table.

Moments later, Mci Ling minced onto the stage. Barb stifled a gasp. She scarcely recognized her. She wore a richly embroidered red robe with big flowing sleeves with wide white bands. Her high, jeweled headdress was adorned with pearls and pink pompons. From each side of the headdress long, white fur boas hung to her waist. Her thick platform shoes gave her additional stature. She looked bigger than life.

Lily leaned across the table toward Barb. "They're

telling the story of a lady from the court of an emperor who is being sent off to marry a chieftain beyond the Great Wall. The emperor hopes the marriage will ensure peace between the two peoples."

The story progressed, accompanied by the music of flutes and guitars, the bewildering sounds of big and small drums, a bell, cymbals, and the strokes of a gong.

Barb started at the sound of loud tick-tocks that sounded like a giant metronome—or the ticking of a time bomb. "What's that?"

"It's an instrument called a *ba*. It's really a wooden time beater which does for the orchestra what the conductor does for his musicians back home."

As the performance proceeded, Lily explained, "The girl hates the idea of marrying this man, doesn't want to go."

Entranced, Barb watched as two men entered carrying a litter. Mei Ling climbed into it, and they carried her around the stage. Accompanied by a two-stringed fiddle, she began to sing.

Barb whispered, "I think the fiddle is missing a string or two."

Smiling, Lily shook her head. "That's an *er hu*, like we saw at the Poor Man's Nightclub. Now Mei Ling is saying goodbye to everyone, and you'll see what she sees and feels on her journey."

As the pantomime continued, they watched Mei Ling step down from the carriage. A groom helped her to mount a make-believe horse. Dazzling stage effects that rivaled Speilberg's suggested biting wind, bizarre scenes of mysterious fog and scurrying clouds.

Lily said, "This scene is meant to arouse nostalgia in the audience."

Seated on the horse, Mei Ling began to play the lute and sing of her love for her native country.

In a loud whisper, Lily said, "She's reached an exotic pass on her journey. She longs to return home, but now she's near the frontier. It is too late. Turning back is hopeless. She continues onward to her destiny."

To Barb's dismay, a buzz of talk and laughter filled the room. Diners visited one table after another. The audience acted as if they were attending a football game rather than a musical production.

The curtain closed to polite applause.

Barb said, "Amazing! It's really a combination of grand opera, ballet, acrobatics and history all rolled into one."

"Right. But moral values reign. Many themes are ancient tales that have been handed down till they've become part of the people's thinking."

The girls in the gauzy pastel gowns who had sung at the beginning of the evening floated onstage and began to play and sing in the high-pitched voices that sounded so strange to Barb's ears.

"Is this intermission?"

"You could call it that. Actually, rather than show one entire opera, they are showing excerpts from four operas to make up the program."

The curtain rose on the second opera.

After several minutes had passed, Barb asked, "Where's Mei Ling?"

"Mei Ling isn't in this one, nor the next. She'll appear in the last opera excerpt we see tonight."

"Will she come out and sit with us during the two middle performances?"

"Possibly. She has to shed the costume she's wearing, clean off her lady-of-the-court makeup, then redo it for her role in the last opera. You see, even the makeup of the characters means something. It shows what kind of person they are. A blue face is a cruel one. A lot of red indicates courage, loyalty, straightforwardness; more black denotes impulsiveness. A triangular eye is considered crafty, and so on. Mei Ling won't appear again for at least an hour."

Barb tried to concentrate on the actors' leg and foot, arm and hand movements, and facial expressions, but not knowing what they symbolized made it hard to follow the story. The sets were breathtakingly beautiful—an extravaganza that rivaled the musicals at Radio City Music Hall and any opera she'd ever seen.

During intermission after the second act, Barb said, "Tell me more about Mei Ling. Do you think there's any chance she'll get a troupe together to go on tour?"

"I wouldn't be surprised."

Barb looked Lily squarely in the eyes. "Do you think the tour is really a subterfuge for her to defect to the U.S.?"

"No way."

"Why not? Why shouldn't she join the crowd?"

Lil's eyes slid away from Barb's questioning gaze. Hesitantly, evasively, she said, "Well, because her

entire life has always revolved around the opera.
She never talks about anything or anyone else, other
than her—her admirer. And very little about him.
So between the opera and her lover, she's tied to
Hong Kong."

"What a cloistered life she must lead."

Lily's lips curved in a knowing smile as she regarded Barb over the rim of her teacup. "Not as
cloistered as you might think."

"What's that supposed to mean?"

Lily sighed. "I wasn't going to tell you because
it's a well-kept secret, but I'm sure it won't matter
if you know. Mei Ling has a daughter."

Barb's brows flew up. "A daughter! Where is
she?"

"She lives on a farm in the country, in the New
Territories."

"With Mei Ling's husband?"

"There's no husband."

"Lily, stop talking in riddles. You're dying to tell
me, so go ahead."

"The father of Mei Ling's child was from Beijing. He was a dissident who had gotten in trouble
with the government and had fled to Hong Kong.
When she told him she was pregnant, he abandoned
her.

"Poor Mei Ling was caught between a rock and
a hard place. Having to care for a child could have
destroyed her career. She told the director she had
TB and would have to drop out for six months. He
believed her, or pretended to. She had the baby.
Then, though it killed her to give up the child, Mei

Ling had to work to support her, so she boarded her with a family in the country."

"The father took no responsibility?"

"None. Mei Ling never heard from him again. She was heartbroken—until her protector came along."

"Does her, ah, protector know?"

Lily gave a vehement shake of her head. "She doesn't think he'd take kindly to her having an illegitimate child."

"How old is the child?"

"Twelve. And now that she's grown older, it costs more to feed and clothe her, and the family wants more money. I think that's why Mei Ling is on fire to take a troupe overseas. She figures she can make beaucoup dollars touring the States."

They returned their attention to the stage where the next act was about to begin.

At the end of the third excerpt, Barb hid a yawn behind her napkin and glanced at her watch. Almost eleven. Almost time for Mei Ling to take the stage again.

Lily leaned across the table and whispered, "This is *The Forsaken Wife*."

Mei Ling strolled onstage in the guise of a street singer, wearing pale blue, embroidered robes and a blue turban with ends that hung down to her waist. With a soulful air, she strummed a lute and sang a mournful song.

Mei Ling outdid herself. Every movement of her body portrayed abandonment, a feeling Barb now realized she knew well.

Unlike Lily, Barb was far from convinced that

Mei Ling had no thought of defecting in mind. Clearly, marriage to her lover was not in the cards. Chinese communities in the States would welcome a singer of her talents. And, she could take her daughter with her. But to do that, she would need many dollars, all that a jade horse could buy.

It was past midnight by the time Barb and Lily returned to Winslow Gardens and arrived at the door of Lily's flat. Lily, key in hand, unlocked the door and pushed it open. Barb followed her through the doorway, then stopped short. Without warning, she clutched Lily's shoulder. "Wait!"

Lily wrenched away from her grip. In slightly aggrieved tones, she asked, "What's wrong?"

Barb pressed a finger across her lips. She cocked her head in the direction of the living room. A faint pool of light shone at the end of the foyer. Bending her head close to Lily's ear, she whispered, "I know I turned off all the lights before we left for the opera."

In a normal voice, Lily replied, "Andre may have come home early and left the light on for us. What with trying to keep up with feeding the holiday crowd, he's probably exhausted. I'm sure he's in bed asleep."

"Aren't you going to check?"

"Yes, in a minute." With a slightly sheepish grin, Lily said, "I'm going to pop into the living room and straighten the fringe. And I'll turn off the light."

"Right. I'm hitting the sack. See you in the morning."

Barb was halfway down the hall to her bedroom

when she heard a scream that surged through her body like an electric shock.

She whirled around and dashed down the hall, through the foyer, into the living room. She stopped dead in her tracks. The room was a shambles.

"No, no!" Lily wailed, as though by denying the havoc before her, everything would fly back into place.

Dumbstruck, seething with outrage and anger, Barb surveyed the room. It was a disaster. The drawers of the end tables and writing desk had been pulled out, their contents rifled. The cushions on the chairs and couch lay strewn on the floor.

"The horse," Lily wailed. "Someone was searching for that blasted carving."

As Barb looked around the room, something struck her as odd.

"Lily, listen. If someone were looking for the horse, they'd have had to move at least one or two figures to be sure the horse wasn't there. But they're all still standing in their normal places. Don't you think it's strange that none of the figures on the shelves have been touched?"

"I think the whole thing is strange." She ran into the kitchen and gave another howl.

Barb followed after her. Here, too, drawers were pulled out, cabinet doors opened and their contents a jumble. As if on signal, they ran from the kitchen, down the hall to the bedrooms. Both doors were wide open. Both rooms had been ransacked.

Pounding a fist on the doorjamb, Lily shrieked, "This makes me furious. Some low-down lowlife, breaking in here, making a shambles of my place!

I could throttle him with my bare hands." She sank down on the edge of her bed, shoulders slumped, head bent, the picture of despair.

Gently, Barb said, "It's okay, Lily, I'll help you clean up. It's okay."

Tears of rage and frustration shimmered in her eyes. "It's okay! Once was bad enough, but *twice!*"

"I know," said Barb soothingly. "I understand, I really do. Listen, I'm going to call the police."

Lily's voice rose, on the verge of hysteria. "And call a locksmith, tell him to change the locks. I'm not waiting any longer for the manager to have it done!"

"I will, first thing in the morning. What about the doorman?"

Lily snatched up the phone. "I'll call him right now. Maybe he saw someone, something suspicious."

But the doorman, who swore he hadn't closed an eye all evening, had seen no one who didn't belong here in the tower.

"Anyway," Lily groaned, "the damage is done. The thief is long gone."

"Actually, nothing seems to be missing."

Lily's head jerked up. "Your horse!" she exclaimed, as though struck by lightning. "We never took it to the bank. Oh, I knew we should have put it in the safe-deposit box right from the start instead of waffling around. It's gone. I know it's gone!"

Barb raced from the room, down the hall into the kitchen. She snatched the lid from the big pasta jar and plunged her hand inside. Frantically, she sifted through the noodles.

Lily, following in her wake, shouted, "What do you think you're doing? Quit messing in the noodles! Your hands are covered with germs. You're a—a health hazard."

Barb withdrew her hand and opened it under Lily's nose. In her palm, lay the jade horse.

Lily's eyes bulged in astonishment. "Good lord! What's that horse doing in my noodle jar?"

"I'd left it in my shoulder bag after we showed it to the professor at lunch. I intended to take it with me tonight, but I was carrying my new Gucci bag and it wouldn't fit inside; so I ducked into the kitchen and stuck it in the jar."

"Well, thank heaven it's safe. Tomorrow, for sure, we'll pop it into the bank."

Barb nodded. "God willing and the creeks don't rise."

"Even then," said Lily, stressing each word, "we will stash it in a safe-deposit box."

"Right. Come on, I'll help you make order out of chaos."

As they straightened the rooms, putting things away, it occurred to Barb that they hadn't seen any sign of a break-in.

While Lily was on her hands and knees, straightening the fringe on the carpet near the sliding glass doors, Barb moved on into the foyer and examined the lock on the front door. There were no scratches, no sign of forced entry. And as the Hong Kong police would probably say, the credit card trick must have worked once again.

On the flip side of the coin, strangers had already searched the flat and determined that the horse wasn't there. Why would they search again? An unpleasant thought took root in the back of her mind. Mei Ling needed money. Mei Ling had given Lily tickets to the opera. Mei Ling had a key. Mei Ling had a good hour between the first opera and the time she would have to appear on stage for the fourth opera. More than enough time to hop a taxi, scour the flat and return to the Dynasty.

For that matter, Peter Chang lived right here in Lily's tower, and he wanted money to leave the island, emigrate to America. Where was he tonight? And Andre surely did not cook or supervise the underchefs the entire time he was in the Parisienne. He could have ducked out of the kitchen, taken a cab to the flat, searched it and returned to work. But that made no sense. After all, the man lived here. He could search the place any time he chose. And besides, he had no motive, did he? Except that he wanted to own a restaurant. But a jade horse did not buy even one small intimate French restaurant.

Shortly two uniformed Hong Kong police arrived, looked over the flat, took down pertinent information, and left. Twenty minutes later, they returned. They had checked out the employees' entrance on the ground floor of the tower and discovered that someone had failed to lock the door after leaving at the end of the day. Anyone could have entered the tower at any time.

Lily heaved a discouraged sigh. "That just about ties it." Standing with feet astride, hands planted firmly on her hips, she said, "I've made an executive decision."

Barb grinned. "I can hardly wait to hear it."

"I'm going to call in a practitioner."

"You're calling in a what?"

"A *feng shui* expert. He'll know how to deflect these malevolent forces."

Barb gave her a long, level look. She started to say, "Forget it!" But Lily was a believer. *And who am I,* Barb thought, *to disabuse her of one of her fondest beliefs.*

Barb sank down on the couch and stared abstractedly at the two jade-colored lounge chairs that flanked a teakwood lamp table and stood with their backs to the sliding glass doors. It struck her that for anyone seated on the couch, this arrangement blocked the view of the harbor and a direct path to the terrace.

Turning toward Lily she asked, "Did you park those chairs and table in front of the doors because you knew heights made me loopy and you thought blocking out the view would make me feel safer?"

Lily said, "Sorry, I wasn't that thoughtful. They are there because I read a book about *feng shui.*"

"*Feng shui* being Cantonese for interior decorating?"

Solemnly, Lily said, "*Feng shui* is an ancient Chinese science. It's written *f-e-n-g s-h-u-i,* but it's pronounced *fong shway* and actually means 'wind and water.' The Chinese believe the forces of nature represent the physical evidence of the cosmic energy flow called *ch'i. Feng shui* tries to harness this energy."

"A bit fuzzy, if you ask me."

"Not really. Think of a sailboat. When the sails are angled right, the wind drives the boat smoothly across the water. When the sails are askew, the boat capsizes. In *feng shui,* the boat represents your life. Through the proper placement of furnishings and proper interior design, *feng shui* strives to channel *ch'i*—like the wind in the sail—in a positive, curving path throughout your house. Affecting the *ch'i* flow in turn influences your life, similar to the way the wind affects the sailboat."

"Hum," Barb said. "No comment."

"Feng shui is about finding the balance of *ch'i* so that your life can benefit from it. You have to align yourself with the pulse of the earth. In the Orient, people don't do anything without *feng shui."*

Barb, doubting the evidence of her own ears, said, "Are you telling me you believe in this, in these superstitions?"

Lily regarded Barb with a stern gaze. "Just because you can't see something like *ch'i,* doesn't mean it doesn't exist. It's like ESP, or electricity or wind. We can't see it, but we know it exists."

Barb, still skeptical, asked, "But *how* does it work?"

"I can't explain how or why. All I know is, *feng shui* principles work.

"A lot of *feng shui* is symbolic." Lily nodded toward the black, inlaid-ivory and jade coromandel screen. A folding screen helps the financial side of your life."

Barb grinned. "All this time I thought you'd bought that screen because it was exquisite and had set it there to hide the card table and chairs."

"Did you notice the octagon-shaped mirror over the stove?"

"Sure."

"The mirror doubles the number of burners. Food is symbolic of wealth. Twice as many burners means you can feed twice as many people."

"You've got to be kidding."

"You know my paintings of the tiny fishing boats at Guilin, the fishing village at Aberdeen and Victoria Harbour?"

Barb nodded.

"Flowing water. Indicates wealth."

"You were already in money up to your knees."

"Sure. But my money's invested. When the stock market took a plunge, I could have lost everything—but I rearranged things in the flat, and the market came back."

"How do you know it wouldn't have come back anyway?"

"I don't. But I know that instead of losing money, my securities rose in value. In addition, my career took off."

"What about the marriage side of this—this *feng shui?*"

Lily waved a hand in the air, and when she spoke, she sounded defensive.

"At the moment Andre says he has family responsibilities he can't ask me to share. When they are over and done, I'm sure he'll ask me to marry him."

Barb wanted to say, "But, Lily, my friend, family responsibilities are never over and done." Instead, she said, "I hope so, if you think he can make you happy."

Softly, Lily said, "I'm happy now, Barb. Very happy."

Barb felt a shiver of apprehension, as if she somehow sensed that Lily's happiness was to be short-lived.

Twelve

Ho Kar Wei took a deep breath and clenched his jaw in an effort to hold his anger in check. He had rolled and tossed all night long seething with impatience, waiting for morning to come, waiting until he could call and report, and now he was suffocating here in the red phone booth. Worse, he would be late for work and his supervisor would be very angry. There would be a reprimand, a black mark against his record. But it could not be helped, for he couldn't reach his contact until nine-thirty.

He dialed again, holding his breath, willing him to answer.

He almost jumped when a soft voice in his ear said, "Yes?"

Ho Kar Wei took another deep breath. "I call you about the object for sale."

"Yes."

He swallowed hard, then blurted, "Is not in flat."

"You idiot. It must be there."

"Is not there, I say. I look everywhere she could hide it."

In harsh, exasperated tones the man asked, "Where else would it be?"

"She must carry with her."

There was a long moment of silence. "Then do what you have to do."

"I try again."

"No!" the man fairly shouted. "*Try,* is not good enough. You promised me the carving. Produce it."

Ho's palms began to sweat. The phone stuck to his hand. This job, which had seemed so simple at first, was turning into much more action than he had bargained for.

"I take great risk if I have to harm the woman. You will pay more."

"Fool!" the man shouted. "You made an offer. Do not make offers unless you can come through. I must have it. I think I have a buyer, maybe two. I'm putting it up for auction." A sly laugh escaped him. "Silent auction."

"I understand."

"Good! And I must have it quickly. By Sunday night at the latest." The phone clicked as the man hung up.

Thirteen

The *feng shui* master appeared at their door shortly after nine the next morning. To Barb's astonishment, he looked like an ordinary business-man, as conservative as an accountant: clean shaven, wearing a white short-sleeved shirt and black slacks. His black hair was clipped short, brushed straight back, and dark eyes sparkling with intelligence peered through rimless glasses.

He carried a black leather briefcase and a large circular mechanism that looked like a box compass with a magnetic needle that rotated on a horizontal dial. The dial was inscribed with the twelve signs of the Chinese zodiac and other strange symbols. He strode into the living room with the air of a physician called in to diagnose a mysterious illness and set his box and briefcase on the coffee table. Lily, who had taken the morning off, greeted him profusely.

"Thank you so much for coming to our flat rather than insisting that we come to your office." Lily gave a small, apologetic smile. "My friend is not a believer, you see, but I know you will convince her."

Lily pulled the Chippendale desk chair over to

the coffee table for the master and sank down beside Barb on the couch.

The master glanced at Barb with a slightly surprised expression and in kindly tones said, "I do not attempt to convince anyone. *Feng shui* is there, it exists." He paused, lowering himself onto the chair.

"I do believe in ESP, extrasensory perception," Barb said pleasantly, "but when it comes to controlling my life by rearranging the furniture, I'm a little skeptical."

Solemnly, he said, *"Feng shui* is much more than rearranging furnishings. It is the art or science of manipulating the environment. Our fate is determined by unseen currents that swirl around the surface of the earth, and by dragons that sleep beneath the ground. Neither of these forces must be disturbed by people."

"I understand what you're saying," said Barb, just as solemnly. "I simply find it hard to believe."

The master's dark eyes gleamed with the conviction of his beliefs. "I do not understand. If you believe in ESP, you must believe in unseen forces or currents . . ."

Vehemently, Barb insisted, "ESP is different from *feng shui*. ESP involves the reach of the mind."

Clearly wanting to avoid further discord, Lily said in firm tones, "I wish we had time for further discussion, but since we haven't, we'd better get on with it."

The master's intense gaze switched to Lily.

"Before I arrived at your flat, I studied the site

of this tower to be sure it does not lie on a sleeping dragon."

He turned to face Barb. "You can certainly imagine the wrath of a sleeping dragon who wakes to find a high-rise apartment block on its tail."

"Absolutely," agreed Barb, thinking, *If here be dragons, I'm convinced they do not wish to be disturbed.*

From his briefcase, the master withdrew astrological charts. "First, I must determine your fortunes."

He began by scrutinizing their faces minutely, then after asking their birth dates, cast their horoscopes.

Despite her cynicism of the man's powers, Barb perched on the seat of the couch feeling both tense and curious as she watched him consulting his astrological charts.

Lily, also watching intently, told Barb, "You'll be amazed at how much the master can divine from studying the course of the stars."

Doubtfully, Barb said, "That's as may be, but I'm not so sure I want to know what the future holds."

Lily gave her a reassuring pat on the shoulder. "Look at it this way, if you know your future, then you can change it if you want to."

Barb's dark, crescent brows rose to new heights, and her lips thinned, turning down at the corners. Slowly she shook her head, thinking, *Then his prediction wouldn't be my future, would it?*

To Barb's amazement, the master picked up on various aspects of their lives. Though Lily had not told him Barb's profession, he said, "You are a healer." With a small, disapproving frown, he went on, "Further, you are evading an important commitment. It is imperative that you make a decision, lest the opportunity be lost. A Leo," he said, "you were born to blaze, but you prove to be your own worst enemy. Finally, the stars indicate that you have a long journey ahead."

Pretty obvious, Barb thought. Altogether, she felt his pronouncements could have applied to many aspects of her life and in the lives of people who were looking for reassurance and hope that there would be happier days ahead.

When it was Lily's turn, the master told her she was deeply involved with a man who could not marry her.

He has that right! Barb thought, taken aback.

As he went on, his expression became grave, and his eyes reflected a deep sadness. "I fear you will suffer a brush with death." He could not, or would not, say whether she would survive.

"Oh, but I've had a brush with death!" Lily exclaimed. "It happened years ago."

The master's features set in a closed expression. Swiftly, he got to his feet. "I am here to make certain all is in order, and to do so, I will examine your flat to discover anything that might disturb the spirits."

From his briefcase he extracted an eight-sided symbol, explaining, "This is a *bagua*. Each sector is assigned directions, colors, elements and life situations: marriage, fame, wealth, family knowledge, career, helpful people and children. I will align the *bagua* to the north of each room. Then I can determine what is missing in the space and in your lives.

Lily hung on his every word as they followed him through the rooms of the flat. Nervously, she whispered to Barb, "I'm afraid he'll suggest something drastic, like redecorating the whole place."

Barb shook her head. "He'd lose too much business if he insisted on redos."

In Lily's room he directed that the mirror over her dresser be moved to another wall so that it would not face the bedroom door and drive benevolent spirits away. She went straight to the mirror and lifted it down.

The master turned toward Barb. "Mirrors are the *feng shui* equivalent of aspirin. Properly placed, they can right many wrongs in a home by redirecting the energy."

He scowled at a picture of storm clouds and lightning over the misty, cone-shaped mountains of Guilin. He glanced at the *bagua*. "This is the southwest corner. No marriage will occur as long as that picture hangs in this place."

Without a word, Lily crossed to the picture, took it down and shoved it far back inside her closet.

In Barb's room he said, "I am pleased to see the view of Victoria Harbour from your window." Turning toward a wall on which hung a watercolor painting of fishing boats at Guilin, he nodded in approval.

"Water indicates wealth in *feng shui,* and a picture of flowing water in the southeast corner of your home keeps things moving." He strode into the hall and passing the open bathroom said, "Keeping commode lids down and bathroom doors closed will prevent your money from going down the drain."

He walked briskly down the hallway to the kitchen and stood in the doorway again nodding in approval. "Tsao Kwan, the kitchen god, is good, and the mirror over the stove. The kitchen is the heart of the house. However, I suggest you keep the door closed between the dining room and the kitchen to block negative *ch'i* from entering the room."

He turned and backtracked to the archway between the foyer and the living room. "Wind chimes," he said. "You need wind chimes here, fluttering in the breeze to move the *ch'i* in a positive direction. Living objects, like plants, are also useful in helping realign *ch'i* to flow in a positive direction. Colors, too, have special properties. You must plant red and yellow flowers in front of your flat. Red symbolizes happiness, warmth, strength and money. Yellow signifies longevity."

He stood still, his eyes sweeping over the living room, as if studying the arrangement of the furniture.

"The placement of the chairs and lamp table is good—will keep your luck from going out the glass doors."

Barb eyed him skeptically. "It's intruders barging through the front door that we worry about."

The practitioner gave a sympathetic nod. "I understand. Bells hung inside the doors will protect occupants from intruders. So will a red clock or ribbon."

Barb felt that bells hanging inside the front door

had nothing to do with the balance of *ch'i,* or spirits, good or evil, keeping intruders in or out. If she were an intruder and opened a front door and bells started ringing, she'd run like crazy. Still, if it worked, why not?

A grave expression came over the master's face, and he looked at Lily pityingly. "It is most unfortunate that you live on the fourteenth floor, in flat four. However, you can redirect the negative energy by mounting small, *bagua*-shaped mirrors on the outside walls and placing a curved, half-moon-shaped mat at the front entrance."

With that final bit of advice, he took his leave.

Lily was exultant. Grinning, she told Barb happily, "I will now take control of my life."

"Great!" Barb said. "First, you'd better fortify yourself with a quick cup of coffee."

In the kitchen over coffee and toast Barb asked with elaborate casualness, "What time did Andre get in last night?"

Lily gave a helpless sigh. "Not till sometime after one, and he left earlier than usual this morning. Poor guy sure works hard."

At what? Barb wondered. Why hadn't Andre been in bed asleep last night when they came home from the opera, as Lily had thought he would be? What in the world could he have been doing till after one in the morning? She started to ask Lily, but that would imply that she doubted Andre's integrity. Lily was so bedazzled by the man, Barb couldn't bear to put her on the spot.

Barb said no more, but slathered strawberry jam

on a second piece of toast and began to scarf it down.

Over the rim of her coffee cup, Lily murmured, "Don't forget to give me the horse."

Barb nodded. "It's in my room."

"Are you sure you don't want to go to the bank with me?"

Barb threw out her hands in a helpless gesture. "I'd trust you with my life and my money, why not my horse?"

Lily drained her coffee cup and rose from the table.

"Okay, I'm off."

Barb eyed her Mickey Mouse tee shirt and black sweats. "You going as you are?"

Lily's smooth features contorted in a mock scowl. "Don't I wish." She retreated to her room to dress for work.

Barb retrieved the horse from among the folds of a heavy beige coat sweater in her dresser drawer. She had just finished wrapping it in tissue paper when Lily appeared at her door wearing a tailored gray suit, white silk blouse, and a black leather shoulder bag and heels.

"I'm ready to roll."

As if it were the most fragile of artifacts, rather than the toughest stone imaginable, Barb pressed the horse into her outstretched hands.

"Here's old mutton fat. I feel as if I'm handing over one of my best friends. So guard him well."

Lily opened her tent-sized bag.

"Not to worry. I'll lock him in a safe-deposit box the minute I walk through the hallowed bronze doors of American Fidelity." Gently she stashed the horse deep inside her purse.

"What's on your agenda this morning?"

Barb groaned. "One of my most unfavorite things: shop till you drop. I'm heading over to Kowloon and doing Nathan Road. I hope to find something wonderful for Mom, Dad, Hank, Amy, Anna Lee—everybody—with one fell swoop."

"If you're into jade, there's a little shop where they have good prices, and so far, whatever I've bought there has been the real thing."

"Show me on the map."

"I'll write down the address for you. The quickest way to go is to take the subway and get off at Mong Kok."

Barb shook her head. "Everybody's told me that whatever I do, don't miss the ferry ride from Hong Kong to Kowloon. I've wanted to do this ever since I got here, and today's the day."

"Good luck. Watch out for pickpockets. They're thick as fleas."

After Lily had gone, Barb hurriedly donned dark green slacks, a gold polo shirt and Reeboks. Armed with her new Gucci purse, she locked the door of Lily's flat and punched the button for the elevator. The doors slid open, and she stepped inside.

"Cheers."

Barb did a double take. If he hadn't spoken to her first, she wouldn't have recognized him. He wore a navy golf cap, the brim pulled low over his forehead, aviator sunglasses that concealed most of his face, tan slacks and a navy golf jacket with the collar turned up around his neck.

"Pete, is that you?"

"The same—I think." He sounded unsure, and his normally cheerful mien was gone, replaced by a dour expression.

As she continued to study him in the dimly lighted elevator, she noted a faintly reddish-purple tinge around the area of his right eye. She also noticed that he hadn't shaved for a day or two, but then realized that his five o'clock shadow was covering a wicked bruise. From where she stood, the side of his face looked puffy and swollen, the skin mottled. She started to blurt out, "What happened to you?" and thought better of it. Instead, she said, "I'm sorry to miss your t'ai chi sessions."

"Oh, right." He gave a little chuckle. "You're not going to believe this, but I—uh—ran into a door."

"Bad joss," Barb said, straight-faced. "Doors do have a way of blocking progress." Now, with startling clarity, she recalled Lily's dim sum brunch, and afterward asking Lily how she thought Pete had lost his laughing Buddha. And Lily saying she thought he'd "lost" it paying off a gambling debt on one of his trips to Macau, where gambling was big business; that here in Hong Kong, gamblers took gambling debts very seriously. They didn't mess around. When you lost, you paid up, either out of your wallet or out of your hide. Had Lily's prediction that someday Pete would push his luck too far come true?

The elevator stopped at the lobby, and the doors slid open.

Casually, Pete asked, "Where are you off to so early in the morning?"

She smiled up at him. "Nathan Road, an obligatory shopping trip for my family."

As though struck with an idea, he said, "I'm an expert shopper. How about if I tag along?"

Barb stepped quickly out of the elevator. "Oh, no thanks. I shop much better alone."

"But I insist." His tone was jovial, cavalier, as if he'd found a long-lost friend. "Beautiful young American women should never walk the streets alone. You need an escort."

Barb laughed. "Surely not in Hong Kong, one of the most sophisticated cities in the world."

Pete made no reply, but took her elbow in a firm grip and fell into step beside her. As he did so, she caught a glimpse of his eye from the side. A shiver went through her. It looked like a small, decayed fish.

"Really," Barb protested, "there's no need for you to come with me. I don't want to put you out."

Quickly, too quickly, he said, "You won't put me out. I want to be with you."

He gave her elbow a little squeeze and drew her closer to his side. As they crossed the lobby, Barb nodded to the doorman, hoping he'd say something, anything she could comment on to start a conversation, but he waved them on. Clearly, she couldn't wrench free of Pete's grip without making a scene. And there was no point in making a scene. Once outside, they set out at a brisk walk toward Albert Road, where they caught a cab to the Star Ferry Pier.

It was a photo-op day, perfect, Barb thought, for a calendar illustration for the month of October.

Brilliant sunlight gilded the harbor and glinted off high-rise mirror buildings. Her foreboding of the night before faded.

Pete broke into her thoughts. "What did you do last night?"

Barb hesitated. She could tell him about the flat being ransacked, but she had no desire to go over it all again. After all, no harm had come to Lily or herself. They were probably lucky they hadn't been there. Her fertile imagination soared: They could have been held up at gunpoint, beaten up, tied up— or worse. Who knows what might have happened? But what was the matter with her, imagining all these horror scenarios? She had never been a fearful person.

Enough, she told herself sternly. *Get a grip.* Instead of telling Pete about the break-in, she said, "We went to hear Mei Ling sing in the Chinese opera. It was incredible—breathtaking—the costumes, the scenery, the music, the acting, we loved it."

"Humm," he murmured distractedly. "Sometime I'll have to give it a go."

When they arrived at the busy, crowded pier, Pete bought high-priced tickets, all of thirty cents, for first class seats on the upper deck of the green and white Star Ferry. Once on board, Pete led her past the rows of wooden seats other passengers had scrambled to commandeer, onto the open-air deck where they stood at the guardrail surveying the harbor.

The sky overhead was a pale porcelain blue, with puffy, white, gilt-edged clouds. In the distance beyond the hustling, bustling city, the undulating mountain peaks of the New Territories loomed like gray ghosts.

Barb lifted her chin and breathed deeply of the morning air. It felt cool and damp against her skin. A brisk breeze ruffled her hair. Blasts and hoots of whistles and horns bounced across the dark, choppy waters. Sampans flitted around the harbor. Pleasure craft plowed the waters beside container ships that swept slowly eastward.

Without warning, she felt Pete's arm curve snugly around her waist, and he rested his cheek lightly atop her head. Her heart flipped over, more from surprise than excitement. She pulled back, looking up into his face, wishing she could see past his dark glasses. He gazed down at her with a fatuous grin.

To make conversation, she asked "Where were you last night?"

"Last night?" He sounded vague.

"You asked where *I* was. Where were you?"

"With friends," he said easily, "knocking about, stopped for a pint here and there."

Gently, she said, "It appears to me that *you* were knocked about."

His lips curved in an ingratiating smile. "Let's not talk about me. Let's talk about you, something pleasant, like your little jade horse."

Sharply she looked up at him. She started to ask him to take off his glasses so she could read the expression in his eyes. But, of course, he wanted to conceal his shiner. Instead, she said, "What about my horse?"

"What do you plan to do with it?"

He seemed unduly curious, but then she supposed, because he had grown up with a father who had exported objets d'art and a mother who was an interior decorator, it was a natural question.

"I haven't decided."

"I'll be glad to take it off your hands."

Barb laughed. "It's not exactly a burden."

He threw out his hands as if conceding the point.

"Naturally not. But to you it's simply a—a curio. While to me, well I'd place great value on it."

Barb's brows rose. "Oh, what value?"

"Are you interested in selling?"

Now she was curious, wondering how far he would go. "Maybe."

As if he were offering her a fortune, he said, "I'll give you two hundred more than the dealer's appraised value. I will give you one thousand HK dollars."

"One thousand?" Barb repeated as though she couldn't believe her ears.

"One thousand," he said magnanimously. The rest of his words came out in a rush. "Actually, I'm a bit short on cash at the moment, but I expect to be flush within a week or two. Then I'll send you a cashier's check. Meanwhile, you give me the horse and you'll no longer have to worry about anyone stealing it—won't have to bother stashing it away in a safe-deposit box—you haven't put it away, have you?"

If he thought she'd go along with such a cockamamie deal, he was out of his mind. In Barb's mind, a spark of suspicion kindled and grew. Where was Pete before he'd gone boozing with his so-called friends and gotten beaten up for fair? Calmly, she said, "You can't be serious."

"Never more serious in my life." Misconstruing her meaning, he went on, "I realize one thousand HK dollars is a very generous offer, but I would never take advantage of a friend." He put an arm around her shoulders and, hugging her close, kissed her forehead. "We are friends, aren't we?"

"Not the way you mean."

"Don't be shy."

"I'm not."

"I know you're not." He bent his head to hers and nuzzled her ear. Softly, he whispered, "We speak the same language, you and I." His low, confident tone implied an intimacy between them that did not exist.

She jerked her head aside. Resentment made her voice sharp. "Then you should understand when I tell you the horse isn't available, and neither am I. Now let me go."

Instead of releasing her, he hugged her closer to his side and dropped another kiss on her forehead. "You don't really mean it."

"I do mean it." She jerked backward and, flattening her hands against his chest, tried to push him away. At the same time, over Pete's shoulder, she saw a short, husky Oriental man wearing a baseball cap and a gray bomber jacket, standing partly behind a post watching them with interest. For a fraction of a second, their eyes met. Instantly, the man wheeled about and, bolting inside, ran to the stairway that led down to the lower deck.

"Pete, stop making a fool of yourself, we're being watched."

His arms dropped from her sides. He spun around, looking every which way. A frightened expression crossed his face. "Where? What does he look like?"

"Short, husky, Oriental. He's gone now."

Pete ran his tongue over his lips. His voice sounded shaky. "Are you sure he was watching us?"

"Absolutely."

"Hang on. That may be someone I want to see. I'll be back in a minute." Before she could ask what it was all about, he strode quickly away.

Barb strolled to the bow of the ferry and stood leaning against the guardrail. As the boat churned across the harbor, before her rose a forest of tall, narrow buildings that reminded her of the blocks in a child's Lego set. Huge signs—Philips, Yashica, Samsung, Motorola—identified several of the many businesses that thrived in the concrete canyons. A luxury liner, *Star of Orient* had docked at Ocean Terminal.

Without warning, two strong hands gripped her shoulders. A wave of fear engulfed her. She gave a terrified cry and lurched forward, trying to wrench from the hands that imprisoned her. For a moment it seemed the hands were propelling her forward; then abruptly, they let go. Off balance, she lurched and almost toppled over the guardrail into the dark, swirling waters below.

She heard Pete's laughter, felt his strong arms encircle her waist. Swiftly he pulled her back against him, pressing her tightly against his body.

"You don't think I'd let you drown, do you? Now I've saved your life. You owe me."

White-faced, breathless, she shouted, "I owe you nothing, you oaf. That wasn't funny! Let me go!" At the same moment, she brought the heel of her shoe down on his instep as hard as she could.

Pete let out a howl, flung her from him, and began hopping around the deck, clutching his foot.

"Oh, come off it, Pete. It's not that bad. You're lucky I wasn't wearing heels."

Scowling, red-faced, he said, "You come off it! You've got a twist in your knickers."

"A *what?*"

"You heard me. It means you're—you're out of sorts."

"Oh, *I* see. You scare me to death and *I'm* out of sorts."

In a sudden about face, he held his hands up before his chest, palms out. "Truce, truce. I apologize."

"Accepted," she murmured. "Did you find your friend?"

"No," he said shortly. "And he's no friend." As if to close the subject, he clasped her upper arm and turned her to face the Kowloon shoreline.

"See that huge pile of dark red marble over there? That's the Regent Hotel, very elegant. And that abstract-designed concrete building is the space museum, and next to it is the Hong Kong Museum of Art and the Cultural Centre." He continued to point out landmarks until the boat docked with a thud at the Star Ferry pier. To Barb's surprise, the trip had not taken more than twelve minutes.

When they alighted from the ferry, Pete followed close on her heels, his hand on her shoulder, guiding her through the cavernous terminal. As they reached the street, she gazed about her. It was then she saw him again, the husky figure in the gray bomber jacket and baseball cap, his dark gaze fixed on the two of them.

She turned and grabbed Pete's arm. "There he is again, the man who was watching us. He's standing just inside the doorway of that souvenir shop."

Pete's head whipped around. At the same moment, the man darted out of the shop and, shoving his way through the throng of passengers disembarking from the ferry, ran outside the terminal. For a moment Pete stood perfectly still, as though anchored to the floor. If she had not known better, Barb would have thought he was immobilized by pure terror. He turned to face her and in a low, tense voice said, "Oh, look, Barb, I'd like to help you out today, but I have a little business to finish up here in Kowloon. See you later."

Nonplussed, she watched him stride away and disappear into the crowd. Something had gone very wrong in the life of Pete Chang. She only wished she knew what it was.

Barb allowed herself to be swept along with the tide of people going about their business. Suddenly it was thrilling to be here in Hong Kong, to be part of the frenzied crowd rushing everywhere, bent on accomplishing whatever mission drove them. A feeling of euphoria stole over her. The world was her oyster and Hong Kong was the pearl. No wonder Hal had loved it so, had thought it was the most fascinating city in the entire world. How she wished they could have enjoyed it together.

"Whoa," she told herself. It would be so easy, seduced by the glamour and excitement of this city, to be lulled into a false sense of security. "Forget euphoria, be ever-vigilant."

Though it didn't look far on her map, Mong Kok was a far hike on foot. She flagged down one of the fire engine red taxis that darted through the streets and showed the driver the address of the shop Lily had recommended. Tooting his horn, dodging in and out among cars and busses, he charged up Nathan Road, past sidewalks swarming with people, and let her out at Mong Kok.

The tiny jade shop was one of countless mom-and-pop businesses that lined a dark, narrow side street and spilled out onto the walk. A tiny, shrunken woman in a faded, cotton print dress and black cardigan sweater, looking infinitely careworn, tottered out of the shop. Wispy white hair escaped from a knot on top of her head. She smiled at Barb and nodded at the trays of jade jewelry displayed on tables in the entrance to the shop.

Barb returned her smile, then turned to look over the dazzling array: rings, pendants, bracelets, a collection of unset stones, pale pink, creamy white, but most in various shades of green. She picked up a ring, studied the gold mounting. It looked like the perfect gift for Amy.

"Good price, cheap," chirped the old woman. Her

dark, imploring eyes met Barb's. "Only four hundred dollar Hong Kong."

"Four hundred dollars!" Barb repeated, mentally dividing by eight. "That's fifty American dollars?"

The old woman, evidently thinking she was protesting, said, "Four hundred dollar, okay, okay?"

Barb shook her head. She had no idea what the ring was worth, but Lily had cautioned her not to pay the first price asked, for part of the joy of shopping was haggling. Barb hated to haggle. She slipped the ring on her finger, turned it toward a ray of sunlight that poked into the narrow street and rubbed the surface of the stone. It felt smooth and warm under her fingertips. She liked it. And if she liked it, Amy would like it. Feebly, she countered, "Two hundred dollars?"

In the voice of an outraged parrot, the woman screeched, "No two hundred. Three!" She held up three fingers and shook them under Barb's nose. "Three hundred dollar, last price."

Again, she divided by eight. Thirty-seven dollars and fifty cents. At the same time, she became aware that she had an audience, that several people had gathered to watch the bargaining and were hovering in the background. She felt a warm flush of embarrassment creep up her face into her hairline.

She cast a quick sidelong glance over her shoulder. The roof overhead cast a shadow on their faces so she couldn't see their features clearly, but there was something about the shape of the head, the set of the shoulders of one of the men, that seemed familiar. Yet she knew no one here in Hong Kong other than Lily and her friends. Maybe the man reminded her of someone back home. More than once she had met clients outside the clinic and failed to recognize them. Maybe he was a resident she had seen at Winslow Gardens, or possibly an employee. And, she thought dispiritedly, maybe she was just plain paranoid, imagining people were following her.

In any case, whether the ring was true jade or not, she liked it. To her, it was worth thirty-seven-fifty. Besides, the old lady looked as if she needed the money so badly that Barb hated to haggle further. She dug in her purse and brought out three one-hundred-dollar Hong Kong bills. Faster than the speed of sound, the fragile old lady whisked them from Barb's hand and, nodding and smiling, shoved them into a sweater pocket. She slipped the ring inside a pink tissue sack and gave it to Barb.

Barb tucked the sack in a zipper compartment inside her purse and took out her map again. Another "must see," according to Lily, was the bird market on Hong Lok Street off Nathan Road. Eagerly she retraced her steps to Nathan Road.

She wended her way through the throng of sightseers and shoppers past street stalls where everything imaginable, from white ducks in crates, snakes and frogs, to silk blouses, tee shirts and leather goods, was offered for sale. Craning her neck to see the street signs, she finally discovered Hong Lok, which turned out to be a dark, narrow alley crammed with stall after stall of vendors.

She could hear the birds before she saw them. As she moved forward down a narrow aisle, a deafening chorus of chirps filled her ears, and the yeasty smell of seeds and droppings filled her nose. Both sides of the aisle were stacked with hundreds of bird cages. Small orange plastic cages housed tiny birds; big red plastic domed cages were home to colorful parakeets and white cockatiels. All sorts of bird paraphernalia, along with foods and medications, were displayed for sale. Two of the vendors were feeding the birds, poking live crickets and grasshoppers inside the cages with chopsticks.

She could see that here on this small island where six million people were crowded into hundreds of high-rises, a bird was an ideal pet. She slipped past several shoppers who were shaking their heads and chattering, evidently bargaining with hawkers to buy a bird, and continued down the narrow aisle.

Luckily, the mass of shoppers all flowed in one direction. It wasn't till she came to an aisle that ran across the alley, that she saw a second aisle parallel to the one where she was browsing. If she continued in the direction she was going, the aisle would loop around, leading to the way out.

She passed racks of dresses, and blouses and skirts draped from the sides of the stall and the ceiling. Bolts of silk yard goods were stacked high on tables. Other stalls offered plastic kitchen tools, toys, transistor radios and countless souvenirs: replicas of Buddhas, dragons, white painted porcelain vases and sets of mah-jongg tiles. She paused before a spinner filled with watches and picked one up for a closer look.

A lean, long-faced young man wearing a yellow Hard Rock Cafe Beijing tee shirt, eyed her hopefully. "You buy? Fi' dolla', American."

Barb shook her head. "Just looking."

He shrugged, drifted across the aisle and started
talking with a young girl with sparkling eyes and
a wide smile who was hawking colorful silk shirts.
Barb continued to examine the watches. Finally she
found one with a gold face and faux diamonds for
numbers that appealed to her. She smiled to herself,
thinking, *For five dollars, how could you go wrong?*

She looked around for the shop owner, who had
disappeared from sight among the crush of shoppers. She glanced up and down the aisle and, from
the corner of her eye, caught a quick flash of movement. Her gaze fixed on a man's black-shirted back,
evidently a shopper who had had a sudden change
of plans and decided to turn around and buck the
flow of traffic. There was something faintly familiar
about the shock of straight, ink black hair cut
straight across the back of the rounded head, and
the square set of the narrow shoulders. But then,
people said all Asians looked alike, didn't they?

"Get real," she told herself. "Of course they
don't all look alike, any more than Anglos do." Still,
the fact that the man seemed familiar made her uneasy. Why couldn't she place him? Usually, she was
very good at recognizing people she had met only
once. Although, if the truth were known, she was
better at recognizing dogs and cats she had met only
once. Could this man be one of the onlookers at
the jade shop? Even if he were, so what? He had
as much right to be here as anyone else.

"You buy?" asked a voice at her elbow. She
turned to face the grinning young entrepreneur in
his yellow Hard Rock Cafe tee shirt. Despite Lily's

orders, she absolutely refused to haggle over a five-dollar watch. She dug in her purse for a five-dollar bill and handed it to him, then zipped the watch inside the zipper pocket along with the ring.

Back on Nathan Road, she browsed past the sidewalk stalls and soon filled a gray plastic bag with silk shirts for her dad, her brother and Steve, cloisonné bracelets and a black padded cotton mandarin jacket with matching slacks—for Anna Lee. She stopped short before a booth bulging with souvenirs.

What caught her eye was a straw coolie hat. From the back, dangled a long, shiny, black queue that looked for all the world like human hair. Laughing to herself, she picked up the hat expecting the queue to fall off. To her astonishment, it was fastened securely to the straw. Was this ever a hoot! She could no more resist buying it than she could resist dumping catsup on fried eggs. Elated, she thought, *Perfect, for Anna Lee to wear on Halloween.* It was her find of the day!

Back on Nathan Road, she scanned the teeming street for a taxi. Taxi after taxi flashed past, but all were occupied. Again she looked at her map. The subway station was only half a block away. Could she hack the subway? Why not? As Steve so often said, "Nothing ventured, nothing gained."

The subway was a revelation. It was well lighted, and sparkling clean. How did Hong Kong manage to keep it in this pristine condition despite all the thousands of people who must pass through here every day? She glanced around at the other passengers waiting to board the train. They appeared clean, neat, nicely dressed. No derelicts lurched about, no litter cluttered the concourse, no graffiti defaced the walls. More high marks for Hong Kong, she thought, impressed.

She dropped coins into a machine, and a ticket popped out. Shortly, on silent wheels, a train glided into the station, and the doors slid open. A raft of people jammed on the already crowded cars. She squeezed onto the car in front of her and stood looking out the window facing the platform.

Several latecomers were hurrying down the stairs. Though only the legs were visible, she gave a start. On the finger of one man sparkled a diamond ring. The crowd of passengers shifted as others shoved on. She pressed forward, trying to see past the people who had pushed in front of her, blocking her view. The doors slid closed, and before she could see the man's face, the train pulled out of the station.

A shiver crawled up her spine. Coincidence? No way! All morning, without consciously trying to figure out what it was, she'd had this gut feeling that something wasn't quite right. Once more she was grateful for vet school training, for Dr. Moers who had harped endlessly on the importance of observation.

"Watch! Observe! Look at the eyes, the ears, the mouth, the tail; the body language during examination; the reactions of the animal to the owner, the owner to the animal."

She had watched, observed, and as sure as God made little green apples, she knew she was being followed. The icy fingers of fear seemed to grip her heart, and suddenly she felt cold all over. Had her stalker made it down the stairs? Had he slipped onto the train before the doors closed? She knew he hadn't shoved through the crush of people pushing onto her car, but there were others. When she got off the train he would be watching for her. Somehow she would have to lose him.

She knew what she had to do. She would get off at the next stop and simply wait for the next train. But when the train slid to a stop, another mob of people surged on, forcing her toward the end of the car. Getting off was impossible. She could scarcely move. Her breath was coming in short gasps. Frantically, she thought, like sardines packed in a can, she was trapped in the midst of countless bodies pressed against her own. Now she recalled that to the Chinese, the idea of intruding on another person's space was incomprehensible. No one had his own space. But the thought made her feel no better.

After stopping for what seemed only a fraction of a second, the train moved on. At the next stop, more passengers pushed on. And the next and the next. *Oh, lord,* Barb thought distractedly, *is every last body in Kowloon going to the Hong Kong side?*

She stood stiff and tense, trying to think what she would do when she reached the end of the line. The one thing she definitely did not want to do was go directly to Lily's empty flat.

Though the train was lighted, the short trip through the dark tunnel under the harbor seemed endless. When they reached the far side of the harbor, the train stopped, but only a few passengers alighted. At the next stop Barb bent down, peering through the window at the names of the stations. Suddenly there was a lot of movement, a shifting among the riders. Several stood up, as if poised for flight. She leaned down again, peered through the window and caught the word "Central" before the train slid to a stop. Like the outgoing tide, people flowed toward the door in a mass exodus.

This is it, Barb thought. *Stay in the middle of the mob and you're out of here.* She moved with the crowd, shifting, keeping to the center as much as possible, until she came to the turnstile. People ahead of her were forming a line, and now she saw that they were inserting their tickets in a slot in the top of the turnstile. She would have to pass through it in order to get out of the station. The ticket. What had she done with it?

Quickly, she shifted her package under her arm and opened her purse. She rooted around inside. The ticket wasn't there. A feeling of panic closed her throat. She felt a hand against her shoulder, a hip shoved against her own, as she was pushed along by the press of passengers in back of her. The line moved quickly. It was her turn to pass through the turnstile.

"Take your time, think," she told herself. She closed her purse and stuck her hand in her pocket. She let out a shaky sigh of relief as her fingers clasped the flimsy ticket. She whipped it out and slipped it into the slot. As the turnstile gave, she bolted through it and ran up the stairs and out onto the street.

But she was not home free. The delay had cost her several minutes. Had those minutes given her pursuer time to spot her in the throng that alighted from the train? Had he found her after all? She dared not look back. Dared not take a chance that he was dogging her footsteps again. If he were, if their eyes met, he would know she was aware that he was following her. And then? And then what? Best he not know.

Breathless, she paused for a second to get her bearings. Across the street sprawled Chater Gardens, an oasis of green lawns, trees and statues where Filipina girls gathered on Sundays to gossip, picnic, write letters and do each others nails.

She turned toward the tram line on Des Voeux Road. Where it joined Queen's Road, stood the ultra-modern Hong Kong and Shanghai Bank building overshadowed by the elegant glass Bank of China Tower that rose beside it.

A green double-decker tram trundled down the street, bell dinging. It screeched to a stop and the doors flew open. Should she jump on, ride wherever it took her? The hair on the back of her neck prickled. Without volition, her head swiveled around. For a fraction of a second she was unable to move.

He was coming after her. Though he had donned dark glasses, still she recognized him—round head, black patent leather hair, black shirt open at the throat—he was elbowing his way through the crowd leaving the subway. His thick, dark brows were drawn in a determined scowl, his mouth an angry slash.

She bolted off the curb toward the tram. Inches from the door, it slammed closed and, bell dinging, the tram continued on its way down the track. She wheeled around. Her black-clad stalker was running across the sidewalk. A taxi slid up beside her and slowed, melding with the traffic. Unmindful of whether it was free, she flung open the door and dived inside.

Fourteen

"Hey! What the devil do you think you're doing?"

Barb landed in the lap of a lanky, long-legged man with a tropical tan and a Southern accent that wouldn't cut butter.

She plunged off his lap onto the seat beside him and found herself facing a wide-eyed woman with bobbed brown hair who wore a green pantsuit, a wedding ring and an incredulous expression.

The driver whipped around and began shouting at Barb in a long, excited stream of unintelligible syllables.

Quickly, the woman flapped a hand in an airy gesture of dismissal. "It's okay, okay."

Apparently mollified, the driver returned his attention to the road.

Breathless, Barb panted, "Sorry. I didn't realize—I mean, there was no time—"

As if the woman sensed Barb's distress, she said kindly, "Take a few deep breaths, honey, then you can tell us all about it."

Barb swallowed a few quick gasps. She felt her face redden with embarrassment. It was unlike her to be so unnerved, but then she'd never had to deal with a stalker.

"I apologize, barging into your cab this way, but you see there's this man—he's been following me all morning. Just now he followed me out of the subway, and I saw him standing on the curb watching me. He started toward me, so when your cab pulled up, I jumped in . . ."

The woman reached over and patted her hand. "You did the right thing, honey."

Her husband eyed Barb with a skeptical expression.

The woman went on, "I'm Ginny Morrison and this is my husband, Bill."

"I'm Barb, Barbara McKee."

Ginny's voice took on a note of pride. "We're going to visit our son on Okinawa."

Amused, Barb thought, clearly their son was at the top of their list of attractions.

"Our son *lives* on Okinawa. He's a computer programmer and works for—"

Abruptly, Bill Morrison broke in. "Where do you want to go, Miss uh—McKee?"

Barb beamed her best "new client" smile, hoping he wouldn't throw her out of the taxi. "I'll be happy to go wherever you're going." She turned her head and peered through the rear window, scanning the faces of the pedestrians for her pursuer.

"Is it all right?" Ginny asked. "Do you see the man who was following you?"

Barb shook her head and let out a long, relieved breath. "I think we've lost him, I hope." Facing Ginny, she went on, "I'm so grateful to both of you for letting me share your cab, I can't thank you enough."

Ginny let out a bubbly laugh. "That's just Southern hospitality, honey. We're from Memphis. And I bet you're from the Midwest, I can tell by your accent—"

Gently, patiently, her husband broke in, "Sweetheart, the point is not where she is from. It's where she is going." His gaze swiveled to Barb.

"We're going to ride the tram to Victoria Peak."

"Great!" Barb agreed. Though she'd have preferred to see the Peak under different circumstances, she was so grateful that they hadn't thrown her out of the cab, she'd have gone anywhere they suggested.

When the cab driver pulled up before Peak Tram Station, Barb insisted on paying the fare. They slid out of the cab, strode past a fountain that bubbled over a tier of steps, and made their way up a ramp past a gift shop. Although Barb was sure she had shaken her pursuer, she could hardly wait to get on the tram, out of sight, just in case he had managed to hail a cab and was combing the streets for her. Her spirits sank when she saw that a line of smiling, chatting tourists had already formed before the ticket booth. Nerves still on edge, she kept glancing over her shoulder, and to her relief, the man did not appear. At last, tickets in hand, everyone surged aboard the two bright red cars that made up the tram. Barb bolted aboard the first car with the Morrisons on her heels.

A narrow aisle bisected the rows of seats, three on one side, two on the other. Barb spotted a young Asian girl in one of the double seats and quickly slid into the empty seat beside her. She wanted to make it clear that she had no intention of latching on to Ginny and Bill Morrison.

A recorded spiel gave a brief history of the tram, built in 1888, 1800 feet above the harbor. As the cars crept upward at a forty-five-degree angle, Barb could hear the metallic meshing of the cogs, and tried not to think what would happen if they were to give way. The tram slid past elegant old mansions and high-rise concrete towers set down among a jungle of foliage. As it climbed higher and higher toward Victoria Peak, Barb had the eerie sensation that she was floating among the clouds.

Twelve hundred feet above sea level, the tram paused to give passengers a bird's-eye view of the harbor. Barb's breath caught in her throat at the sight of the incredible panorama spread out below. A vast fringe of skyscrapers bordered the shore, and ships from all over the world plied the whitecapped waters.

At the last stop, Barker Road, everyone stepped from the tram onto a black-and-white checkerboard stone terrace. Nervously, Barb glanced over her shoulder to make sure her stalker hadn't somehow caught up with her and boarded the second car. She let out a long, relieved breath. She saw no sign of him.

In the center of the terrace a fountain spurted with a loud thud, thud, thud. After saying goodbye to Ginny and Bill Morrison, Barb strolled onto an orange-roofed pagoda with a small balcony that offered a spectacular bird's-eye view of the city, the harbor, and beyond, the islands of the South China Sea.

Hundreds of ships at anchor, hundreds of ships under steam, stretched farther than she could see: immense cargo carriers, tramp freighters, supertankers, and holiday cruise liners; hydrofoils, Hovercraft; sailing junks, lumbering container ships and tug-drawn lighters. A hawk floated in the thermal updrafts, head swiveling, eyes scanning for unwary prey. A shiver coursed through her, and her knees threatened to give way.

A gusty wind whipped across the Peak ruffling her hair, and raucous rock music blasted in her ears. Swiftly she turned from the dazzling view of the harbor and left the pagoda. She wandered among the milling tourists across the terrace to the Peak Market, a gift shop that displayed the red Chinese junk symbol which guaranteed the merchants' reliability and honesty.

The huge, rambling store boasted counters, tables and shelves laden with every sort of souvenir imaginable. Tee shirts, toys, figurines, books, even tables piled high with jars of exotic foods, teas and candies. From the top shelf of a candy display, she picked up a Cadbury's almond chocolate bar. She turned it over, looking for the price tag, and as she did so, her eyes met those of a man standing on the opposite side of the table staring at her. Her heart seemed to leap into her throat.

Slowly, deliberately, he took off his dark glasses. Her stalker's dark, penetrating eyes reflected instant recognition. His intense, evil gaze struck her with the force of an electric shock. As if the candy bar were suddenly burning her fingers, she dropped it on the counter and spun around.

Dodging through the crowd of shoppers, she fled toward the back of the store and around a corner where a variety of clothing was offered for sale. She wound her way through racks of silk jackets and slacks. If only she could find a restroom, she could dash inside and lock the door.

She glanced over her shoulder. Her heart skipped a beat. She saw her pursuer weaving from side to side through aisles clogged with people browsing before the displays. Frantically her gaze swept around the walls, searching for a door that bore a female silhouette. There *had* to be a restroom. And there it was, far back in a corner.

She dashed to the door, twisted the handle. Locked! She could feel panic rising in her throat. Determinedly, she pushed it down.

"Think!" she told herself. "If you don't move, he'll trap you here in this corner at the back of the store."

She spun around and faced the wall of windows that overlooked the terrace. For one wild moment she was tempted to pick up a heavy brass candlestick and break the glass, a move sure to get everyone's attention. She was so rattled she almost missed it: a glass door at the end of the wall of windows.

Crouching low, hidden behind the racks of jackets and slacks, she scuttled crabwise across the room toward the glass door. Hampered by her plastic bag of gifts, she paused, hunkered down, and quickly slipped a man's maroon silk print jacket from a hanger and looped the plastic bag over the hook. She hung the jacket over it and shoved the hanger back on the rack.

At the door, she stood upright and, palms flat against the glass, gave a mighty push. The door flew open. On her right stretched the broad black-and-white checkered terrace. On her left loomed the entrance to an enclosed shopping mall.

She bolted through the doorway into the entrance of the new Peak Tower, where she saw a Haagen-Daz ice cream store and a long escalator leading to a second floor. The normal thing to do, she decided, would be to run down the wide corridor and duck into one of the shops. It would take her stalker all day to search each one to try to find her. And while he was looking in another shop, she could leave the one where she was hiding and board the tram down the Peak. Swiftly she scanned the long corridor lined with shops, then shaking her head, asked herself, "What's wrong with this picture?"

Scowling, she stared down the long, dim length of the mall. For one thing, shoppers were as scarce as hen's teeth. But it was the dimness of the lights that clued her in. Several shops were completely dark. Others had lighted windows, but no lights shone inside. It struck her then that almost all of the shops were closed. Thoughts flew around in her mind like birds in a cage. She envisioned herself tearing down the mall desperately looking to find a shop that was open. By the time she found one, her enemy would be on her like a duck on a June bug.

She plunged toward the escalator and began to run up the moving stairs. Halfway up to the second floor, she looked over the side and froze. He was standing below her, his head moving jerkily, this way and that, scanning the mall. Just then he looked up. His eyes locked with hers, and as though shot from a cannon, he raced toward the escalator.

Run, she thought, *run, run!* At the top of the escalator, she almost collided with several pots of hot pink azaleas. On her right she glimpsed a placard on an easel advertising the Peak Cafe on the third level of the mall. A voice in her head said, *Go for it! A cafe will have a restroom, a manager, and waiters or waitresses who will get this maniac off your back.*

She sprinted off the escalator, and onto the one that led to the third level. She looked over her shoulder, and for a second she thought her heart would stop beating. The head and shoulders of her black-shirted enemy rose relentlessly into view as he ran up the escalator below her. His venomous gaze locked with hers.

Run! shrieked the voice in her head. *Run!*

She raced up the remaining stairs, and looked desperately around the mall for the cafe. All of the third-level shops were dark. Many, totally empty, had obviously never been occupied. Not a shopper in sight. She wheeled about and finally spotted the glass-walled cafe at the front end of the mall. Glass windows overlooked a garden terrace. She raced toward the cafe, then stopped short. Chairs were stacked on top of the tables. No one was moving about inside. The place was deserted. Without warning, two strong arms encircled her from behind, enclosing her in a pincerlike grip.

She screamed, screamed again, though there was no one to hear her. Her captor's arms closed more tightly about her, pressing her hard against his chest. She almost gagged at the smell of stale cigarettes and sweat.

At the top of her voice, she yelled, "Let me go!" She dropped her purse, laced her fingers together and brought her clasped hands down hard on his wrist. At the same time she got off a vicious kick to his shins with the heel of her shoe.

"Ei-ee!" he shouted, and abruptly released his hold. She stumbled and almost fell. He bent down, scooped up her purse from the floor and ran.

At the top of her voice, she shouted, "Stop! Stop, thief!"

She took off running after him, down the long, shadowy corridor, past the dark, empty shops. Suddenly, he disappeared. Though her rationale told her it was impossible for the man to simply disappear, she kept on running. Unexpectedly, as she raced past the last shop, the corridor made an abrupt right angle. She rounded the corner shop and on her left saw two elevators. As she skidded to a stop, the shiny metal doors on one of them slid closed.

She jabbed at the buttons on the wall. The light over the elevator in which the thief had slipped away flashed red, descending. The other light flashed green, on its way up.

"Damn and blast!" Barb muttered, enraged.

She wheeled about, dashed down the corridor and hit the escalator running, downing three steps at a time. She raced down the second escalator and across the mall lobby past the Haagen-Daz shop and out the door. On the terrace, she halted, her furious gaze sweeping the faces of the tourists. All of a sudden, she saw him, squeezing onto the second car of the red tram about to make its descent.

She plunged toward him, waving her arms and shrieking, "Stop, thief! Police! That man stole my purse!"

It seemed to Barb that every person on the terrace froze, and stood staring at her with shocked eyes. Nobody, but nobody, moved. Just before the tram door closed, the thief threw her purse onto the stone terrace.

As if galvanized into action by this defiant act, a sedate-looking, elderly Oriental gentleman bent down and picked up her purse. With dignified strides, he crossed the black-and-white checkered terrace, and with a small bow, he handed it to her. Other onlookers crowded around her asking where and when and how the thief had stolen her purse. Another bystander offered to go and find the police. Several minutes later, seeming to materialize from nowhere, two khaki-uniformed Hong Kong police appeared at her side.

Polite, efficient, concerned first for her safety, one of the officers asked if she was hurt. She assured him she was unhurt, and that all her attacker wanted was her purse. They fired routine questions at her, and as soon as she explained what happened, one of them said, "We will call the terminal and have the tram stopped at the other end. You may go down and identify the culprit."

"Fine. I'll be happy to. But I do have my purse. Although the man grabbed it, he threw it from the tram as it started downhill."

"Nevertheless, we do not permit visitors to be

accosted in Hong Kong. The culprit must be apprehended and punished. I will have the tram stopped, at once." He strode away across the terrace.

His companion said, "We are thankful that he did not steal your purse, but I suggest you check the contents to see if anything is missing."

Hastily, Barb flipped open her purse. Grasping both sides and spreading them wide, she rummaged through it.

"It's empty," she exclaimed. "He stole all my money, and my map, my phrase book, everything!"

"Sorry, very sorry," he said earnestly.

At that moment, the other officer returned, looking glum.

"I regret to say, we were a hair too late. The tram had that minute opened its doors, and the passengers quickly alighted and dispersed."

To Barb's disappointment, they gave her little encouragement as to their chances of finding the thief, for her description would fit hundreds of young Asian men who frequented the streets of Hong Kong.

The officers obtained her promise to appear at the station to fill out the necessary forms, and politely refrained from saying that the mugging had occurred as a result of her own carelessness. The fact that they were most sympathetic and concerned made her feel a little better, but not much.

They left her with a stern warning to heed the signs posted in public places to beware of pickpockets and purse snatchers.

She stood there in the sunlight, alone, with no money, stranded at the top of Victoria Peak, debating what to do. It was a long walk down, and a longer walk to Winslow Towers. Desperately, she glanced around her. If she walked out to the road, and if she could find a cab, she could ride to Lily's bank and—she gave a start as a hand came down on her arm, and a kind Southern-accented voice asked, "Need any help, lady?"

She turned to see Bill and Ginny Morrison standing beside her, their eyes filled with concern.

Ginny said, "We were inside the gift shop when we heard all the commotion. What happened?"

Barb had scarcely finished filling them in, when Bill pulled out his wallet and handed her three hundred Hong Kong dollars.

Mingled relief and gratitude surged through her. Impulsively, she threw her arms around him and gave him a hug.

"You saved my life. I can't thank you enough. And as soon as I get back to my friend's flat, I'll write you a check and drop it off at your hotel."

"We're not worried about the money," Ginny assured her. "What about you?"

"I'm fine as frog's hair. In fact, things aren't as bad as they could be because I changed purses this morning and left my billfold, passport, everything, in my old shoulder bag. I only had Hong Kong dollars in this one," she said, giving the bag a pat. As she did so, an unpleasant thought struck her. "Maybe I spoke too soon." Quickly she opened her purse, reached inside and unzipped the side pocket.

"What?" Bill asked, clearly mystified.

Grinning, Barb held up her five-dollar watch, the

pink sack holding her jade ring and a key to Lily's flat. "I was afraid he'd taken these as well, but he must have been in too much of a hurry to search the inside pocket."

They chatted a few minutes longer, and after she bid them goodbye, Barb hurried inside the gift shop. Fervently she hoped no one had picked up the jacket hiding her plastic bag of gifts. She ran back to the clothing section of the shop and grabbed the hanger off the rack. It was still there, nestled safely under the maroon silk shoulders of the jacket. She rolled her eyes heavenward, murmuring, "Thank you, Lord."

She walked out to Barker Road and, after waiting almost twenty minutes, boarded a double-decker bus. Still shaken by the mugging, she sat unseeing as it lumbered down the narrow road around hairpin turns, past palatial villas almost hidden among stands of bamboo, sycamore and locust trees, past beds of white hydrangeas, crimson and gold cannas, and red, pink and purple bougainvillea blooming in gay profusion along the roadside.

When she alighted from the bus, she still felt unnerved, as if violated by the man's attack. Dreading the interview, but anxious to get it over with, she took a taxi to the Hong Kong Police Station and filled out the proper forms. They gave her several books of photos of criminals to page through, but none of them looked like her attacker. By the time she left the station, she felt more upset than before. Who was this creep? What did he want with her? Suppose he was waiting for her at Lily's flat? All her nerve endings tingled. She felt that at any mo-

ment she would fly into a million pieces. She would
have to stop thinking such thoughts or she would
drive herself crazy. What she needed was action,
something to calm her nerves.

She set off at a brisk walk down the Queensway.
Striding down the wide boulevard, she tried to drive
fearful thoughts from her mind, forced herself to
watch the passing scene: the double-decker trams,
the taxis whizzing by, the endless parade of Rolls
Royces. She passed the Museum of Teaware and the
new supreme court building and farther along, Pacific Place, a complex of five-star hotels and a multi-
level luxury shopping center. As though propelled
by some unseen force, she entered the spacious, airy
lobby and rode an escalator up to the shopping mall.

Still walking with no destination in mind, she
came to a restaurant and stopped short. The familiar
red and yellow decor drew her inexorably inside.
Like a robot, she passed through the cafeteria line
and emerged with a tray loaded with french fries,
a Big Mac and a chocolate milkshake. As she
sipped the shake, pigged out on crisp fries and
munched her hamburger, her nerves quit jumping.
It was time to return to Winslow Gardens.

Shortly after three-thirty she took out her key and
let herself into Lily's flat. She had closed the door
and set her package on the table when she realized
she was not alone. She stood very still, listening.

A voice drifted into the foyer from the living
room. A man's voice. Andre's voice. Then silence.
Why did no one answer? Was the man talking to
himself? *Maybe he's the most interesting person he
knows,* she thought wryly. Should she walk in and

interrupt his private, personal conversation with himself?

He began speaking again, and this time the words were loud and clear.

"Darling, I know you need money. I understand, *cherie*. I'm doing my best to get it together." There was another short silence; then Barb heard him going on in a tense voice, "One does not find forty-eight hundred francs lying around on the ground. I can send you half now and half next week." There was a long pause. His voice grew louder, sounding angry, indignant. "Of course I can't borrow it from Lily. Are you out of your mind?" Another silence, then, "Sorry. You will have to wait until the seventeenth."

Another woman, Barb thought. This was incredible. Andre was keeping another woman. Now his voice turned soothing, placating. "All right, all right, I'll be paid on the fifteenth, and I'll telegraph the full amount to you the same day." After another short pause she heard him say softly, *"Au revoir, cherie. Je t'aime."*

Barb's brows flew up. *Je t'aime?* I love you! Maybe it wasn't blackmail after all. Maybe Andre was involved with another woman! A wave of fury surged through her. How dare he accept Lily's hospitality, let her think he loved her, then turn around and betray her? Should she tell Lily her Mister Wonderful was stringing her along? Then thinking of the king who beheaded a messenger bearing bad news, she thought better of it.

In the first place, Lily would be infinitely hurt. Hurting Lily was the last thing she wanted to do.

As for herself, being beheaded by her best friend was not acceptable. On the heels of that thought, it struck her with the force of a blow that Andre Durand needed money, not only to buy his own restaurant, but for a more pressing demand. He needed it badly and he needed it now. She pushed the dour thoughts to the back of her mind to mull over later.

Quickly she tiptoed back to the door, turned the knob noisily, held the door open for several seconds, then slammed it shut.

"Anybody home?" she called from the foyer.

"Andre," he replied. "In here."

When she sauntered into the living room, he was still seated before the phone at Lily's writing desk. Now he rose to greet her, flashing his best Crest smile. When he spoke, his accent made his English words sound as fluid as French silk.

"To meet you here is an unexpected pleasure."

She forced a return smile. "Thank you," she said stiffly. "I didn't realize this was your day off."

He met her gaze head on. "It isn't, but today I had some personal business to attend to."

Barb crossed to the jade lounge chair and sat down, thinking, *You can say that again.* At least he hadn't trumped up some feeble excuse for being there. She gave him a point for that.

In carefully neutral tones she said, "I hope I'm not interrupting."

"Not at all," he said smoothly. He slid a cigarette pack from his shirt pocket and fished a silver lighter from the pocket of his slacks. Crossing to her chair, he held the pack out to her. She closed her eyes and shook her head. She wished he wouldn't smoke.

She hated that dry, dead-leaf smell. Usually, she would speak up, ask the smoker to please cease and desist; but this was Lily's flat, and evidently she didn't mind. Moreover, even though Andre paid half the rent, he was Lily's guest. *And much more,* thought Barb ruefully. She pressed her lips firmly together.

He sank down in the chair across from her, shook a cigarette from the pack and slid the pack back in his pocket. Flicking on the lighter, he regarded her thoughtfully over the flame before he touched it to the tip of his cigarette. He inhaled deeply, then leaned back in his chair, very much at ease.

"I thought you'd be out sightseeing," he said conversationally.

You bet your life you thought I'd be out, she thought, *so you could have a private conversation with your French paramour.*

"I went shopping along Nathan Road."

He leaned forward, light eyes wide with interest. "Did you make any purchases?"

She sighed inwardly. Now that she had discovered he was two-timing Lily, the last thing she wanted to do was to sit here making small talk with him.

"A few things—for my family."

"Your family?"

Oh, lord, she'd thrown him a conversational rope. "Lily tells me you have a grand, loving family."

Right, she thought, *flattery will get you everywhere.* "Yes, well, we consider Lily one of our own."

He smiled and nodded knowingly. "Lily speaks

so often of your family, I feel almost that I know them. There are your mama and papa who have a big farm in Idaho—"

"Iowa," Barb broke in quickly.

"Iowa, forgive me—and you have also the brother and a sister?"

"Sister-in-law." Why did she find herself resisting his efforts to be charming?

Carefully, he flicked his cigarette over a cloisonne ashtray. "Please, do tell me about them."

Trapped! she thought. How could she deny her family? "Well, my brother Hank is a computer programmer. He's married to a super girl, Amy. They have one daughter, Anna Lee, twelve."

"You and Lily were friends as children?"

"No, we met in college. We were roommates."

He gave her a benevolent smile. "Lily told me what a good friend you have been to her."

For a moment Barb was taken aback. But of course Lily would have told him about the accident, when Lily had been driving and had been struck by an approaching car head-on. The accident that had killed Lily's parents. Had she also told him that night after night during their freshman year at State she had awakened screaming from the nightmare of reliving the accident? How Barb had stood by her, helped her work through the guilt that consumed her?

"I only did what anyone would do under the circumstances." She looked him square in the eyes, and in a low, tense voice full of emotion, she went on. "Lily is like a sister to me. She is very vulnerable. I would not like to see her hurt, ever again."

He leaned back in his chair and regarded her with a long, level look. "Nor would I."

It occurred to Barb that Andre had been asking all the questions. Normally, it was she who asked the questions.

"What about you?" Barb asked. "How did you meet Lily?"

Coolly, he said, "We met in the line of business—at American Fidelity."

His answer gave her a jolt. Lily had told her he was a distant relative on her grandfather's side. The bank was another ball of wax. Lily was a loan officer. Why had Andre been borrowing money?

As if reading her thoughts, he asked, "Have you a problem with that?"

Barb felt her face flush. "No. I just thought there was a family connection."

"We are distantly related, it's true. But we had never met until I called on Lily at the bank." Looking straight at her, he said, "I always have thought there was more to you than meets the eye."

With a bright smile she replied, "I hope so. And I've always thought the same about you." With a small stab of satisfaction, she saw a red flush stain his cheeks. She rose to her feet. "If you'll excuse me, I have things to do."

He looked up at her, an odd expression on his face, as if trying to decide whether she was friend or foe. Graciously, he said, "Of course, madame."

She went to her room and, minutes later, heard the front door slam shut.

Fifteen

The boat rocked to and fro, waters lapping at the sides. He hoped the jerky motion would not wake his uncle from his nap. His hand began to sweat. Clutching the cellular phone tightly, he said in a low voice, "Chow here."

The voice on the other end growled, "Who is this that disturbs me at tiffin, and allows my tea to get cold?"

"I tell you, I am Woo Chow. I would not disturb you, but this is very important."

"What is it this time?"

His mouth grew dry, and maddeningly, when he spoke, his voice shook with excitement.

"There has come into my possession an artifact, one you are extremely interested in obtaining."

It was only a small lie, for at any moment he would have it in his possession. And by announcing that he already had it, he would insure that other interested parties would stop looking for it.

The man's voice grew hard with impatience. "Are you going to tell me what it is, or am I to guess?"

As though announcing a victory at the end of a long battle, he said, "It is a small jade horse. A gem of a horse from the Sung dynasty. Very rare piece, very fine workmanship."

There was a long silence on the other end of the phone that made Chow nervous. His hand grew damp. He squeezed the phone tighter.

"Does this horse happen to be a recumbent horse of mutton fat jade?"

Chow stiffened. How could the man know this? "Yes," he said, uncertainly, now not quite so sure of himself.

"You are the second person who has offered me this item."

Chow, suddenly alarmed, began to grow angry as the man went on in lofty tones.

"I have a buyer, but naturally I must see the merchandise before I can make any offers to buy it for my client. Where is it?"

Chow smiled to himself. His go-between was not above sending someone to steal it from him. Did he think Chow was stupid? That he would not realize that the man would make a much higher profit if he could get it without paying for it? But Chow would make certain no one would steal it because no one would ever find him here among the hundreds of boats in the floating village at Aberdeen.

"I have given it to my uncle for safekeeping."

Testily, his accomplice said, "When may I see it?"

Taken aback, Chow stiffened. Who was this second person who dared offer the horse for sale? And then he realized if a rival had the horse in his possession and had shown it to his go-between, his go-between would not be asking to see it.

"I will bring it to you."

"When?"

Chow licked his lips nervously, playing for time. Finally, he said, "Day after tomorrow."

"Why not today?"

Chow smiled at his own cleverness. "I have someone else who wishes to make an offer. Today I will show him the horse."

His go-between's voice took on a sharp edge. "You will not sell it to anyone until you have shown it to me?"

"Naturally not. I am an ethical businessman."

"Then I will see you at four on the Friday."

Chow hung up, more than pleased with himself, thinking, *That one will tell everyone the horse is within his grasp. Then others will stop searching for it. I will be free to search without worrying about competition or interference, and I will be first to find it.*

Sixteen

Barb stared down at the small mutton fat horse Lily held in the palm of her hand.

"I can't believe it!"

In vexed tones, Lily said, "I mean it, Barb. Bank regulations. They won't let me stable the horse in the bank. Won't let me rent a box in your name and put the horse inside. You have to be present."

"Humm. Could you rent a box in *your* name?"

"I have a box, and I could have put the horse inside, but suppose something happened to me. If I were run over by a tram—hit by a bus—you couldn't get in the box."

Barb sighed inwardly, thinking sometimes Lily carried this "no risk" obsession too far. She took the horse from Lily and set it down on the coffee table, then sank down on the couch.

"The problem is, I've signed up for a city tour tomorrow which begins at nine-thirty. I won't have time to go to the bank first."

A pink flush of annoyance colored Lily's pale features. "That's ridiculous. Listen, Barb, first things first. Putting the horse in a safe place is more important than a city tour. You can take a tour next week."

"Next week," Barb explained patiently, "I want to see the New Territories and take a water tour to Lantau and the other outlying islands, and you promised to take a day off to go to Macau. There may not be any time next week."

Lily sat down beside Barb, picked up the horse and handed it to Barb. "Please, Barb, put this animal back in your purse and take it to the bank with me tomorrow. If we leave here at eight-fifteen, we can be there when it opens at nine. We'll call the tour agency, tell them you're on your way. They never leave right on the dot anyway. I'm sure it will be okay."

With obvious reluctance, Barb got to her feet, swept up her shoulder bag from the desk and tucked the horse back inside. "Okay, okay. I'll stop by the bank and do the drill."

"First thing in the morning, right?"

"Right."

As if eager to move on to a safer subject, Lily asked, "What kind of luck did you have shopping?"

Barb returned to the couch and sat down across from Lily. "Good shopping, bad joss, my friend. Very bad joss. Your *feng shui* practitioner is off the wall. My life forces are all askew."

As Barb recounted the tale of her stalker, his attack outside the cafe and snatching her purse, Lily was alternately incredulous, furious and sympathetic.

"And there's no chance they can ever track him down?"

"Not really. When I stopped by the police station, they let me leaf through a few books of mug shots, but none of them looked like the thief. And that's not all. Something else strange happened. This morning I met Pete Chang in the elevator. He looked as if he'd been put through a grinder."

Lily gave an astonished gasp.

"He was covered up from head to toe, mirror sunglasses and all. But I could see he had a granddaddy of a shiner and his poor face looked swollen and bruised. When we got off the elevator, I could see his eye from the side. It looked like rotten meat."

Alarm filled Lily's eyes. "Did you ask him what happened?"

"No, I figured it was none of my business. You know how the Brits are about Americans always asking questions. But for some reason he felt compelled to explain. Said he'd run into a door." Barb's mouth curved in a wry grin. "He must think I rode into town on a turnip truck. And, he insisted on going shopping with me, but as soon as we got off the ferry, he said he had business to take care of and left."

"No explanation?"

Barb shook her head. "Unless—he was ticked off at me because I refused to sell him my horse."

Lily's eyes widened in an incredulous stare. "I can't believe him! How could he buy it? He has no money."

"He said he'd pay me later—one thousand HK dollars."

"How much later?"

Barb shrugged. "I told him I haven't decided whether or not I'll sell it.

"Another odd thing, on the ferry someone seemed to be watching us. It was after that he decided to take off. Do you think it's possible that his gambling friends roughed him up, that they were sending him a message?"

Lily's expression turned somber. "There's not a doubt in my mind. No wonder he cancelled t'ai chi. He's probably one big bruise and aching in every bone in his body."

Barb gave a sympathetic sigh. "Poor Pete. His joss is no better than mine."

"The reason you have bad joss," Lily explained, "is that we've not done everything the practitioner recommended. *Voila!*" She picked up her purse from the coffee table and, from its voluminous depths, pulled several white plastic bags.

By ten o'clock that night, red ribbons were tied on the front door handle. In the living room, a lucky red bird perched in the branches of a six-foot areca palm that Lily had ordered delivered from a nearby shop. Brass wind chimes that Lily had hung in the archway chimed cheerily, stirred by the breeze that wafted through the open glass doors.

Outside on the terrace, bloomed huge pots of yellow and rust chrysanthemums. Small, octagonal mirrors flanked the doors on the outside walls, and a mat that resembled a cluster of waterlilies lay before the door.

Experimentally, Barb opened the front door. A peal of bells rang through the flat. Smiling at Lily, she said, "If an interloper is at all superstitious, we're safe as the gold in Fort Knox."

Lily scowled at the door. "Except that we still

don't have a dead bolt on the door, and no one has changed the lock."

"Don't tell me it's superstition at work—the unlucky four."

"Afraid so. I'll keep hounding the locksmith."

The next morning Barb accompanied Lily to American Fidelity Bank, where Lily introduced her to the floor lobby services manager, and after unraveling an incredible amount of red tape, Barb locked the horse away in a safe-deposit box. She arrived at the tour agency breathless, with only minutes to spare.

Now, seated in a big, comfortable tour bus loaded with sightseers, she gazed eagerly out the window. Their guide, Sue, a short, slender girl with straight black hair and a fringe of bangs, a graduate of Hong Kong University, pointed out sights of interest. The bus crept through Wan Chai, lined with shops, restaurants and bars and along Harbour Road to the Hong Kong Arts Centre. After exploring the Arts Centre, they drove along Harbour Road past the Academy for Performing Arts and stopped again at the Convention and Exhibition Centre. They circled around Wanchai Sports Ground, admired the Royal Hong Kong Yacht Club jutting out into the harbor and continued on to the Sino Tower and the World Trade Centre.

Shortly before noon, the bus parked a block away from the Excelsior Hotel. Everyone filtered out of the bus and walked to a small garden in the center of which stood an ancient cannon.

Sue, in her light, rhythmic voice, explained, "In the late 1800s cannons were fired in salute to the head of the firm of Jardine, Matheson and Company, a great British trading company, upon his return from a trip. The company was reprimanded by the British authorities because such salutes were reserved for the governor and senior naval officers. As penance, the company was ordered to fire a cannon once every noon until further notice. Since no one ever cancelled the order, except for the duration of the Japanese occupation, the noonday firing of the cannon has taken place ever since."

The tour group waited patiently until, precisely at noon, an attendant pulled the lanyard, and the boom of the ancient cannon reverberated across the island.

They stopped for lunch at a nearby restaurant where they were seated at big, round tables. To Barb's delight, each table was dominated by a lazy Susan, where they served themselves from a variety of exotic dishes. After lunch, they viewed the Causeway Bay Typhoon Shelter, the site of a floating fishing village where Sue told them generations of families had lived, some never leaving their boats to go ashore.

The highlight of the afternoon tour was their visit to a jade factory. The "factory" was an old, shabby-looking building on the corner of what appeared to be a rundown residential district. Inside, stood two rows of tables. Carvers, male and female, of all ages, were seated before each table. A bulb with a white, cone-shaped metal shade, which hung from a wall arm, shed a bright light over the table.

Barb approached an elderly man who sat, shoulders hunched, head bent close to his work. In his left hand, he held a small, pink animal which Barb decided must be a turtle. In his right hand he held a drill. On the wall before him a spigot held a hose from which extended a tube. From the tube poured a thin stream of liquid which Barb realized was an abrasive.

On the man's left, a rust-colored bowl held several pieces of various colors of jade. Beside the bowl, four other animals awaited further carving under the old artisan's drill. Barb eyed them curiously: a pale pink bird, a phoenix perhaps, an orange and yellow tiger, a bright green dragon, and a mutton fat carving that looked like a unicorn.

At first glance, she thought she'd seen it somewhere before. After staring at it a moment longer, she realized it was the position, the shape of the animal, that was familiar. The recumbent pose, the head turned over one shoulder, called to mind her jade horse.

Struck with an idea, she crossed to Sue, who was standing at the gift counter chatting with a salesgirl. It would be fun to buy one of these small jade carvings for each of her friends and even one for herself. She scanned the figures on the counter and those in the lighted case below. Quickly, she decided on a turtle, a rabbit, and a dragon. She looked for the unicorn which had captured her fancy, but there were none in the case.

Smiling at the clerk, she said, "I'd like to buy a unicorn, please."

The girl immediately began searching through the

figures in the display case, then shook her head. "Sorry. No unicorns. They are most popular. You come back tomorrow, maybe unicorn."

"I don't think I can come back tomorrow."

Turning to Sue, Barb said, "Will you ask the clerk if it's possible for me to buy the unicorn one of the carvers has on his table?"

"Of course."

As soon as she asked, the girl shook her head and rattled off a few words which Sue translated. "She says it is not finished."

"Oh."

The girl must have heard the disappointment in her voice, for she said, "You like tiger, dog, bear?" She pointed to each one.

"No, give me a camel instead."

After the tour ended at four, Barb strolled down the Queensway to American Fidelity and found Lily in her office. As they stood waiting for the bus on their way home from the bank, Barb told Lily, "It's incredible, really ironic, that such a small animal can create such havoc. I feel as if a fifteen-hundred-pound horse has been lifted from my shoulders."

Lily gave a long, happy sigh. "All I can say is, thank God that beast is no longer living in my flat."

Thinking that was rather a strong reaction, Barb turned to look at her, brows raised in mild surprise. "Maybe we should put up a sign: NO ANTIQUE HORSE INSIDE."

Lily gave a light laugh. "Not a bad idea. The thing is, I felt responsible for it."

"But by now, anyone who searched your flat knows it isn't there."

For a long moment Lily was silent. Finally, she said, "Maybe."

"Whaddya mean, 'maybe'? You don't think one of your friends has an eye on it, or do you?"

Lily seemed to be staring very hard at the changing colors on a traffic light across the road. The light flashed red, and a cavalcade of cars ground to a screeching halt.

"Lily?"

For a long moment she remained silent.

The traffic light changed to green, and as if prompted by the cars charging forward, Lily said, "I keep thinking about Pete Chang saying he *lost* that laughing Buddha. Nobody just *loses* an object as valuable as a laughing Buddha. I mentioned it to Mei Ling, and she, too, thinks he lost it gambling. Mei Ling says he's up to his eyeballs in gambling debts—she doesn't know how many thousands of dollars—and that last week he went to Macau to try to recoup, but got in even deeper."

Barb felt a tremor of mingled shock and sympathy run through her. Shock that a man who appeared to be the picture of British integrity would allow himself to fall into such a trap, sympathy for Lily that her friend was in such deep trouble.

"He has a big-time problem. I really feel sorry for the poor guy."

Lily, avoiding Barb's gaze, said, "True, Pete has problems, but none that money won't solve."

Barb looked at her sharply. "Are you saying you think Pete was after my jade horse?"

Lily hesitated. "I don't want to think that, but . . ."

The rest of her words were drowned out as the bus roared up to the stop. The door flew open and Lily got on.

As Barb followed her onto the bus, Lily's words pounded in her ears: "I don't want to think that, *but . . ."* That tiny word said it all. There was no point in pursuing it further. Privately, she wondered why Pete would offer to buy the horse if he had intended to steal it. It didn't make sense. Unless, having failed to steal it, he thought he could buy it and sell it at a whopping profit.

All during dinner and for the rest of the evening, Barb tried to put thoughts of Pete as the would-be thief from her mind, but they kept coming back and back again. It was the same as someone saying, "You can't have any bread," and after that, all you can think about is bread.

Shortly before eleven, Lily flicked on the TV and turned the dial to the English news channel. As if on signal, the phone gave a loud, demanding shrill.

Barb leaped up from her chair. "I'll get it. It's probably Steve."

"At ten A.M.?"

Barb grinned. "The man has no respect for time. He says he loves me every hour of the day, and I guess this is his way of showing it."

She crossed to the writing desk and picked up the white princess receiver. Filled with anticipation, she said in a lilting voice, "Hello. Barb here."

Without preamble, a muffled voice said, "I'm interested in purchasing a small jade artifact you have in your possession."

"Who is this?" Barb demanded.

As though she hadn't spoken, the voice went on, "I will pay the highest price on the market."

Instantly, on the defensive, she said, "I don't know what you're talking about."

The voice came again, low, and husky, and sounding far away, so that she couldn't tell whether the caller was a man or a woman—or a heavy smoker.

"Oh, I believe you do. It's a small, recumbent horse, mutton fat jade. Does that jog your memory?"

Barb sank down in the chair before the desk. What was jogging her memory was the pattern of the caller's speech—not the one or two abrupt phrases uttered by other anonymous callers, but complete sentences. And more telling, the words themselves, artifact, recumbent, mutton fat, all showed some knowledge of the horse. If she could stall, keep this creep on the phone. . . .

Again she asked, "Who is this?"

She strained her ears listening, hoping to detect any kind of an accent.

"That isn't important." He bit off the words in impatient, staccato tones.

Heatedly, she said, "It is if you want to buy my carving. How do I know this is a legitimate offer? How can I sell it to you if I don't know who you are?"

The voice grew stronger, verging on anger. "Who I am is not important. When we agree on a price, arrangements will be made for pickup and payment."

An old adage leaped into her mind: *Those whom the Gods wish to destroy, they first make angry.* In airy tones that indicated his offer was of no importance, and not worth considering, she said, "I'm afraid that's impossible."

"Impossible!" The voice sputtered with outrage.

"Impossible," said Barb with finality. "I don't have it. The horse is no longer in my possession."

Anger, cold as steel, seemed to flow through the line. The caller's next words were snapped off as if spoken through clenched teeth.

"You had best get hold of it and quickly." His tone turned menacing. "If not, you will meet more trouble than you can ever imagine, for I mean to have the horse."

A hot rush of fury surged through her. In low, evenly spaced tones she said, "Don't you threaten me. If you think you can intimidate me, you'd better think again!"

She slammed down the receiver, then lifted it off the hook in case the caller tried to ring again.

Lily had switched off the TV and sat staring openmouthed at Barb. "What was that all about?"

Barb recapped the conversation and, when she had finished, asked, "Who do you think it could be?"

Lily gave a Gallic shrug.

"For one thing, whoever it was didn't sound one iota Oriental. Does that give you a clue?"

She paused, waiting for Lily to mention any one of her friends. But Lily sat there, shaking her head.

Barb could feel her temperature rise. Lily must have some idea who the caller was. Why couldn't she take her part? That Lily wasn't more loyal dismayed her. But then, wasn't Lily being loyal to her other friends by not naming names?

Right, she thought, sighing inwardly. *Okay, Lil, I'll handle it myself.* She waited until after Lily had gone to bed, then tiptoed into the living room and leafing through Lily's address book found five phone numbers. Quietly she pressed number after number. People who were likely to be at work, she called at home. And those apt to be at home, she called at work. If anyone answered the phone in person, she would hang up. But as she had expected, everyone was either at work and unable to come to the phone, or not at work until business hours resumed tomorrow morning. She smiled to herself. She would be forever grateful for answering machines.

Seventeen

By ten-thirty the next morning Barb, dressed in a gray polo shirt and black slacks, came to a halt before Man Mo Temple on the corner of Hollywood Road and Ladder Streets. A shiver ran through her. The wide sky was obscured by a gunmetal gray overcast, promising a sullen morning that threatened a downpour. In the street beside her, a coolie seated on the footrest of a red plastic rickshaw dozed under a straw hat while awaiting a tourist who would pay for a ride in the almost extinct two-wheeled vehicle.

From here, she had an excellent view of the doorway of the antique shop across the street. It occurred to her then that anyone approaching the shop had just as good a chance of seeing her, and would wonder why she was here. She took several steps forward until she stood almost hidden behind the shoulder-high red pillar postal box on the corner. In her head she replayed the whispered message she had left on four tape recorders:

"The item we discussed is now available. If you are still interested, be at my shop at eleven A.M. tomorrow morning."

Feeling like a spider spinning a web, she smiled

to herself. Leaving the messages at night meant there was almost no risk. Mei Ling was performing Peking Opera excerpts at the Dinner Theatre. For Andre, who was officiating in the kitchen of La Parisienne, she had left a voice mail message. The curator had long since left the museum and would discover the message on his machine when he arrived this morning. True, Peter Chang could have answered the phone in person. Calling him was a calculated risk, even though Mei Ling had said Peter spent his nights gambling. If he had answered, she'd have hung up and called back later. But her luck had held. Peter had not answered. Her grin widened. As Lily would have said, "Good joss!"

The fifth message, of course, had to be slightly different from the others. This morning, when Duncan MacGregor played his messages, he would hear a low, husky voice saying, "I wish to purchase a rare object you have for sale. I will see you at your shop at eleven o'clock tomorrow morning."

For the fifth or sixth time she glanced at her watch. Five till eleven. She didn't have long to wait. She felt a tingling feeling of mingled curiosity and anticipation. Who would show up at Dong Po MacGregor Antiquities? The next moment a huge green tour bus drew up before Man Mo Temple, blocking her view. All she could see was the tour company name and Beijing printed on the side of the bus. The doors flew open disgorging a crowd of passengers. They swarmed about like ants at a honey pot. Though the temple was closed, several intrepid sightseers strode to the doors and peered inside. But most of the tourists fanned out across

Hollywood Road like an invading army and disappeared inside the antique shops.

She stepped around the red pillar letter box and stood poised on the curb. She glanced to her left, beyond the rickshaw, up the wide, steep stairway called Ladder Street. Little light penetrated the narrow street squeezed in between tall buildings. Six or seven people were climbing the shadowy stairs. Only one person, a young man, hands shoved in the pockets of his black leather jacket, strolled downward. She turned to her right and glimpsed shoppers pausing at stalls and other items for sale, spread out on the ground that lined the street. Several pedestrians were climbing the stairway toward Hollywood Road. She recognized no one.

Uneasily, she glanced at her watch again. Ten after. Had she missed her mark? Had the caller who had threatened her mingled with the throng of tourists and entered the shop unobserved? It would be risky to enter the shop before the caller arrived. If he, or she, saw her there, the game would be up. Barb's jaw set in a determined tilt. Nothing worthwhile was ever gained without some risk. And there was only one way to find out whether her quarry had slipped inside the shop.

With brisk steps she crossed the street and paused before the shop window to the left of the doorway. A thin layer of grime obscured her view. The window could do with a wash, she thought, frustrated. She tried to see inside the shop, past the displays of vases, screens, Buddhas and other artifacts cluttering the window, but it was too poorly lighted. Under her breath, she muttered, "You'd think the old skinflint could afford more than a sixty-watt bulb."

She ambled farther along the street and peered in the window to the right of the doorway. She could see only dim figures moving about.

Resolutely, she pushed open the door and stepped inside the shop. A faint, musty smell permeated the air. Swiftly she crossed to stand behind a tall, lanky man with wide, bony shoulders wearing a white shirt and black trousers. He carried a long, thin stick bearing a yellow pennant that marked him as a tour guide.

She glanced quickly around her. Duncan MacGregor was nowhere to be seen. A young girl with shiny black, silken hair cut in a wedge was standing behind the glass counter showing a pair of silver filigree earrings to a customer. Barb eased away from the guide and stood in the shadow of a massive blue and white porcelain jardiniere that gave her a wider view of the shop.

Her intense gaze swept past rosewood and black-wood furniture, paintings and curios to the far corner of the room which was dominated by an eight-panel, black coromandel screen inlaid with ivory and jade, half again as large as Lily's.

She recalled, from having poked around during her previous visit to the shop, that an area devoted to Duncan's office was hidden behind the screen. She had seen a scarred, mahogany kneehole desk, the top littered with papers, a blue and white porcelain teapot and two cups, a green leather chair and several filing cabinets. She particularly remembered a pair of white Staffordshire dogs with glass eyes perched as if on guard atop a chest-high, gray steel safe.

Purposefully, she threaded her way through the milling shoppers toward the screen. Shielded by one of the black panels, she peeked through a slit where two panels were hinged together. Her heart seemed to jump into her throat. Duncan, wearing his red plaid cap and a rumpled, brown tweed jacket, was seated in the leather chair, leaning forward, his hands gripping the edge of his desk.

Facing Duncan, his back to her, stood a rotund, bald-headed figure wearing a black and beige, diamond-patterned silk shirt. His head was thrown back at a defiant angle; his hands at his sides were bailed into fists. Professor Fais! The last person she had expected to swallow her bait. Quickly, she turned her head away. Standing as close to the screen as possible without knocking it over, she pressed her ear to the slit between the panels.

Professor Fais spouted a string of words in Cantonese.

"Please," Duncan hissed. "We will speak only English, unless you want every tourist from Beijing to overhear our conversation."

"In English, then," he snapped. "I do not understand why you do not permit me to see the figurine."

In tones that conveyed one-upmanship, Duncan said, "Ah, but you have already seen it, have you not?"

In a sharp voice Professor Fais replied, "I want to make certain you have in your possession the object you offer for sale."

"It is in safekeeping," Duncan said confidently. "It is the price that is open to negotiation."

"No!" The word burst from the professor's lips like a small explosion. "No negotiation. Eighty thousand Hong Kong dollars."

Ten thousand, U.S., Barb thought. *Surely Fais can offer more than that!*

There was a long moment of silence. Barb turned her head and peeked between two panels of the screen. Duncan, his face utterly without expression, had picked up the blue and white porcelain teapot and was pouring tea into the cups on his desk. A small cloud of fragrant steam rose from the cups.

Duncan nodded toward the teapot. "English breakfast tea."

Stalling for time, Barb thought. *Good ploy.* The silence stretched on. She felt as though she were watching an intensely competitive game of chess.

At last Professor Fais blurted, "We have every right to own the jade horse because it never should have been taken from our country. It belongs in China."

"This is Hong Kong."

The professor's voice rose to a whine. "Do not play the game with me. Soon Hong Kong will be China. Soon all will be one."

The Scotsman's burr thickened. "If I sell you the jade for eighty thousand Hong Kong dollars I will make nothing. My—ah—supplier demands ten thousand American dollars, which is eighty thousand Hong Kong dol—"

Professor Fais raised a hand, cutting him off. "May I please to remind you, the horse *is* stolen property. You could find yourself in much trouble should the Hong Kong Police be told that you are selling stolen artifacts."

Duncan's sand-colored brows flew up as he gazed at Professor Fais over the rim of his teacup. "My dear man, the entire island knows I sell stolen merchandise. Stolen from ancestors, stolen by employees from former residents who have long gone, stolen at ridiculous prices from owners who simply wish to unload items they no longer want. How do you think we stay in business? It is a way of life. I can let you have it for thirty thousand, American."

Barb stifled a gasp.

Professor Fais picked up his cup of tea and, holding it in both hands like a bowl, sipped at it noisily. Softly, he said, "Are you not required to supply provenance for the antiquities you sell?"

Duncan's lips curved in a sly smile. "Naturally. And I do."

Professor Fais drained his cup and, as if in a parting gesture, set it down on Duncan's desk. He gave a long, loud sigh. "I will give you twenty thousand, American. If you do not accept my generous offer, you may never hear another. There is merit in the ancient adage, 'Bird in hand is the value of two birds in bush.' "

Duncan's smile broadened. "Funnily enough, I have two birds in hand. I have another buyer. This is why the price is open to negotiation. My best price—twenty-five thousand, American, two hundred thousand, Hong Kong."

With obvious reluctance, Fais said, "I will speak with the director at my museum. However, funds for new acquisitions are limited. I assure you, you have received our best offer, twenty thousand American dollars."

Duncan MacGregor's gray-blue eyes turned steely. "Your best offer is not acceptable." He leaned back in his green leather chair and regarded Professor Fais with an indulgent smile. "It's no use you know, your being stubborn. This opportunity to bid on the horse will not be open forever, my friend. I will hold it until noon of the fifteenth of this month. At that time, the horse will go to the highest bidder."

Professor Fais made a stiff little bow. "Good day, Mr. MacGregor."

Before he could turn around, Barb quickly stepped away from the screen. Elbowing her way through the crowd of shoppers, squeezing past browsers, she strode toward the door. It wouldn't do for the professor or Duncan MacGregor to catch her slinking about the shop.

Once outside, she hurried down Hollywood Road, turned down Ladder Street and ran down the steps, dodging pedestrians and shopkeepers who darted toward her, pleading with her to buy.

Breathless, she arrived at Queen's Road Central and grabbed a taxi. She glanced at her watch. Eleven-thirty, too early to meet Lily for lunch at the tea house. Then, on impulse, she told the cab driver, "American Fidelity Bank."

She had waited only ten minutes in the marble and glass lobby when Lily's office door opened and an elderly Asian gentleman with a cane and a long white beard appeared. Lily held on to his elbow, walking at his side, as he tottered out into the lobby.

Barb gave her a little wave. Smiling, Lily motioned her into her office. Barb sank down in a royal blue armchair beside Lily's desk. Shaking her head, Lily sat down on a swivel chair behind her desk. "It's been a bad hair day. Everybody wants to borrow money to escape from Hong Kong while they still can, and most of them can't possibly qualify."

Barb gave her a sympathetic smile. "Sorry, my friend. I myself have had a fascinating morning."

Lily leaned forward, her eyes alight with curiosity. "What, what?"

"Well . . . I just happened to be in the vicinity of Dong's Antiquities and wandered inside. Actually, I was swept inside by a tide of tourists from Beijing."

Lily's eyes twinkled. "Come on, Barb, get on with it. Can't you see I'm coming apart at the seams with curiosity?"

"Oh?" Barb said, feigning surprise.

Lily, sliding the papers on her desk into a manila folder, shot her a threatening look. "Give!"

"So I was standing next to this huge coromandel screen that hides Duncan's office and what should I hear but voices in back of the screen."

Lily laughed. "You just *happened* to be standing by the screen, right?"

Barb's chin rose, and her mouth quirked at the corners. With mock reproach, she said, "I'm going to ignore that uncalled-for implication that I deliberately eavesdropped. Unless you don't care to hear what was being said . . ."

Lily's brows flew up, her eyes opened wide. "Tell, tell!"

"There were two men trying to strike a deal."

"Who? Who were?"

"Duncan MacGregor and—"

"Barb, the guy's a shopkeeper. Whaddya expect?"

"What I don't expect is for one of them to be Professor Fais."

"Fais! You've got to be kidding."

"Would I kid about something like this? And another thing I don't expect is to hear the two of them haggling over a small jade horse."

"Horse talk doesn't mean they're haggling over *your* horse. There must be countless horses around, like those galloping polo ponies, that big rust-colored Tang horse, and those little—"

Barb leaned forward and looked her straight in the eyes. "It was *my* horse, believe me."

"How do you know?"

"Because Duncan said he had the horse in his possession, in a safe place."

"If Fais believes that, I have a terra-cotta warrior I'd like to sell him. He *can't* have it in his possession, you know that. We put it in the safe-deposit box, remember? I think you're losing it."

Sometimes Lily's passion for facts irritated the bejeeze out of her. Softly, she said, "Lil, my friend, don't you ever go with your gut feelings? Obviously, he intends to get the horse, one way or another. And so does dear Professor Fais."

Lily's lips thinned. She opened a drawer, dropped the folder inside a hanging file, then leaned her arms on the desk and folded her hands.

"Now tell me exactly what they said."

As clearly as she remembered, and she remembered almost word for word, Barb repeated the dialogue between Professor Fais and Duncan MacGregor. Finished, she frowned slightly.

"There was something off-key about their conversation, something not quite right that I can't put my finger on. The most obvious thing, of course, is that Duncan was offering the horse for sale as if he had it stashed away in his big steel safe in his office."

"But we know he hasn't, so what makes him so sure he can produce it if a buyer comes up with the money?"

"Beats me." Anxiously, Barb ran her hand through her hair. "This whole thing is driving me crazy.

"Another thing that really nags at my mind, is Professor Fais'—I guess you'd call it his persona. He seemed to be an entirely different person from the dapper, confident expert we met at the tea house. Today he was so—so confrontational."

"That figures. He was trying to negotiate a deal, and Chinese businessmen are noted for cutting a tough deal."

"But why wasn't the museum director in on the discussion, or haggling at the bargaining table—or whatever?"

"That's easy. It would be a tall professional feather in the professor's cap if he were to be the one to find and buy the jade horse. It would probably be one of their most important acquisitions. A big coup for a small, private museum."

"Right," Barb agreed. But whether it was a gut feeling or the fact that she'd been trained to observe body language, and the intensity of reactions in both animals and humans in various situations, a voice in her head told her that something was rotten in Hong Kong.

Lily grabbed her big black purse from under the desk, rolled her chair back and stood up.

"Let's do lunch."

Over dim sum at their favorite tea room, Lily demanded that Barb go over the entire morning's scenario. When she finished, Lily shook her head. "Your brain needs a change of venue. Tonight Mei Ling and our friends will be playing mah-jongg at my flat, and I'm going to let you sit in in my place."

Barb laughed. "I haven't the foggiest idea how to play the game."

"I know. That's why you're going to sit in. We'll teach you."

"I think that's biting off more than I can chew at this moment in time."

Lily gave her a sweet, implacable smile that Barb knew from past experience meant that nothing short of the atom bomb would deter her from her purpose.

Barb gave a small, resigned sigh. "Okay, you're on."

That night, long after she'd gone to bed, Barb lay wide-eyed and sleepless. She could still feel the shock of Mei Ling's stunning revelation at the mah-jongg table.

The evening had started out innocently enough. Barb dragged out the table, covered it with a green felt cloth, and set up four padded metal chairs. Lily had set out the white bone tiles, racks to hold them, a pair of dice, counters for scoring and a small brass bowl for the "kitty." The scene was set for a pleasant game of mah-jongg with Lily's good friends, or so she thought.

Mei Ling was first to arrive. She made her usual dramatic entrance garbed in a bright, multicolored tunic that reminded Barb of a Matisse painting, worn over black silk slacks, and high-heeled, platform-soled sandals. Gold hoop earrings dangled from her ears, and a tall, fan-shaped, ivory-carved comb guarded the chignon on the back of her head. But rather than her usual ebullient manner, she was strangely quiet and subdued.

Close on her heels came Cecile and Connie Wu, two sisters who looked to be in their late twenties. Cecile wore a powder blue blouse and Connie a white V-neck sweater. Both wore floral-patterned slacks. Cecile, shorter of the two, with long, curly black hair and sparkling eyes, a Hong Kong tour guide, gave her a dimpled smile. Connie, slender, with short, silken black hair and bangs, who taught English at the university, covered her mouth with her fingers and bobbed her head in greeting.

Introductions over, Lily nodded toward the table. "Mah-jongg, anyone?"

Mei Ling and Cecile immediately pulled out two chairs and sat down at the table. Connie held back, saying shyly, "Let Dr. Barbara play in my place. I will assist her."

Barb smiled and raised her hands, palms flat, in a gesture of refusal. "No, no, thank you. I appreciate your offer, but I much prefer to watch and listen while you and the others show me how to play."

Connie bobbed her head again, and sat down at the table. Lily spread out the tiles, and everyone began turning them facedown and shuffling them around the table.

"There are many ways to play this ancient 'game of the four winds,' " Lily said, "but we favor the Chinese system."

Barb pulled the chair from the writing desk over to the table and sat watching intently as each of the women drew tiles and began to build a wall two tiles high and eighteen tiles long before her rack. They pushed the four walls together to form a square; then each in turn threw the dice to determine who would claim the title of East Wind and be first to play. Mei Ling won the throw. Cecile explained that the other players were known as South, West and North Wind. Mei Ling threw the dice again to determine which wall would be opened for drawing tiles and where it would be broken, then quickly swept them up and set them on her rack. Turning to Barb, she said, "I'm picking up my luck."

Cecile, who was South Wind, opened her wall and swung it toward the center of the table. Each of the players in turn drew tiles and discarded, tiles clicking, hands moving so quickly that Barb could hardly follow them, until Connie finally won the hand.

Connie rose to her feet. "Barb, you take my place."

Barb shook her head. "Thanks, but no thanks. I'll jump in when I know how to play the game."

Lily smiled. "You never know all there is to know about it. It's impossible to play this game without constantly learning something new. That's the secret of its fascination."

When they finished the hand, they threw the tiles into the center of the table and, with a loud clatter, shuffled, and rebuilt the walls for the next one. After a round of four hands, Lily became East Wind and the game went on.

When they finished the second game, Lily served tea and bowls of rice porridge with noodles which she set on stands next to their chairs. Chopsticks firmly in hand, they helped themselves. When their turn came to play, they set down their chopsticks and returned to the game, except for Mei Ling. Mei Ling ate nothing, but sipped at her tea, finishing it quickly in what Barb knew was considered to be impolite haste. Barb, pleased with herself that at last she had conquered the wayward chopsticks, dug into her bowl with the best of them.

It wasn't until after they had finished the third round of the third game that Cecile smiled across the table at Mei Ling and said gently, "You do not seem yourself tonight, Mei Ling."

At once Barb realized it would not be polite to ask Mei Ling what was wrong, and that Cecile was giving her an opening to say what was bothering her if she wanted to confide in them. Surreptitiously, Barb eyed Mei Ling. Her chin rose in a defensive tilt, and Barb saw her swallow hard. Quick moisture shone in her eyes, and she looked away across the room. *Something's really getting to her,* Barb thought.

Mei Ling murmured dully, "I guess I didn't pick up my luck after all."

Connie said consolingly, "It is unusual for you not to mah-jongg, not even once."

Lily, clearly concerned, said, "Don't you feel well? Do you want to stop playing?"

Mei Ling shook her head and sighed. "No, I'll finish the game. Let's play the last round."

In gentle but firm tones, Cecile said, "Mei Ling, Connie and I are your good friends. Is there anything we can do? If so, you must tell us."

As though some inner dam of self-assurance had suddenly given way under the pressure of a great flood, Mei Ling burst out, "It's Jasmine. The time has come."

Lily appeared bewildered. Connie, looking suddenly stricken, nodded knowingly. Cecile shook her head hopelessly from side to side and in low, agitated tones said, "Oh, no!"

Mei Ling took a deep breath and let it out slowly. Turning toward Barb she said haltingly, "When Jasmine, my daughter, was three, the doctors told us she had an inoperable brain tumor—that she probably would not live past puberty. Now I see signs. Today we had an appointment with the doctor. He could not say for certain, but he gave her six months at most . . ." Choking over the words, she was unable to go on. Her eyes filled with tears.

"Oh, Mei Ling!" Barb exclaimed. "I'm so sorry, so very very sorry."

Cecile reached across the table and covered Mei Ling's hand with her own. "The tumor was thought to be inoperable years ago. Since then, there have been many advances in medicine. Surely there is something someone can do. Why not ask for a consultation?"

Lily produced a tissue and dabbed at the tears staining Mei Ling's cheeks. "Yes, by all means, do have a consultation."

With a hopeless shake of her head, Mei Ling said, "Here there is no one. Jasmine's doctor says there is a doctor in America, in the state of Arkansas, who has done this surgery, extracting a tumor that was wound around a child's brain. It took many hours and cost many thousands of dollars."

Barb felt a tremor of shock from her head to her toes. She had discarded Mei Ling as a suspect because she thought Mei Ling's talk of a tour to the States was a pipe dream, a fantasy, or at the most, a goal to be realized far into the future. But Mei Ling needed money desperately and she needed it now.

Eagerly, Connie said, "Don't despair, Mei Ling. We will take up a collection. I will set out boxes around the university, and here in the Gardens. And we will pass them around during intermission at your performances."

Morosely, Mei Ling shook her head. "We will never collect enough for such a surgery."

"You have another long-time friend, Zia Jin-Fang. Will he—?"

"No, never!" Fresh tears flowed down her rouged cheeks. "He doesn't know Jasmine exists. How can I ask him?"

Connie leaned to one side and put an arm around Mei Ling's shoulders. Softly, she said, "Don't cry, Mei Ling. If he truly loves you, and he must, you've been together so many years, he will understand about Jasmine. He will want to help you."

Mei Ling gave a vigorous shake of her head, and the chic, ivory carved comb tumbled from her chignon, struck her shoulder and fell to the floor. Barb bent down, picked up the comb and handed it to Mei Ling. With trembling fingers, Mei Ling tucked the comb back into her chignon.

Cecile said flatly, "Even if Mr. Zia wanted to help, he would never have enough money to pay for such a surgery. There has to be some other way."

There was a long, dreadful silence while they tried to think of another way to help Mei Ling. Finally, Lily, glancing at her watch, said, "It's getting late and we all have to work in the morning, so let's not play any more. Let's all go home, and tomorrow we will ask everyone we know to try to think what's to be done for Jasmine."

After everyone had left, and Lily and Barb were tidying up the living room, Barb said, "Did you know about Jasmine?"

Lily, setting the bone tiles back in the box with a clatter, nodded. "Only about her child out of wedlock, as they put it. I knew nothing about the tumor."

Barb folded each chair seat up with a snap. "How terrible it must be for Mei Ling, to know her child is going to die."

Lily snapped another chair seat closed. "She must be beside herself, absolutely desperate."

"Of course," Barb said softly. "Absolutely desperate."

Eighteen

On Saturday, because Barb and Lily were gone all day long, they didn't hear the bad news until shortly after six, when they returned to Lily's flat.

Early that morning Lily had hired a savvy, young taxi driver she knew to tour the New Territories. As they drove through the lush green, rolling countryside, time and again they passed big, square, two-story concrete houses set amid fields of stubble.

"Who lives in these houses?" Barb asked. "Looks like the high-rent district."

To Barb's surprise, Lily replied, "Farmers. Farmers here are well-to-do because their products are always in demand." They passed another conclave of houses bordered by a series of ponds populated by hundreds of ducks.

Grinning, Barb said, "I didn't know there were so many ducks in the entire world."

"They're very lucky," Lily said, "all bound for glory, to appear on restaurant menus as Peking ducks."

As the driver drove on, Barb was further impressed by the sight of new satellite towns and resettlement estates.

They visited a Buddhist temple at the foot of Tai

Mo, Hong Kong's tallest mountain, a traditional Chinese market and a bird sanctuary with a marvelous view across the waters to China. After stopping for a Chinese-style lunch in Sha Tin in a restaurant that overlooked picturesque Tolo Harbour, they made a stop at the Sha Tin racecourse, then headed back to Kowloon.

Well pleased with their day, Barb and Lily returned to the flat shortly after six. Once inside, Lily made a grab for the *South China Morning Post* which Andre had left on the table in the foyer.

Barb poured glasses of chablis for Lily and herself and carried them into the living room, while Lily stretched out on the couch and pored over the paper. Barb, seated at the desk, was catching up on her journal when Lily burst out, "Ei-ee, listen to this!

" 'Last night an elderly man, believed to have been a fortune-teller at the Poor Man's Nightclub at Yau Ma Tei, lost his life when he fell into a pool at the zoo. The pool is surrounded by a low stone wall with a waist-high Plexiglas shield. In the center of the pool stands a small rocky island which serves as a sunning beach for crocodiles. Because of the mutilation of the body, positive identification has not been made. The police suspect suicide.' "

Barb spun around to face Lily. "How horrible! Just the thought of it makes my stomach turn over. There are better ways than that to commit suicide. I think it must have been an accident."

Lily tossed the paper aside. "Poor old thing probably had terrible eyesight and stumbled into the pit in the dark."

Barb's eyes narrowed. "How could he? Isn't the zoo closed at night?"

"Yes, but people still wander through it."

"You'd think the wall would have prevented anyone from falling into an exhibit."

Lily shook her head. "You would think so. But sometimes people climb on them, and lean over the Plexiglas shield."

Barb put down her pen and closed her journal. "I think we need to make a trip to the Poor Man's Nightclub."

Lily cocked her head to one side, as if doubting her hearing. "Excuse me?"

"I said, I think we need to go to the Poor Man's Nightclub."

Lily's eyes opened wide. "Why?"

"To see if our friendly fortune-teller is still telling fortunes."

"Come off it, Barb. There are millions of fortune-tellers in Hong Kong and Kowloon."

"Millions?" Barb challenged, looking Lily square in the eyes.

"Well, hundreds, maybe. But the chances of the old guy who fell into the moat being our fortune-teller must be one in a million. The police aren't even positive he was a fortune-teller."

In a voice edged with suspicion, Barb persisted. "I still think we should check it out."

"Is this another one of your famous gut feelings?"

"You've got it. And it's getting stronger every minute."

Lily gave a hopeless shake of her head. "Barb,

you're my best friend in all the world, but damn if you're not as stubborn as a runaway horse with the bit in its teeth."

Grinning at Lily, Barb rose to her feet. "Right. And that's what keeps me from giving up on animals that are at death's door. And what keeps me going is that most of them live. Let's go *now*."

"*Now!*" Lily groaned. "We haven't even had dinner."

"There are enough food stalls in the place to feed an army. We can eat there, buffet style, stall to stall."

Lily closed her eyes signaling defeat. "Okay, okay, we're outta here."

The Poor Man's Nightclub was bedlam as usual, teeming with people. Bare light bulbs bloomed like white moons in the velvet darkness. The parking lot had again been transformed into a circus of color, a cacophony of music and voices and mouth-watering smells of food cooking.

The moment they set foot on the converted parking lot, Lily said, "I'm starved. Let's find the dim sum stalls."

"First things first," Barb said, and plunged ahead through the crowd. When at last she found the fortune-tellers' enclave, she stopped short in mingled shock and surprise. Only a few fortune-tellers were there. Turning to Lily, she asked, "What's going on? What's happened?"

Lily shrugged. "Hang on." She walked over to a flat-faced woman dressed in black seated beside a

sign saying, Tarot Card Readings. A long, black po-
nytail hung over one shoulder. In fast Cantonese,
Lily asked when the fortune-tellers would appear.

When she returned a moment later she said
cheerfully, "Sorry to disappoint you, my friend, but
the lady says we're too early. Most of the soothsay-
ers don't show up till around eight. We'll have to
come back later."

"I'm more uneasy than disappointed, and it
makes me crazy that there's nothing I can do about
it."

"Food is the only answer," said Lily flatly.

Once again Barb and Lily wended their way
through jam-packed aisles. They stopped at several
food stalls where they bought dim sum wrapped in
special paper, wonton noodles, porridge, clams in
black bean sauce and sweet bean desserts, eating
while they browsed past the shops. At an outdoor
cafe on the edge of the parking lot, they sat down
at a rickety wooden table, sipped green beer, nib-
bled caliche nuts and watched the passing parade
of people. Fascinated, Barb studied their faces, noting how different each one was from every other.

Suddenly she clutched Lily's arm. "Look, Lil,
doesn't he look like old Poon's nephew?"

Lily's head swiveled right, left and back again.
"Who? Where?"

"There, that stocky fella with the crew cut, walking fast, on the other side of that couple with the
three kids. See, the kids are all carrying balloons."

Lily leaned forward, squinting at the crowd. "I
see the balloons, red, green and yellow, but I don't
see—"

"It's too late. He's gone. You missed him." Barb stood up and slid the strap of her black leather bag over her shoulder. "Come on, let's roll."

Lily took a final sip of beer and got to her feet. "Okay, but don't rush in there like the midnight express asking if the old man has bitten the dust."

Barb grinned. "Not to worry. I won't ask, because I don't speak Cantonese. You will."

Lily shot her a heavy look. "Over my dead body."

Barb smiled. "I hope not."

They strode on, past countless stands bearing signs advertising various Chinese food specialties. Without pausing to watch sideshows featuring jugglers, acrobats and musicians, they elbowed their way swiftly through the milling crowd. Barb craned her neck to see above their heads. She let out a relieved breath when, farther along, she glimpsed the white banner that read Y. K. Poon, fortune-teller. She wanted to shove aside everyone who blocked her path and run as fast as she could to see if the old man was safe.

Moments later she halted before Y. K. Poon's stand. Her eyes narrowed as she surveyed the scene. There was the wooden table. There were the cards. There were the little brown birds. Where was Y. K. Poon? Bewildered, she stood looking around her.

Lily came tearing after her. "Good lord, Barb. This isn't some kind of blasted marathon, after all."

"Sorry." She threw out her hands in a helpless gesture. "Poon's stand is here, but he isn't. Nobody's here."

"Okay, okay. I'll ask."

She crossed the aisle to the black-garbed, flat-faced, ponytailed tarot card reader, spoke a few words and returned to Barb.

"She says to wait. Poon's nephew always sets up the old guy's stand, and Poon will probably be along any minute."

Lily continued to visit with the woman across the way.

Leaning against a pole at the edge of Poon's space, Barb stood first on one foot then the other, looking up and down the aisle.

Without preamble, a voice behind her said, "You seek fortune, miss?"

Barb started, spun around. Before her stood the pudgy man with the crew cut and stony eyes who had taken their money when Y. K. Poon had told their fortunes, the man Poon had said was his nephew.

"Actually, I'm looking for Mr. Poon."

His dark eyes were hard and unfriendly. Though she'd been here only three nights ago, he was acting as if he'd never seen her before. And there weren't that many round-eyes scoping out the Poor Man's Nightclub. But then, she thought, why should he remember a couple of *gwailos?*

"Poon not here. I Woo Chow. I read fortunes."

Barb gave him a friendly smile. "Thanks, but I don't want my fortune read. Where is Mr. Poon?"

In a flash, his expression changed to one of infinite sadness. He folded his hands under his chin, as if in prayer.

"Misser Poon meet with accident."

Lily, who had returned to Barb's side, asked, "What kind of accident?"

For a second or two, he shook his head from side to side, as if unable to speak. Then, abruptly recovering his speech, he said, "Bad, bad accident. Uncle Poon have bad joss."

Barb gazed at him with genuine sympathy.

Lily said more forcefully, "What happened?"

Barb was sure he would tell Lily it was none of her business. To her astonishment, his sorrowful expression faded, replaced by a belligerent stare.

"How you know my uncle?"

"He read our fortunes a few nights ago. He told my friend she had an object which was of great value. Don't you remember?"

In the harsh light from the bulb strung up over his head, Barb saw a rush of color suffuse his face, and the light of knowledge glistened in his eyes.

"No, I not remember," he said quickly and turned away.

He *knew,* Barb thought. He knew all about the horse and the priceless value his uncle had placed on it. Now she recalled how he had hovered around them while Poon told her fortune.

"Wait," said Lily in a loud voice.

Slowly, he turned back to face her.

"You still haven't said what has become of Mr. Poon."

"Uncle Poon ah—" he paused for a fraction of a second—"fell into the pool of the crocodiles at the zoo."

Barb felt a chill tingle down her spine. Even the thought of what had happened next appalled her. She couldn't bear to think about it. Placing a hand on Lily's arm, she shook her head from side to side and mouthed the words, "Stop! Don't ask."

As if once wound up, he couldn't make himself stop, the man continued, "The crocodiles—found Uncle Poon."

His eyes, filled with resentment, bored into them, almost as if he thought they personally had pushed Uncle Poon to his death.

"I'm sorry," Barb said, "truly sorry about your uncle."

He said nothing, but stood there looking at them. Resentment faded from his eyes, replaced by pinpoint fires of anger.

Suddenly she understood. They were intruders, invading his privacy.

Quietly, in Cantonese, Lily said a few words which Barb gathered from her tone expressed her condolences.

Barb leaned over and whispered in Lily's ear. "There's nothing we can do. Let's chill out."

They sauntered around the market for another hour, but Barb's heart wasn't in it. She couldn't get Y. K. Poon off her mind. All the way home, rocketing through the darkness of Kowloon, through the Harbour Tunnel to their stop on the island, she puzzled over the death of the old man.

Turning to Lily she asked, "Why would Y. K. Poon do away with himself?"

Lily shrugged. "I've no idea."

"Do you think he gave someone a reading that was way off base, truly impossible, and they accused him of being a fake? So he lost face, couldn't bear the censure of the world and took his own life?"

Lily yawned. "He's bound to have made more than a few wrong predictions down the road. So what's one more? If he felt he'd lost face when he made a mistake, he'd be long since gone. Besides, he'd have chosen a neater, cleaner way to go."

Barb mulled that over. "Well, do you think he predicted a fortune for someone that that someone didn't want to hear, and that someone became angry with him and decided to get even by shoving him into the pool?"

"I doubt it. The Chinese are more philosophical. They know their joss can change, and that fortune-tellers aren't infallible."

"I'm convinced the old fella was too smart to lean out over a display and fall in. Besides, he could see well enough to read the cards the bird picked out. So he should have been able to see a pool. Do you agree?"

"Yeah, sure." Lily was staring out the window at lighted station signs. "We get off at Central. Next stop."

"I don't think you're taking this very seriously."

"I am, I am! But after all, I'm not married to him. I'm not even a distant cousin."

"And why would he choose to do himself in, especially so far from his home base?"

Lily turned to look at her. "Whaddya mean, his home base. We don't know where he lives."

"You said the zoo is on the island-side, near the Mid-levels. His fortune-telling stand is in Kowloon all the way up at Jordan and Temple."

"But he could still *live* anywhere. You can't read anything into where his stand happens to be."

"I suppose you're right. But if a dissatisfied customer didn't do away with him, and he didn't fall into the pool by himself, and he didn't do away with himself, that leaves only one conclusion."

Lily stared at her, her gold-green eyes filled with skepticism. "What?"

"Someone murdered Y. K. Poon and for an altogether different reason."

Lily threw back her head and gave a derisive hoot. "That's the dumbest thing you've ever said. Who in the world would want to murder a defenseless old man—and why?"

Barb's full lips curved upward in a Cheshire cat smile. "Exactly."

"Exactly? Exactly what?"

"Why *would* a defenseless old man be murdered?"

"Not for his money, that's for sure."

"There has to be a reason, and my instincts tell me it has something to do with my carving."

Lily rolled her eyes upward and in low, sing song tones said, "That old gut feeling has me in its spell, that old gut feeling that I know so well—"

Barb's brows drew together in a mock scowl. "Laugh if you will, but it wasn't till we came along telling him about the jade horse that trouble came to stay."

"You could chalk it up to coincidence."

"I could, but I don't believe in coincidence." In tones that rang with conviction, she said, "I believe in cause and effect."

Lily's eyes widened in an incredulous stare. "You honestly believe that because you inherited a jade figurine, the old man was killed?"

"They're connected. Believe me. When we were quizzing the nephew, you weren't watching his reactions. He acted somewhat sad, sort of, and tense and nervous, and evasive, and he clearly wanted us to chill out."

"You amaze me. You picked up on all that in less than five minutes?"

"I watch animals' and people's actions, reactions, their intensity, and their body language. All that tells me something."

Lily's lips curved in a warm smile. "Barb, my friend, *you* should be the fortune-teller."

"And I predict everything's connected. I'm thinking back to your flat being searched and nothing being taken. Now it's obvious. Someone was looking for the jade horse."

"But there was no way the old man could have known who we were or where we lived."

"Someone could have followed us home."

Lily laughed. "You really are pigheaded."

Barb grinned. "It goes with the territory." Struck by an unpleasant thought, she stopped, recalling the nephew's voice. "The voice of our caller on the phone was all wrong. No way could it have been Y. K. Poon's nephew."

Lily cocked her head, watching Barb with a curious, questioning gaze. "Then who? Who would know who we are and where we live?"

With a determined set of her jaw she said, "That's the question. And I mean to find the answer."

Nineteen

Restless, unable to settle down to writing in her journal, Barb tossed her pen aside. Normally, by ten o'clock on Saturday night, she and Steve would be boot scootin' to some good ol' country western music at the Traildust Steakhouse. But now, nine A.M. back home, he'd be covering for her at her clinic, open till noon on Saturdays.

She ran a hand through her hair, trying to think, trying to recapture details of today's tour of the New Territories in her travel journal, but words wouldn't come. Her mind kept flipping back to old Poon. The reason he kept niggling at her mind, she finally decided, was that she was used to hashing things over with Steve. Lily wasn't very receptive to her gut feelings, whereas Steve, even if he doubted them, had learned to respect them. What would he think about Poon's demise? she wondered. She longed to call him, but she hated it when he started worrying about her. Worse, she didn't want him flying out here like a bat out of a cave to rescue her. Maybe she could simply slip Poon casually into the conversation and listen for his reaction.

She turned to look at Lily. "Mind if I give Steve a call?"

Lily smiled, stood up, and flicked off the TV. "Of course not, I definitely think you should call him. I'm going to bed and leave you two to settle the problems of the world in private. Tell Steve hi. See you in the morning."

She left the living room, and the sound of her heels tapping on the parquet floor faded as she walked through the foyer and down the hall. Barb picked up the phone and dialed.

To Barb's surprise, Karen's caring tones saying, "Animal Hospital, how may we help you?" didn't come flowing over the line. A bad omen. Instead, Steve, sounding breathless and distracted, answered, "Animal Clinic, whaddya need?"

Barb, bracing herself for bad news, said, "Sounds as though you're the one who needs help. Where's Karen?"

"Oh, Barb!" he huffed. "It's you. Good to hear from you, love. Karen's in the back, and I just walked in the door. You won't believe where I've been."

"Try me."

"I've just finished examining three hundred, get this, three hundred hissing, quacking, quarrelsome ducks. Right from the start, I told the bonehead manager I don't do birds. He got sort of testy. Said nobody in this town does birds except you and he has a contract with you."

Relieved that there was nothing more serious wrong, she wanted to laugh, but sensing that after checking out three hundred ducks, Steve would not be amused, she said, "Rings a bell. Marlowe Ag Products, Ink?"

"Right. They've developed a new product, a spray for corn fields. They're meeting the EPA requirement that they send a report on environmental impact. Since ducks are part of the environment, they have to be sure, if the ducks eat the sprayed corn, it won't affect the development of their eggs or their offspring. Marlowe houses two birds to a cage on their farm, and ten of them are sick—vomiting—and their crops are mushy. I brought four back for necropsy. I'm giving them routine blood tests and taking seven tissue slides on each of them."

"Good move. Sounds like duck plague."

"The thing is, they have a couple hundred quail they're testing, too, and they're all okay."

"Better pack up a quacker and send it overnight mail to the university for analysis. I want a second opinion. Anything else critical?"

"One lead poisoning—a rotty lapped up water dripping from a chain-link fence—we saved the rotty; Maggie Leidy has autoimmune hemolytic anemia that we're working on, and we have the usual injections, spays, neuters. What's with you?"

"Ah, well, ah, we've been looking at ducks, too."

Steve laughed. "On your dinner plate, I presume."

"On the webbed foot, to sell to restaurants and markets. They raise huge flocks on farms in the New Territories."

"The new who?"

"Territories. It's an area north of Kowloon that was leased to the British in 1898 for ninety-nine years."

"And in '97, ownership reverts to Red China?"

"Correct, along with Hong Kong and some two hundred smaller islands which were ceded to the Brits in perpetuity in 1842—" she took a deep breath—"as well as Kowloon, a sliver of the Chinese mainland, ceded in 1856."

"What other good news do you have to tell me?"

"You'll be thrilled to hear that the jade horse has been deposited in a safe-deposit box."

"By whom? You or Lily?"

"Me. The bank lobby service manager wouldn't let Lily do it for me."

"Wise man."

"Good lord. Surely you don't think Lily's a horse thief."

"Never. But she does talk the side off a barn, and the fewer people who know about the horse, the better."

"I'm beginning to have second thoughts about it myself."

"What's that supposed to mean?"

"It's just that my keeping the horse is sort of like the Brits hanging on to the Elgin Marbles they found in Greece. The marbles are a national treasure, and really belong in Athens."

Steve gave something that sounded suspiciously like a snort. "Nothing personal, but your horse is hardly a national treasure."

"I know, but I think about this little museum trying to preserve a few antiquities, and the horse would be a big feather in their caps, so to speak. I can understand why Professor Fais is dying to get his paws on it."

"I doubt one horse will make or break the museum."

"For want of a nail a kingdom was lost."

"Excuse me?"

"You know, during some historic battle, for want of a nail the shoe was lost, for want of a shoe the horse was lost, for want of a horse the king was lost and for want of a king the kingdom was lost."

"Who said that?"

"My grandfather. He's always said it."

"Yeah, right," Steve said dryly. "Any more threatening phone calls?"

Barb laughed. "Only from me."

"From you? Give!"

She told him about the trap she'd set and about the messages she'd left on the answering machines; how Professor Fais had sprung the trap and how he'd tried to make a deal with Duncan MacGregor.

"Duncan faked him out, claimed he had a second buyer. But his entire routine is ridiculous since the carving is locked away in the bank—unless he thinks he has some way of getting it out."

Steve said, "You're too clever by far, my love." But he sounded more worried than approving. "Promise me that from here on out you'll stick to sightseeing."

"I'll do my best."

"So what else is new?"

"A weird thing happened yesterday."

"Weird, how?"

Thinking about old Poon, she swallowed hard, forcing out the words. "An elderly man fell into a pool at the zoo and was—well, it was alive with crocodiles."

"Oh, my God, that's terrible! You didn't see it happen—did you?"

She tried to keep her voice calm and even. "No, but it turned out the victim was the old man who told our fortunes at the Poor Man's Nightclub."

There was a long silence. Finally he said, "He *fell* into the pool?"

"That's what the paper said, *fell*, over a stone wall with a Plexiglas shield."

"Was he walking on the edge? Standing on the edge watching the nutcrackers in action? What?"

"The paper didn't say that. If so, someone would probably have seen him tottering on the brink, and a reporter would have picked up on it, done an on-the-spot interview."

"Why would a guy who was evidently enjoying a long and happy life suddenly jump into a croc-infested pool?"

Barb smiled to herself. "My thoughts exactly."

"Why do I think there's more to this tale than you're telling me?"

"It's just such a coincidence that this man tells our fortunes and a few days later he dies."

"It doesn't sound like any coincidence to me. The guy actually has no connection with you," he paused, and when Barb said nothing, he asked, "has he?"

"Only in that he was a close friend of Hal's. He also said I had come into a treasure and to guard it well."

"Did you tell him what it was?"

"No."

"Well thank the great juju in the sky for that."

"Lily told him."

"Great! Who else knows about it?"

Barb's lips curved in a rueful smile. "Well, there's the opera songbird, Mei Ling; and Peter Chang, the t'ai chi expert; and Professor Fais, the museum curator; and Duncan MacGregor, the antiquities dealer; and the bank lobby services manager; and Rosa, the Filipina maid; and Lily's significant other, Andre Durand. I think that about covers the waterfront—except for my mystery phone callers who could well be hirelings trying to scare me into selling."

"That animal must be the world's worst kept secret."

"Everyone's desperate for money. Rosa once told Lily she'd go back to the Philippines if only she had the money. But I doubt Rosa knows an artifact from an artichoke, and besides, if she were a thief, there's plenty of stuff around here she could have stolen long before now if she'd had a mind to."

"Who else?"

"Yesterday during the mah-jongg game, Mei Ling blurted out that Jasmine, her secret daughter, has what her doctor told her is an inoperable brain tumor. But apparently there's a doctor in Arkansas who has performed such surgeries, and she needs money to take the child to the U.S. That would take a boatload of Hong Kong dollars."

"What about the bank lobby services manager?"

"I warned Lily not to discuss the horse with him, but she couldn't resist telling him the bank was harboring a horse. I interrupted, told him it had great sentimental value. So I don't think he has a clue as to its true value."

"Next?"

"I overheard Andre talking on the phone the other day, and from what I heard, I think he's carrying on with some greedy Parisian female."

"Have you told Lily?"

"No. It would break her heart. I'm hoping he'll give himself away or give up the paramour."

Barb envisioned Steve shaking his head, heard the sympathy in his voice. "That's a damn shame."

"Moreover, the woman evidently has an endless love—of money."

"And the t'ai chi jock wants money to emigrate to America, right?"

"Right, but more telling, Mei Ling says he's snowed under with horrendous gambling debts that he can't possibly pay. In fact, when I saw him the other day, I wondered if he'd been in a car wreck. The right side of his face was one big blue, black and purple bruise, and his right eye looked like a rotten oyster. He said he'd walked into a door."

"Hum. Not much originality under the eyelashes. Heard any more from the antique dealer?"

"Nary a word, but then I wouldn't, since he thinks he's got the horse locked up. I think he's the kind of guy who rides onto the battlefield after the battle is over and shoots the wounded."

"What about your friendly curator?"

"I don't think robbery is his style. Anyway, the museum has allocated funds for new acquisitions. He doesn't need to steal the horse."

"But didn't you tell him it's not for sale?"

"True. The thing is, I've got to find out who wants the horse enough to kill for it."

"Who wouldn't?"

"I have to start somewhere."

"Cherchy (sic) the *femme,* as we say in old Paree."

"French is not your forte, Lindsey."

"I'd still start with the French chef."

Her voice rang with exaggerated enthusiasm. "You're on."

"Fine. Great! *Magnifique!* As soon as I mail off the duck, I'll throw a few duds in my backpack and board the big bird for Hong Kong."

Barb almost shrieked, "Steve, no! This is time-out time, remember?"

In loud, forceful tones he said, "You need me. I can sense it. I want to be there for you. Always."

"Steve, darling. You are wonderful to offer, and I love you for it, but I'd rather—"

"I know, you'd rather do it yourself. Why you have to be so cussed independent, I'll never know."

Through gritted teeth, she said sweetly, "It's my nature. Why do you have to be so—so macho?"

In lofty tones he announced, "I'm going through my mid-life crisis."

"You can't!" she exclaimed. "You're not old enough."

In that superior tone that he knew always made her hackles rise, he said, "I'm mature for my age."

"Steve," she said with mock sternness, "wrap it up."

"Gotcha! Love ya, Doc." He lowered his voice.

"Look, a guy just walked in holding a satanic-looking red chow on a chain in one hand and a baseball bat in the other. Gotta go."

Before she could reply, the phone clicked off. Shaking her head, smiling in spite of herself, she hung up. "I love you, too," she murmured softly, "I love you, too."

Cherchez la femme, Steve had said. That wasn't easy, considering that *la femme* probably lived in Paris. However, Barb mused, maybe seeing Andre in his lair might reveal more about him than she'd been able to glean from the few times she'd seen him in Lily's flat.

On Sunday evening, shortly before eight, Barb, with Lily as her guest, strolled into La Parisienne. The maitre d' seated them across from each other in Louis XIV chairs covered in rose-colored brocade. Pink carnations and freesias bloomed in a crystal vase in the center of the white damask-clothed table. Barb breathed deeply of the aroma of the sweet, fragrant freesias and admired the gleaming silver and crystal glasses that sparkled under the glow of a magnificent multitiered chandelier.

Enchanted, she surveyed walls adorned with gilt-framed paintings of scenes from life at the French Court at Versailles during the reign of Louis XIV and Marie Antoinette, and halted at a huge Grecian urn mounted on a marble table in the center of the room that held a massive flower arrangement.

A waiter handed them a menu and suggested specialties of the house. After he had taken their order, the sommelier appeared at their table and, speaking to them with a deference that made Barb feel they were royalty, said that Chef Durand had asked him to suggest wines for their dining pleasure.

After a gourmet meal of *les escargots a la Bordelaise, fonds d'artichouts Bayard, filet en brochette Medicis,* that ended with *crème brulee* and café au lait, the maitre d' escorted them back to the kitchen.

Andre, smiling a welcome, greeted them with open arms. As he showed them around, the first thing that struck Barb was the cleanliness of the kitchen, the shining pots, gleaming utensils, spotless worktables and white tile floors. White-garbed underchefs worked quickly and efficiently, stirring steaming soups and sauces on big ranges, chopping vegetables, carving rounds of beef, cleaning fish. Tempting aromas of mouth-watering creations mingled with each other.

The second thing that impressed Barb was the ambiance. Everyone exuded an air of goodwill. And from the warm way the staff responded to Andre when he introduced Lily and her, it was obvious that they thought highly of their master chef.

The only fly in the ointment occurred when Lily asked, innocently enough, Barb thought, "When will you be home?"

Andre's jovial expression faded; his face seemed to close.

"I'm not sure."

Lily smiled up at him. "We'll wait for you if you're leaving any time soon."

He gave a slight shrug. "That is impossible to say. If a guest orders a special dish, I must be here to prepare it."

"Andre, surely you've whipped up a few dishes ahead of time . . ."

Watching, silent, Barb thought, *Why is he being so evasive? He's acting as if he doesn't want to come back to the flat.*

An impatient note crept into his smooth Gaelic tones. "At La Parisienne, all selections are prepared to order, cherie."

"Can't anyone else fill in for you?"

He folded his hands behind his back, and from where she stood Barb saw his fingers laced tightly together, as if he were trying to hang on to his patience.

"I have regular customers, gourmands who expect their dinner to be prepared by me. That's the reason they patronize La Parisienne. You know that."

Good lord, Barb thought, *how high and mighty can we get?*

Lily nodded, "I see." Though she said no more, disappointment shone in her eyes. She glanced away.

For a long moment Andre was silent. At last, gazing at Lily with what Barb called Spaniel eyes, he said smoothly, "Cherie, you are truly much more to me than any of my gourmands." He put one arm around Lily's shoulders and the other around Barb's.

"Come with me, ladies, we will find the taxi and go home."

The sound was so faint that if Barb had been asleep, she probably wouldn't have heard it. But she had stayed up to finish writing in her journal. Still dressed in the cranberry paisley silk blouse and forest green suit she'd worn to dinner, she had kicked off her shoes and perched on the side of the bed. Pen poised over her journal lying open on the nightstand, she heard the soft thud of a door closing. Flicking off the light, she crossed the moonlit room, eased her door open a crack and peered into the hallway.

In the thin drift of moonlight that crept into the foyer from the living room, she saw Andre tiptoeing down the hall. Strangely, he had changed into a black turtleneck sweater, black slacks, sneakers and carried a flashlight.

She saw him pause and stand very still, head up as though listening. She held her breath. Carefully, quietly, he inched open the front door, stepped into the corridor and closed the door after him.

Barb snatched up her purse and slipped into her loafers. Bolting from her room, she sprinted down the hall after him and flung open the front door. Halfway down the black carpeted corridor she saw the brass elevator doors slide closed. She slipped out the door, dashed down the corridor and jabbed the button on the wall to summon the elevator.

Once inside, she stared at the panel of white lights blinking the number of each floor as the elevator descended, willing it to go faster. When the doors opened onto the lobby, her gaze swept around the spacious, airy room, past the lighted torchiers, the leather chairs, the tall potted palms. Her hopes sagged. Andre was nowhere in sight.

She dashed across the lobby, through the glass doors and outside. She ran down the walk past shoulder-high oleanders, thick, dark rhododendrons and tall pine trees. Overhead, wispy clouds floated in a dark sky, lighted by a milky-rose cloud reflected from the city below. She shivered against a chill breeze that stirred the damp air and smelled like wet earth.

She rounded a curve in the walk and emerged on the edge of the road. She stopped short, caught her breath, wondering which way to turn. Maybe Andre hadn't gone down the hill. Maybe he'd gone for a stroll in the gardens. Why had she assumed he was taking off somewhere? Frantically, she glanced around her. All at once, she saw him, a lithe, wiry figure, hands jammed in his pockets, pacing back and forth beside the bus stop.

Swiftly she stepped into the shadows of a snow pine and stood watching. A low, churning sound and a squeak of brakes heralded the arrival of a bus. The doors snapped open and Andre clambered on.

Had he forgotten to do something at the restaurant? Barb wondered. But he could have called and asked someone else to do whatever it was. Or was he simply checking up on his staff—making sure they had turned off the oven, she thought wryly. Or was he going to meet someone—someone whose identity he didn't want to share with Lily? The big, yellow double-decker bus roared away into the night.

She raced down the hill to the main road and stood on the corner, waiting, tapping her foot in a frenzy of frustration. The bus was now well ahead of her. But life on the streets of Hong Kong never missed a beat merely because the sun had set. Within seconds a taxi pulled up beside her. Feeling like an idiot, she jabbed her finger in the direction of the receding bus, shouting, "Bus, bus, go for it!"

"Okay, okay, lady. Don't shout. I talk English." He gave a chuckle as though pleased with himself. "You top banana?"

Disconcerted, intent on not losing sight of the bus ahead, she blurted, *"Oui. Si.* I mean, yes. I'm top banana and you follow bus. Okay?"

Now, at almost one A.M., Hong Kong was as bright as day, a neon jungle of garish lights. *At least they're not blinking,* Barb thought. Blinking lights, Lily had told her, were prohibited by law, because of the airlines. Pilots approaching Kai Tak Airport could easily confuse them with landing lights. Blinking or not, Barb still had the feeling she was cruising around a Chinese Las Vegas.

Skillfully, the driver wound in and out among a river of other taxies, Mercedes Benz and Rolls Royces. Barb closed her eyes, unwilling to watch the receding bus, but her lids flew open at each stop. She had to watch to see if Andre had gotten off. When the taxi driver finally pulled up close to the rear of the bus, she said, "Stay in this lane, back of the bus. I'll let you know when I want to get out."

"Okay, okay. You top banana." He gave another chuckle.

She bit her lip, wishing he had never heard the phrase "top banana."

At the Queens Road Central the bus churned to a stop, and a gaggle of passengers stepped off. She craned her neck searching for Andre's dark head, a face with ruddy cheeks, fair complexion, round eyes and sculpted features. She gave a start. There he was, almost hidden behind two Oriental men clad in expertly tailored business suits, white shirts and striped ties.

The bus pulled away from the curb. The taxi driver gunned the motor and tailed the bus, enveloping them in its exhaust fumes.

"Stop!" she commanded. "Stop right here."

Startled, he slammed on the brakes.

Barb glanced at the meter and fumbled in her purse for money. "I need to meet someone who got off the bus."

As if he hadn't heard her, he drove on. "Too much cars. Top banana be run over. You wait. We stop by sidewalks."

"Stop, *now!* Please! My—uh—friend will get away."

She reached across the back of the seat and shoved several bills over his shoulder.

"Here, take the money. Keep the change."

He made no reply, but continued down the street for several more yards until he found a space next to the curb and jolted to a stop. He turned to face her and with a broad smile grabbed the bills. "Thank you. Top banana okay."

"Okay." She wrenched open the door and jumped out of the taxi. Turning back the way they had come, she almost ran toward the corner where she had last seen Andre. At nighttime, even under the glare of the bright red, green, blue and yellow neon signs, everything looked different. She struggled to get her bearings, hunting for a landmark. She did a double take. Half a block away, on the far corner, overhead loomed a hot pink neon sign: *La Parisienne. Fine Dining.* She recalled having seen the sign earlier, outside the prestigious Hong Kong Crown Hotel.

She tried to run faster, thinking, Why would he go back to the restaurant when he had left there less than two hours ago? Was he keeping an assignation with someone? At the end of the block, she started to cross the street toward the hotel. As she stepped off the curb, she caught sight of Andre loping down a dark, narrow alley that ran behind the hotel.

Why would he go around to the back? But maybe even master chefs didn't use the front entrance. In fact, dressed as he was, like some ne'er-do-well, the doorman would probably have tossed him out on his ear. Breathless, gasping, she reached the end of the alley just in time to see him step inside the rear entrance of the hotel.

Determined to see this through, she marched down the alley. On her left loomed the fifteen-story hotel. On her right rose the high walls of what looked like a tenement. Glancing upward, she saw rows of tiny porches, many with wash hung from a pole. Through the windows, lights flickered like fireflies. As her gaze dropped to the ground, she halted abruptly.

In the dimness she made out a collection of wooden boxes and boards standing on end. On the boxes were seated people, silent, wary, watching her. An old crone with sparse hair, wearing a tunic and black slacks pulled above her knees, grinned at her. A young woman in blue-and-white-checked slacks and top clutched an infant to her breast. Beside her stood a child of perhaps four years with a bowl-style haircut wearing a floral print top and pants. Two big, woven bamboo baskets with boards across the top that evidently served as a table held three dingy white enamel pots. Beside the table stood a blackened square can with a metal pot perched on top that served as a stove.

On the walls hung big, brown burlap sacks, baskets and paper-wrapped bundles that evidently contained all their worldly belongings. Other shadowy figures huddled against the walls along the alley. With a jolt it struck Barb that here was the alleyway home of the Chinese immigrants Mei Ling had mentioned, living a hand-to-mouth existence.

Her heart went out to them as she glanced around her. Outside the hotel stood green plastic bins that overflowed with trash and gave off a nauseating stench of rotten food and fish. Abruptly the door opened, and silhouetted in the square of light behind him stood Andre. Swiftly Barb backed into a shadowy doorway.

In his arms Andre held a huge iron kettle. Mystified, Barb watched. The restaurant had long since closed. This must be leftover food that Andre was dumping. But why Andre? Why not one of the clean-up crew? When he stepped out onto the stoop, Barb stifled a gasp, for suddenly people seemed to come out of the woodwork and converge on him like ants at a picnic. Everyone carried a bowl and a big spoon or ladle. He had scarcely set the kettle down on the stoop before they began dipping into it. Barb thought she had never seen people so ravenous, so desperate for food.

What struck her as strange was the unearthly silence that pervaded the alley. There was no loud talk or laughter, or joy at receiving food. Nothing but a low hum, like the buzzing of bees at a honey pot.

Within minutes they had emptied the kettle.

Andre went back inside, and his starving recipients faded away.

She could scarcely believe the evidence of her own eyes. At the same time she felt overcome with mingled embarrassment and guilt. She had leaped to conclusions, thought the worst of the man, never once giving him the benefit of the doubt, only to find he was bent on feeding the homeless and hungry of the world. The least she could do was wait for him to leave and offer an apology.

Moments later he reappeared, carrying a giant-sized platter of what Barb took to be rice with bits of meat and vegetables. As if on cue, the homeless horde descended, bowls in hand, filled them and took off. Andre made a third appearance with another platter of rice which disappeared so fast Barb was not sure she'd seen it. He carried the empty

platter inside. A few minutes later the kitchen light
went out, and as he opened the door and started
down the steps, Barb moved out from the shadowy
doorway.

"Andre?" she said softly.

He halted as though he'd been shot, drew back
and in a harsh whisper said, "Barb! What in heaven's
name are you doing here?"

He sounded surprised and angry at the same time.

She could feel a hot flush of embarrassment rising up her face into her hairline. "I—I heard you
go out and I followed you."

In the milky moonlight she saw him scowling
down at her, dark brows drawn into a V. His tone
was cold and sharp.

"And for what reason, may I ask?"

She couldn't bring herself to confess that she suspected him of some indefinable skullduggery. Instead, she said, "I was curious, that's all."

"Do you have any idea how much trouble you
could cause me, following me here?"

"No." Her voice rose, slightly defiant. "I hardly
think it's a crime for me to be here, any more than
it is for you."

"That is the point," he snapped. "It *is* a crime
for me to be here. In Hong Kong there are extremely strict laws against feeding the homeless. It
is highly illegal. The government doesn't want refu-
gees from China to emigrate to Hong Kong. There
are too, too many. There are no jobs for them, and
no housing. Feeding them encourages them to come
here."

Feeling like two cents, she murmured, "I'm sorry. I didn't know. Do you do this every night?"

"No, only now and then. The police would be certain to find out if I did it on a regular basis."

"Does Lily know?"

"Naturally.

"I wonder why she didn't tell me?"

"Because I swore her to secrecy. If the police find out what I'm doing, I'll be arrested at once. Is that what you want?"

"Of course not. But I wouldn't have told them. You should know that."

"I know nothing of the kind. I have sensed that you haven't liked me from the start. How do I know what you will do?"

She looked up at him, not knowing what to say. She couldn't deny that she hadn't particularly liked him. He was astute enough to know she was lying. To tell him she was reserving judgment sounded too lofty, too pretentious. He might well ask, "Who appointed you judge of Lily's friendships?"

Finally, she said, "I don't *dis*like you. I can only promise that I won't turn you in to the police."

He made a mock bow. *"Merci, madame.* May I assume that we have between us a truce?"

"Fair enough," Barb said, forcing a smile. She turned away and began to walk swiftly down the alley.

In two quick strides he caught up with her. "Perhaps you will take the taxi with me?"

Being with him made her feel uncomfortable, but for Lily's sake she would try to build a bridge instead of a wall between them.

"Thank you," she said stiffly. "I'll be happy to share the taxi with you."

Without further words, they walked to the street where Andre hailed a cab.

Privately, she thought, she'd have to give him high marks for being willing to risk his job and his freedom to feed the starving homeless. *But you're still not off the hook, Andre Durand. You're still in desperate need of money.* She could hardly demand an explanation of his involvement with the Parisienne femme fatale, but she would wait and watch this French lover, chef and do-gooder.

Twenty

By ten A.M. on the rainy, windswept Monday morning, Barb, swathed in a yellow plastic hooded raincoat, stood before the entrance to a palatial mansion off Upper Albert Road. A shiny brass plaque beside the door read, Asia House—Museum of Chinese Antiquities. Judging by the tall iron fence surrounding the wooded grounds, the sprawling, white concrete house and the carved teakwood front door, it had once been the home of a wealthy British government official.

Grasping the dragon's head knocker, she gave several brisk raps. Almost at once the door was opened by a thin, gray-haired Oriental man wearing a goatee, a pince-nez and a long, black silk robe.

"Welcome to Asia House," he said in a cordial voice that left no doubt he was pleased to see a visitor.

He motioned her inside the marble-tiled entryway where she stood with rain dripping from her raincoat onto an Oriental carpet. Her host appeared not to notice.

Barb smiled and, shrugging off her raincoat, hung it on a brass rack next to a colorful porcelain fishbowl that held a tall potted palm. The scent of sandalwood pervaded the air.

"I am John Law, director of Asia House," the man said. "You are a student of the antiquities?"

"Not exactly. I'm visiting a friend in Hong Kong who introduced me to Professor Fais. He told me you have a fascinating collection, and I hoped he would give me a tour of the museum."

The director's smile faded. "I regret that Professor Fais is not here on Mondays. But I will be honored to show you our treasures."

Hiding her disappointment, she murmured, "Thank you."

In a voice that glowed with pride, John Law said, "We have displayed our collection with the idea of presenting the long art tradition of a single culture beginning with neolithic pottery from about 3500 B.C. to the last great porcelains of about A.D. 1830." He paused, as if awaiting her approval.

Barb nodded. "Great idea."

Gesturing with his long, thin hands, he went on. "In the rooms on your right, we have a small collection of landscape paintings, Chinese textiles, silver cups and bowls. The rooms on the left side of the museum house twelfth and thirteenth century scrolls and porcelains."

Through a doorway on her left, Barb caught a glimpse of wall hangings and lighted display cases. "I'm particularly interested in artifacts from the Sung dynasty."

"Sung," he repeated. "Not well represented, I'm afraid. We have only a few small plates and flasks and a landscape painting or two."

"Have you jades as well?"

"Jades?" he said, as if he'd never heard the word. "We have several spearheads, a pierced disc and one or two ritual objects. Our ornamental jades include two pendants, some buckles and sword fittings. And there are a few cups, bowls and vases done in the later centuries." He extended an arm in an expansive gesture. "Come, I will show you."

He donned his pince-nez which hung from a ribbon around his neck as if assuming his lecture mode. Slowly he guided her through the rooms of the mansion. He explained each acquisition in reverent tones, ending with archaic jades. As they passed each one, his eyes shone with such pride, such love for the exquisite old artifacts, but, Barb thought, so pitifully few in number. The horse would indeed be the pièce de résistance in this little jewel of a museum.

Barb admired the jade pendants, the disc, the belt buckles, and the sword fittings with appropriate exclamations of praise, then asked, "Are there any animal carvings?"

Looking almost sorrowful, he shook his head. "Alas, we have none. Recently we had an opportunity to purchase a small jade sculpture, but our funds are limited, you see. That we exist at all is due to the generosity of a wealthy benefactor, Madame Ho Tung, descendant of the late Sir Robert Ho Tung, a leader of the Chinese community. Before her death, she instructed the trustees of her estate to limit our purchases to within a certain number of dollars each year. Otherwise, we would dip into our principal."

"Is it possible to raise the rest of the funds from an outside source?"

The man smiled, and gave a hopeless shake of his head. "The price is far beyond our reach. The present owner is asking fifty thousand dollars, American dollars."

Fifty thousand, Barb thought, stunned. Obviously, he could not be talking about her jade horse.

"That seems rather steep. I'm interested to know what artifact could possibly be worth fifty thousand American dollars?"

In hushed tones, he replied, "It is a small, recumbent mutton fat horse."

Barb looked him square in the eyes. "What dynasty is this horse?"

"Sung, which includes the years between A.D. 960 and 1127. That is the reason we are so desirous of owning it. It would be a major drawing card to our little museum. And when patrons realize we are serious collectors, that we want to save and preserve our Chinese treasures, they will donate funds for future acquisitions." He removed his pince-nez and polished the glass on the end of his black silk sleeve.

In carefully casual tones, Barb said, "Perhaps if the owner is eager to sell and you offer twenty-five thousand—?"

"I suggested that possibility, but Professor Fais has spoken with the owner, who insists upon fifty thousand, and not one dollar less." Sadly he shook his head. "The *gwailos* drive a hard bargain."

Speechless, Barb ran a hand through her hair, thinking, *I thought I'd seen and heard everything, but this blows me away. Good old Professor Fais has his own agenda.* He'd planned to buy the horse for twenty-five thou and sell it to the museum for fifty thou. Cool! How cool could you get?

John Law set his pince-nez back on his nose and peered at her with a myopic stare. "Are you unwell?"

"Yes. I mean, no."

"I will give you a cup of Dragon Well tea. Good for the heart and the spirit." He led her into a small room that must have once served as a parlor and now served as a gallery for the display of bronze bowls and sculptures.

A few minutes later, seated before a small table on carved Chippendale chairs that looked as if they had come from a royal palace, Barb sipped hot, fragrant green tea with John Law.

"Do you know Professor Fais well?" he asked.

Barb shook her head. "I've met him only once. My friend has studied under him and thinks he's a fine instructor."

In admiring tones, he said, "Professor Fais is our curator and is unusually knowledgeable on the subject of jades."

"So I've gathered," she replied dryly.

Should she tell him old Fais was trying to pull a fast one? On the other hand, perhaps a mere twenty-five thou commission on the side for the middle-man was standard operating procedure here in Hong Kong. She would keep silent, for now.

She gazed at him over the rim of her teacup. Softly, she said, "Since I, too, am a *gwailo,* perhaps

I could speak with the owner of the horse on your behalf."

He threw up both hands in a gesture of protest. In hushed tones he said, "No, no. Professor Fais tells me the owner is a wealthy physician of great renown in the United States, a Doctor McKee, who would never stoop to haggle over such a treasure."

She set down her teacup with a thud, thinking, *This really ties it.* Should she blow the whistle on the professor here and now? On the flip side, how would she feel if a stranger from a foreign country told her that a highly respected and trusted employee was pulling a fast one? Not nice, not PC, she decided. With an effort, she kept her voice calm and even.

"I suppose not," she agreed halfheartedly.

When she had finished her tea, she felt better, but not much. Now she knew what she must do. She would go back to Lily's flat, look up the professor in Lily's address book, then face him down.

As soon as she opened the door to Lily's flat, she saw it, the small, carved mandarin netsuke sitting in the center of the table in the foyer. She stood stock still. Once again someone had entered Lily's flat, but the intruder had left a gift.

In a loud voice Barb called out, "Hello? Anyone here?" Her voice echoed down the hallway through the silent rooms of the flat. She walked over to the table and stared down at the colorful mandarin. It reminded her of several other mandarins in Lily's collection. Beneath it lay a card on which was written a brief message:

> My dear Lily: A small token of my appreciation to you for trying to arrange a loan of much money. It required a long time to find this mandarin, but now I am happy I was fortunate to find the one you lack to complete your collection.
>
> Mei Ling.

A light bulb seemed to go on in Barb's head. She felt like an idiot. Now it all came together. She remembered Lily telling her she needed one mandarin to complete a series. And she remembered the day she had found Mei Ling in Lily's flat, and Lily's figurines disarranged. Mei Ling must have been looking over the series to see which ones Lily had, so she could shop for the one that was missing. But why hadn't Mei Ling told her what she wanted instead of making up that silly story about the electricity going off? Surprise, that must be it. Mei Ling wasn't sure she could find the mandarin in the first place. And if she could, she had wanted to surprise Lily. Lily would be delighted.

Her thoughts were distracted by the sudden jangle of the phone. She glanced at her watch. Twelve o'clock noon, straight up. Eleven P.M. at home. It had to be Steve, she decided. Her spirits soared. He'd probably been trying to call her all evening. Mondays were always hectic trying to keep up with all the clients whose pets had run into trouble over the weekend. She dashed to the white princess phone on the writing desk and scooped up the receiver. Her heart raced with anticipation. Happily, she said, "Doctor Barb here."

For a fraction of a second, there was silence. Then a whispery voice that sent a chill down her spine said, "The jade, I must have. I pay you much dollars."

"How much?"

"Two hundred thousand, Hong Kong," he whispered.

Stalling for time, she said impatiently, "I can't hear you, you'll have to speak louder." If only she could recognize the voice! But the husky, whispery voice could be anyone: Peter, Andre, Duncan MacGregor, Professor Fais, even Mei Ling.

Louder, still husky, still unidentifiable, the voice said, "You sell me jade horse."

"I—I don't have it."

"You get horse or have accident—like Poon."

Barb stifled a gasp. She could easily envision what remained of Y. K. Poon floating in the dark waters of a pool. Somehow, she had to get this creep off her case. Tell him anything, she thought, anything to get rid of him.

"All right, all right!" she snapped. "Just leave me alone."

"You bring tomorrow, when zoo open."

Zoo! He wanted to meet her at the zoo! A hard knot formed in the pit of her stomach. Her hand seemed grafted to the phone.

"I can't be there that early. I have to get the jade from a box in the bank."

There was a short silence. Finally, he said, "You

come one clock. White tiger cage. Old amah wait. You give horse. Amah give money."

"Yes, okay!" Barb shouted, and slammed down the receiver.

The call unnerved her. She could do a delicate, three-hour surgery, steady on, without missing a beat. But dealing with an unknown, with an enemy she couldn't see, made her crazy. She had to get out of the flat. She snatched up her jacket and shoulder bag and flew out the door. What she needed was a long, brisk hike around the Mid-levels to clear her mind. It was during the third mile that the idea flowed into her mind like a communication from outer space. Why she hadn't thought of it earlier, she would never know. Shortly after five, she returned to the flat feeling as though she could lick her weight in wildcats.

Ten minutes later, Lily burst through the door of the flat and strolled into the living room, asking, "What's news?"

Barb mustered a smile. "The news is that I had a revealing day at Asia House."

Lily sank down on the couch and with a touch of irony in her voice asked, "Grand tour of their collection?"

"That and more, much more." With total recall and suspenseful pauses, Barb regaled Lily with the story of Professor Fais and his scheme to hold up the museum for an extra twenty-five thousand dollars, U.S.

Incredulous, Lily's eyes bulged. "I can't believe it! Fais, on the take!"

"Do middlemen get perks, like a finder's fee?"

"I think they get a commission, maybe ten percent, but surely not fifty percent."

"The police?"

"You'd need proof. You have no proof."

"I intended to go see the professor, to face him down with his double-dealing scheme, but I got sidetracked."

"Oh? How?"

Barb could have bitten her tongue. She had no intention of telling Lily she'd gotten sidetracked by a threatening phone call. For one thing, Lily would demand to know what she was going to do about it, and then when Barb told her, she'd worry about her. Second, Lily would never go along with the program. And third, Lily would tell everyone she knew, and didn't know, and blow the whole deal sky high. Thinking fast, she said, "Food—lunch." That, Lily would understand.

Lily nodded. "First things first. And then?"

Frantically, she racked her brain for a small white lie. "And, uh, and then when I called the professor's flat, he wasn't home." Lord, how she hated to lie to Lily.

"Oh. *I* see."

Inwardly, Barb flinched. Lily's, "Oh. *I* see," usually meant she saw a great deal more than anyone wanted her to. Quickly, Barb went on.

"If Fais continues to acquire artifacts at a fifty percent commission, John Law will eventually catch on—or they won't make many acquisitions."

Lily kicked off her shoes and tucked her legs up under her on the white leather couch. "Best to let the director catch him in the act. You know what happens to messengers when they bring bad news. It's off with their heads."

An unfortunate choice of words, Barb thought, feeling unaccountably threatened.

"Right," she agreed, a little too enthusiastically, for suddenly there popped into her mind a way that would insure that John Law would discover for himself Professor Fais' perfidy.

The hours between dinner and her meeting with the amah at the zoo the next day dragged interminably. She felt like a cat with its tail under a rocker. What if there were several amahs lingering there before the white tiger cage? To Barb, all amahs looked old and wore black. How would she know which one to approach? Maybe the amah would approach her. But to the Chinese, all round-eyes looked alike. Would her menacing caller have described her to the amah? But that would mean the caller knew her, and that meant it was someone she knew! The thought sent a shiver up her spine. A vague enemy with distance between them was one thing. An enemy within a circle of would-be friends, another.

The next morning after Lily left for work, Barb donned an electric blue, green and fuchsia jogging suit, then called a taxi to go downtown. By the time she had tucked the horse safely away, it was nearly lunchtime. Her shoulder bag with its new occupant felt as though it weighed a ton, and she felt as though tiny electric currents were racing through her body.

"Calm down," she told herself. *This will be a simple transaction. After all, the creep didn't ask you to meet him at the croc pit. And an old amah is hardly going to spread the bars of the white tiger cage and shove you inside.*

What she needed, she decided, was sustenance. Good solid food in the bod. And she knew just where to find it. She strode briskly down the Queensway into Pacific Place One, through the spacious lobby of the elegant multistory shopping center that looked like five U.S. malls rolled into one. She rode up the escalator and walked past a row of luxury shops, straight inside the Golden Arches. Again she stood in a long cafeteria line, but the food, like water to a parched chrysanthemum, was worth the wait. She emerged from the line carrying a tray bearing a double Mac, french fries and a chocolate shake.

Half an hour later, feeling well fortified, she left the mall, flagged a taxi and told the driver, "Take me to the zoo."

Still, she felt tense and apprehensive. She couldn't shake a feeling of foreboding as the driver guided the taxi through Hong Kong Park, past the Peak Tram station and along the steep road that wound up the hillside to the entrance to the zoo and botanical gardens.

She alighted from the taxi and stood still for a moment, looking around her. Had she been followed? No taxi pulled up after hers. Everyone around her looked like ordinary tourists. She strolled down a wide path under the shade of tall, leafy trees. She glanced at her watch. Twelve-forty-five. Fifteen minutes till—till what?

A chilling thought struck her. What if there was no amah at all? What if this thug grabbed her shoulder bag and ran off with it? Or worse, grabbed *her* and hustled her out of the zoo? What could she do? She could scream bloody murder, and would. But who would pay attention? She could easily imagine her captor explaining that the *gwailo* was crazy, and the onlookers with downcast eyes would continue on their way. She gave herself a mental shake. Such thoughts were self-defeating. With an effort of will, she put them from her mind.

She emerged from the sheltering trees onto an open, parklike area that overlooked the city and the harbor beyond. At another time, she might have enjoyed the view of the mansions nestled in the thick green foliage below, and the panoramic scene of the busy harbor spread before her. But now, all she could think about was getting this meeting over and done.

Again, she glanced around her at the milling visitors. She thought she had seen one of them, a short, balding Asian man in a faded blue cotton suit, when she alighted from the taxi, and once again she had the sensation that she was being followed. *Cool it,* she thought. There was no reason why she shouldn't see the same people walking the same path she had taken.

Staying in the thick of the crowd, she strolled among families with children, sightseers snapping pictures, and other tourists buying ice cream from a vendor who stood behind a cart. She wandered

on past an aviary, pausing to admire the flamingos
and other exotic birds. She glanced at her watch
again. Ten till one.

As she walked on, she felt as though every nerve
ending was jumping, and the hot, damp air pressed
around her, enveloping her like a wet towel. Earlier
she had spotted signs pointing the way to the large
animal display. Now she followed the arrows around
curving paths, past shy, spindle-legged mouse deer,
smiling orangutans leaping around huge enclosures,
and scowling jaguars pacing to and fro, until she was
within several yards of the white tiger enclosure. She
came to a dead stop.

Clusters of people stood as though transfixed, gazing at the black-and-white striped tiger sprawled on
the floor. Slowly, she scanned the sightseers: a young
couple with four children, one in arms; five Asian
teenagers, three boys and two girls, in blue jeans and
tank tops; a small tour group of senior citizens; two
middle-aged couples, obviously Americans, snapping pictures right and left. No amah.

Barb blew a stream of air through thinned lips.
She didn't know whether to be relieved or disappointed. On the one hand, she was glad there was
to be no confrontation. On the flip side, she'd hoped
the exchange would put an end to the brouhaha over
the horse, once and for all.

The group shifted, and as people moved on, others took their places. She watched intently, never
taking her gaze from the rapt sightseers. She felt
something brush her hip. Startled, her head jerked
around. Beside her stood a tiny, wizened old woman
scarcely higher than her elbow, garbed in black

from head to toe. The woman grinned up at her, revealing a row of broken teeth filled with gold. In her right hand, she clutched a bulging red plastic bag. With her left hand, she patted Barb's hip, as if to determine whether her navy blue jogging pants' puffy appearance was actually Barb or fabric.

Was this the amah she was to look for? Barb thought of patting the red plastic bag to see whether it contained paper currency or something else, but then she had a better idea. She dug in her purse and pulled out a few coins.

With a hand quicker than the eye, the old crone scooped them up with clawlike fingers. At the same time, she croaked, *"Lao-yu, lao-yu, yu, yu."*

"Yu," she knew was the Cantonese word for jade.

As the amah continued to say, *"Yu! Yu!"* Barb did a double take. She had imagined the woman would lead her off the main path to a secluded spot among the thick foliage where they would be hidden from prying eyes, and could make the exchange in private. This meeting was not at all as she had envisioned it. Dealing in the open, making the exchange out here in front of the white tiger and everybody, disturbed her. But perhaps this was the better way, to appear open and aboveboard with no one paying an iota of attention.

Barb nodded and delved into her purse once more. She brought out a small, bulky package wrapped in several layers of pale blue plastic and yards of tape. Again, quicker than the eye, the woman's hand darted out. At the same moment, Barb reached for the red plastic bag. The woman shook her hand, repeating, *"Yu, yu."*

Barb held fast to the horse and pointed at the bag. "Open," she demanded.

The woman shook her head. She either did not understand or pretended not to. Barb said firmly, "Open." Then, still clutching the horse, acted out the word with her hands.

Apparently, at last understanding that she could not have the horse until she opened the bag, the woman flipped it open.

Barb could see that it was filled with bills. Once again she held out the horse and took hold of the bag. When the woman let go, Barb relinquished the horse. Quickly, the woman turned away and scuttled down the path.

Barb spun around, following her with her eyes until she disappeared from sight. In her place, striding rapidly along the path, Barb saw the man in the faded blue suit, the man she suspected of following her. She turned away and continued at a brisk walk until she came to a curve in the path. Heedless of the startled stares of onlookers, she broke into a run. Breathless, gasping, she sped through the zoo entrance, down the wooded hillside, along the blacktopped road.

"Don't look back!" she told herself. At the same time, without volition, her head swiveled around. A tour bus had pulled up before the entrance, spilling out passengers. The man in the blue suit was nowhere to be seen. Behind the bus, a taxi made a U-turn and came barreling down the hill. Barb stepped to the curb and flagged it down.

"Winslow Gardens," she told the driver, then sank back on the seat and closed her eyes. A feeling of relief swept over her along with a slight twinge of apprehension. She put it far back in her mind.

When the taxi driver pulled up before the entrance to Lily's tower of flats, Barb glanced at the meter. Instead of digging in her purse for her billfold and leafing through it, she reached inside the red plastic bag, drew out two bills and thrust them into the driver's hand. As she opened the taxi door, to her astonishment, the driver let out an outraged yell.

"No! No good money! You give Hong Kong dollars, yes!"

He threw the bills over the seat into her lap. She picked one up, staring at it. It didn't resemble any Hong Kong bills she had ever seen.

Red-faced, eyes flashing, the driver shouted, "Paper money Chinese burns for dead."

Anger and indignation surged through her. *They tricked me!* she thought. *How could I have fallen for such a scam!*

The driver, no less outraged than Barb, continued to berate her in a volley of Cantonese invective.

"Okay, okay, I pay!" she shouted, digging in her billfold. She extracted enough Hong Kong dollars to cover the fare and a generous tip for the insult and shoved the bills into the driver's hand. She slipped out of the cab, leaving the red plastic bag of bogus money on the backseat.

She began to smile to herself. She was not nearly as upset as she could have been, considering the circumstances. Her euphoric mood prevailed.

Once inside Lily's flat, she picked up *Wild Swans,* a book she'd been reading, and plopped down on the couch. Deep into the story of a Chinese family during the thirties, she wasn't aware of time passing until the daylight faded and dusk crept inside the room. Startled, she glanced at her watch. Six-thirty! Where was Lily?

Twenty-one

Lily was very late!

Barb jumped up from the couch and ran to the kitchen. Maybe Lily had returned to the flat for some reason and left a note on the message board. Her gaze zeroed in on the white plastic slate hanging on the wall. Wiped clean. Of course, it was possible Lily had some complicated loan deal going and was working late. But if she'd had any idea she'd be this late, she would have called. With trembling fingers she dialed Lily's office number.

Waiting, ring after ring, she stared abstractedly at Tsao Kwan. Suddenly, the kitchen god's smile seemed to twist into a mocking grin that sent a shiver up her spine. After fifteen rings, she slammed the receiver down on the hook.

Unbidden, the word *accident* leaped to mind. A wave of panic swept through her as the thought took root and grew: Lily lying in pain in a hospital bed, her body broken—or worse, at death's door. It didn't bear thinking about. Firmly she banished the thought. Ever-cautious, no-risk Lily could not have an accident. A treacherous voice in the back of her mind said, "But once long ago, she was in an accident through no fault of her own, an accident caused by a careless driver."

"Stop!" Barb told herself sharply. "Stop leaping to conclusions. Stop torturing yourself! Think!"

It was possible that on her way into the tower Lily had run into Peter Chang. And maybe Pete Chang, hoping to chalk up points while Andre wasn't around, had invited her to his flat for a drink, and catching up on each other's news they had lost track of time. Yes, she reasoned, that was certainly possible.

She found Pete's name on Lily's list, grabbed the wall phone and dialed his number. It rang, and rang, and rang five times before the answering machine picked up. Barb dropped the receiver back on the hook.

Her heart began to beat double time. "No reason to panic," she reassured herself. Lily could have stopped by Mei Ling's flat for some reason. Maybe Mei Ling had called, offered her comp dinner theater tickets for tonight, and Lily had to pick them up ASAP. Quickly she ran a finger down the list and found Mei Ling's number.

But when the phone was picked up, a strange voice, a man's voice, said, *"Wa."*

"Sorry, I must have dialed the wrong number. I want to speak with Mei Ling . . ." She faltered, fumbling for Mei Ling's last name.

"You have the correct number."

"Mei Ling, please. May I speak with Mei Ling?"

"I regret, to speak with Mei Ling is not possible." The man sounded genuinely sorry.

"It's very important. It's an emergency."

"Mei Ling has emergency. Cannot speak on phone."

"Who is this?"

"I am Zia Jin-Fang, friend of Mei Ling."

Mei Ling's protector! A sudden chill gripped her. What was wrong with Mei Ling?

"I, too, am a friend of Mei Ling. What's happened? Is Mei Ling ill? Has she had an accident?"

There was a long silence on the other end of the line. At last, in solemn tones, Zia Jin-Fang said, "Mei Ling is resting, after the death of her daughter."

Stunned, for a long moment Barb was speechless. Her heart went out to Mei Ling at the loss of her beloved daughter. She only hoped, now that Mei Ling's secret was out, she would not lose her protector as well. At the same moment it occurred to Barb that of course Lily must be there, comforting Mei Ling.

In choked tones, Barb said, "Please tell Mei Ling how very sorry I am."

"Thank you. I will tell her."

"And please tell Mei Ling's friend, Lily, to stay there with Mei Ling as long as she needs her."

"Only I am here."

"Our friend Lily LeMaitre is not there?"

"Not here."

"Has she been there?"

"Has not been here, sorry. *Joy geen,* goodbye."

Barb heard a click as the line went dead. Her heart beat a rapid tattoo. Where in hell was Lily? She would have to call Andre. He would probably be furious at being summoned to the phone while the kitchen was in a frenzy of dinner preparations.

But knowing that Lily was safe was more important than Andre's culinary creations any day. With trembling fingers she dialed La Parisienne.

Busy! The line was busy! Seconds later, she dialed again. Busy. She dialed a third time. Still busy! She could have screamed with frustration.

On her fourth try, a soft, feminine voice said, "La Parisienne."

"I need to speak with your chef, Andre Durand, please."

The soft, French-accented voice said, "Monsieur Durand is not available at the moment. If you leave your name and number, I'll ask him to call you."

Barb took a deep breath. "This is an emergency." As if saying the words made it so, suddenly it *was* an emergency. "I must speak with him!"

The voice took on an edge. "I cannot leave the reservation desk. If you will leave your name and number, I'll send someone to the kitchen to ask Chef Durand to return your call."

Through thinned lips, Barb said, "Thank you," and gave her name and number. "Will you please send someone to deliver the message *now?* "

"Certainly, madame."

From her slightly sarcastic tone, Barb was not at all sure she would send the message to Andre immediately, but there was nothing more she could do.

Nervously, she paced the floor waiting for Andre to call. When the phone finally rang, the sound went through her like an electric shock. She snatched up the phone.

"Andre?"

"No, I am Celeste. I wish to speak with Andre.

They will not allow him to speak on the phone at the 'otel. I do not wish to leave the message at the 'otel. It is private. So I leave the message at the flat."

Barb felt herself doing a slow burn. Celeste, the Parisian paramour, no doubt. She wanted to say, "Celeste, drop dead." Instead, she said sharply, "Look, any second I expect Andre to call, so—"

"Please, I will leave the message, yes?"

Angry, impatient, Barb snapped, "Yes, yes, just get on with it."

"Please to tell Andre that the money has arrived and *merci beaucoup,* I thank him. I will try to spend carefully until December when another payment is due."

Already tense, nervous, Barb shouted, "Another payment! How long do you think you can go on bleeding this man of every cent he earns?"

"Ah, Lily, I am sorry, but—"

"I'm not Lily, I'm Barb, and if you're so damn sorry, why don't you stop hitting him up for money?"

"I hope December will be the last payment. That should do until the end of May. And then I will find work. And then Andre can begin to send only half as much to my *maman* because I will help, and also in the summer the boys will find work and—"

"Hold it! Just hold it a cotton-pickin' minute. What do you mean the December payment will do until the end of May? Why don't you find a job *now?* And exactly who are the boys?"

"Andre must pay in December because I must

continue my studies for many hours at the Sorbonne."

A college student! thought Barb, enraged. A paramour was bad enough, but the man was robbing the cradle. Through gritted teeth Barb asked, "Have you ever thought of studying less and working more?"

"Non. I must study much so I may finish, so I find the good work to help *Maman* and small brothers."

"And exactly what right do you have to expect Andre to support you and your *maman* and your small brothers?"

"I expect nothing, madame. Andre is helping *Maman* and small brothers because they are poor and need help and he loves them. And he helps me because he loves me, and because I am the *soeur.* The sister."

Sister! The word fell on Barb's ears like the crack of a whip. The woman she had thought of as Andre's scheming paramour was his *sister!*

"Are you here?" Celeste asked.

"Yes, I'm here." The words seemed to catch in her throat. "Does Lily know that Andre is sending you through college?"

"No. He would not tell her because he knew she would insist to [sic] pay. That, he would not allow. But now that we begin the last year, I think it would not matter for Lily to know. So I call him at Lily's flat to say that the money came in time—it was late for the registration, and they—they promised to—to, do you say, put me out?"

Barb felt as though Lily's Oriental carpet had been pulled out from under her. She had leaped to conclusions and she had been wrong. Not only had she misjudged Andre, but she had done him a disservice by judging him in the first place. She had done the same thing with Lily years ago when she had given her more help than she wanted or needed—had given her no chance to heal on her own. Had she leaped to conclusions about Steve as well, deciding he wasn't ready for marriage?

Barb took a deep breath. "I'll let Andre decide whether to tell Lily. And I'll give him your message. Now I have to hang up, so he can get through. Goodbye, Celeste."

"Au revoir, Madame Barbara."

Barb's hand had scarcely left the receiver when the phone rang again. She picked it up and almost shouted, "Andre?"

Without preamble, a low, angry voice snarled, "That was not nice, for you, a visitor in our country, to try to trick your hosts."

A prickle of fear surged through her. "Who is this?"

"Who is not matter. The item you gave the amah is not the genuine article."

Barb shot back, "The money you gave to me is not the genuine article."

"We did not fully trust you. And we were correct not to do so."

Barb ran a hand through her hair. "So?"

"We have something else to trade for the horse. And this time you hand over original carving."

With a cool self-assurance she was far from feeling, Barb said, "Really! I'd say we're even up."

She heard a deep intake of breath, as of one trying to hang on to his temper. "You not understand. You speak with friend. One moment."

Barb supposed his friend spoke better English, and that he hoped his friend would convince her to part with the horse. This conversation was ridiculous, and besides she was in a tearing hurry to get off the phone so Andre could get through. She started to hang up when she heard a small, frightened voice cry out, "Barb, are you there?"

Oh, my God! Barb thought. *These people have already murdered Poon, and now they have my dearest friend in all the world! If they do her any harm, I'll kill every last one of them myself!*

"Lily! Lily, are you all right?"

"Yes, I'm okay, but they want—"

"Quickly, tell me, where are you?"

"I don't know," she wailed. "All I know is that when I left the bank after work, this, this thug grabbed my arm and hustled me into the backseat of a rattletrap car waiting at the curb. Then he tied a dirty, oily rag over my mouth, and the driver drove off and brought me—"

Lily's voice was abruptly cut off, and Barb heard a stream of high-pitched, excited Cantonese flow over the line. Barb closed her eyes and tried not to think what awful threats they could be making.

Then Lily came back on the line and, in a voice that shook, said, "Barb, this thug says to tell you he wants the horse, but he's crazy because he already has the horse."

Barb felt a sinking feeling all the way to her toes.

"Lily, it's a fake. I went back to the jade factory and had them rework a recumbent unicorn that looked like the horse. Bad idea. Tell him I'll give it to him. That the minute the bank opens tomorrow I'll get the real thing."

Lily shouted, "Don't give it to him, Barb, don't! He has a horse." So fast, it sounded like one long word, she threw in, "And a TV, and freckles, freckles, freck—"

Again Lily's voice was cut off. The caller's voice came over the line, soft and menacing.

"Do you understand?"

"Yes," Barb snapped. "What do you want me to do?"

"You go to zoo—to white tiger. Give amah horse. I let friend go."

"No. No way will I hand over the horse until I see Lily in person, safe and sound."

There was a short silence. Finally, the man said, "You come to Aberdeen, wait on dock. Sampan come to you. Bring friend, too. You give horse to sampan driver, driver let friend go. Only you come. Do not bring police to dock, or friend have fatal accident."

Barb's eyes narrowed. Something about that scenario smelled as fishy as Aberdeen Harbour. For one thing, even though he'd told her to come alone, how did he know she wouldn't bring the police with her to arrest the sampan driver on the spot? And if he let Lily go free, she would tell the entire world who her captor was and where he hung out. She knew he didn't trust her. Well, she didn't trust him either. She knew what she had to do.

"Okay," Barb said flatly. "What time?"

Twenty-two

Barb stood before the rattan-framed mirror above the dresser in her bedroom staring at her reflection. Her heart thudded in her ears, and her hands were damp with nervous perspiration. She clenched and unclenched her fists to loosen up her fingers and rolled her shoulders to try to relax.

She scarcely recognized the stranger who stared back at her from the mirror's depths. The arms and legs of the black padded coolie jacket and pants she had bought twelve-year-old Anna Lee stopped short of her wrists and ankles, but they would have to do. A black scarf tied turban style around her head concealed her hair. On her head perched the straw coolie hat with the long, thick black braid dangling down the back that she'd bought for Anna Lee to wear on Halloween. She clutched the loop of cord fastened to each side of the hat, and with fingers that shook, she slid a black wooden bead up under her chin, tightening the cord until the hat sat securely on her head.

She willed herself not to be nervous. When people were nervous, they made mistakes. She could not afford any mistakes. The monsters who would push a harmless old man into a crocodile-infested pool would think nothing of carving up a helpless *gwailo* and tossing her overboard to feed the fish.

She peered closely at her face in the mirror. She looked so obviously round-eyed. Maybe she should slather a layer of the white face paint that Mei Ling had given Lily over her face. Maybe people would think she was a singer in the cast of the Cantonese opera. On the other hand, heavy theatrical makeup on a country farm girl would look out of place, might draw unwelcome attention to herself. She could not afford close scrutiny.

She gave her disguise a final once-over in the mirror. Her gold watch, protruding from beneath the too-short sleeve, caught the light. She glanced at the time. Twenty of five. Still well over an hour before the kidnapper's seven o'clock deadline: the horse in exchange for Lily. Would a poor farm girl be wearing a gold watch? Hardly! She stripped off the watch and dropped it on the nightstand.

This day had been the longest day of her life. She had no doubt that Lily's captor had deliberately set the deadline at the close of the day to give her a full twenty-four hours to worry about what was happening to Lily. In addition, there was the added advantage of meeting at dusk when Aberdeen Harbour was swarming with diners being ferried to the floating restaurants and the shadowy figures of sampan pilots were not easily identifiable in the autumn twilight. She allowed herself a small smile. A meeting at dusk could work both ways.

Early this morning she had gone to the bank and taken the horse from the safe-deposit box. She returned to the empty flat to face a day of waiting for the hours to drag past until she could confront Lily's captor. Every minute seemed interminable, and she could think of nothing but Lily at the mercy of a desperate and unconscionable monster. Was she tied down? Did they give her food and water? Did they mistreat her?

Waiting was driving her up the wall. She could not spend one more minute here in this flat where everything reminded her of Lily. She had to do something to occupy her mind, to keep from going crazy with worry. She hid the horse in a safe place, took a taxi downtown and joined a day tour to Lantau Island Monastery.

Like an automaton, she had followed the tour guide around Hong Kong's largest island, stared unseeing at Po Lin Monastery, and tasted nothing of the vegetarian lunch. The white sands of Cheung Sha Beach, Shek Pik Reservoir and the fishing village of Tai O all passed in a blur.

Back in Lily's flat, she took several deep breaths, bracing herself for the ordeal ahead. Now all she had to do was go. Go and get it over and done. She slung her black bag over her shoulder and hurried into the kitchen. Lifting the lid from the glass pasta jar, she poked through the noodles and gently eased out the horse. She grabbed a handful of tissues from a box on the counter, wrapped the horse and tucked it deep inside her bag. *Wait,* she thought. *Cool it. When have you ever seen a poor peasant girl carrying a black leather shoulder bag?*

She rescued the horse from the depths of her bag and tucked it in her jacket pocket, along with a page from her tour book of handy Cantonese phrases. For that matter, when had she ever seen a poor peasant girl strolling through Winslow Gardens? If anyone stopped her, she would say she was a maid, an amah. But amahs would have gone home by now, unless they lived in. And if they lived in, they would be busy preparing dinner at this time of day. She would have to risk it. Chances were good that most residents were already home from work, relaxing before dinner. Chances were slim, she reassured herself, that anyone would see her. When she stepped from the elevator she would dash across the lobby and out the front doors before anyone could stop her.

She hurried from the flat, locking the door securely after her. In the corridor, she pressed the button summoning the elevator. If it was occupied, she would pretend it was going in the wrong direction and refuse to enter. Silently, the doors slid open. The mirrored elevator was empty.

Relieved, she stepped inside and pushed "L" for lobby. Floor numbers on squares over the doors lighted up as the elevator descended. Thirteen, twelve, eleven, ten . . . suddenly number nine flashed on. Someone was waiting to get on at number nine. The elevator stopped. Quickly, she scanned the bank of buttons beside the doors and pressed "Door Closed." Too late. The doors slid open.

A tall man who carried himself with an erect, military bearing stepped on. Barb noted a shock of white hair and thin lips under a clipped white mustache. The cut of his navy blue suit, white shirt, and conservative red-and-blue-striped tie shouted, "American."

He glanced at her, and instead of looking away, as most people would do, he continued to stare at her. Not meeting his eyes, she looked down at her feet.

"Good evening," he said, but the words were a question rather than a greeting.

She pretended not to hear him.

In flawless Cantonese, he repeated, "Good evening."

She ignored him. Floors flashed by, eight, seven, six.

He frowned and in stern, disapproving tones said, "May I ask what business you have here in this building?"

A feeling of claustrophobia gripped her. She drew a quick breath. She was caught, trapped here in this box. She was dressed as a Chinese woman, but could not speak the language. If she spoke English, he would wonder why she was masquerading in peasant garb, and suspect her of who knows what? If she threw herself on his mercy and said she was lost, he might try to help her find her way. Panic closed her throat. She had no time to let him play good Samaritan. She felt the downward slide of the elevator, and her stomach flipped over. If only she could stall him until they reached the lobby. She kept her head lowered and lifting her hands made several quick motions with her fingers.

"Ah, I understand." The man nodded. "Sign language. You cannot speak."

Barb bobbed her head up and down. She had signed the only words she knew: "Hello, how are you?"

She could almost feel him eyeing her fake braid. In a voice filled with suspicion, he asked, "Do you live here in Winslow Gardens?"

Again she bobbed her head, but before he could question her further, the elevator doors slid open revealing a tall palm tree in a huge cache pot standing beside a long beige leather couch. She darted past the inquisitive stranger and fled across the marble-tiled lobby, past the doorman, through the double glass doors into the gardens.

A woolly, gray cloud cover had moved in obscuring the tops of the tall buildings and creating a nimbus around the jungle of neon lights in the city below. She shivered against the damp chill in the early fall air that seemed to creep into her very bones. Alert to danger, she strained her ears. Had she heard footsteps on the gravel path behind her? Was someone following her? Then she thought, *What of it?* Residents often strolled through the gardens. It was probably the inquisitive American. Still, she had to hold herself firmly in check to keep from running as fast as she could down the long, sloping hill to the outdoor escalator. When she reached the escalator, she stopped short.

"Damn!" she muttered under her breath. The stairs were not going down as she had seen them operate in the early morning. They were moving upward to accommodate the workforce returning home. As fast as she could without drawing attention to herself, she cut over to the sidewalk and made her way downhill to Connaught Road to board a bus to Aberdeen. Waiting amid a crush of Chinese, visitors, tourists and businessmen from the world over, all milling about, she was not nearly so conspicuous. Within minutes a number 70 bus marked Aberdeen pulled up to the curb. She climbed aboard and sat in an empty seat by a window.

"Safe," she murmured, letting out a relieved breath. If anyone had been following her, she had lost him. Thank heaven, luck was on her side. She allowed herself a rueful smile, thinking, *Luck?* She was becoming as superstitious as the Chinese, courting luck.

As the bus moved forward, she noticed that a red taxi had stopped beside the bus. The driver had flung open the rear door, and a man in a black shirt and trousers was leaning down, sliding onto the backseat. He reached out to close the door. Sunlight glinted off the diamond ring on his right hand.

Barb's stomach turned over. Was he the man who had been watching her in the temple and again at the Poor Man's Nightclub and had stolen her purse on the Peak? Of course not. That would be far too great a coincidence. What was the matter with her, jumping at every little thing? Sternly, she told herself, "Quit being so suspicious!"

As the bus reeled around the winding road past the Hong Kong Jockey Club, luxury homes and blocks of glass-and-concrete high-rises, through the Aberdeen tunnel, down through the hilly terrain toward the sheltered harbor on the south side of the island, she tried to prepare herself for the encounter to come. How she wished she could have asked the police for help. But the kidnapper's threat, if she brought the police along Lily would meet with a fatal accident, could not be discounted. She couldn't risk Lily's life by calling on the law.

She had hatched a plan, a calculated risk so daring, so outrageous that it might even succeed. For once, Lily's penchant for prating on had paid off. "Junk" was the key word.

She would go to Aberdeen Harbour early, hire a sampan to take her to the floating village and find the boat where Lily was being held captive. With any luck, Lily's abductor would be gone, would not have returned from his regular job. She hoped to heaven he had one, and that Lily would be left alone on the boat. If not, she was counting on the fact that Lily's keeper, possibly a woman, or the kidnapper himself, would be thrown off guard by her coolie guise long enough for her to go aboard.

She would climb aboard the boat, and before anyone realized what was happening she would find Lily. If necessary, she would bash Lily's guard over the head, and she and Lily would make their escape from the boat onto the waiting sampan. It would be duck soup, if only the fates were with her. She stopped midthought. She had done it again, mentally wooed the fates as if she, like the Chinese, believed in her ability to control her future. Wryly, she chided herself: "It's a wonder you didn't consult the *feng shui* man."

Anxiously she scanned the lowering sky. Dark, greenish gray clouds veined with light, like green marble, cast a pall over the harbor and the dark, distant hills. She would need daylight to carry out her coup. How would she find Lily—how would she even find the boat in the darkness? Resolutely, she put the thought from her mind.

Heedless of bicyclers and pedestrians, the bus churned around a curve and hurtled downhill toward the harbor where deep-sea fishing boats and a fleet of luxury yachts lay at anchor. Ahead loomed the lights of a huge barge, the *Jumbo*, one of three floating restaurants in Aberdeen Harbour. Beads of light sparkled on every deck from stem to stern, giving it the appearance of a seagoing circus. Chinese women piloting sampans shuttled the diners to and from the restaurants.

As Barb stepped from the bus, the odor of fish and exhaust fumes assaulted her. Purposefully she made her way down to the wooden dock at the water's edge and stood watching the sampans swarming around the dark, murky water. Draped with green and blue tarps, they reminded Barb of the pioneers' covered wagons.

Tourists stepped gingerly into the tippy, flat-bottomed boats to be whisked around the choppy waters of the bay on a twenty-minute sightseeing tour given by the male or female pilot. Some of the women poled their sampans; but many had modernized, and the *putt, putt, putt* of their motors echoed across the harbor as the pilots sat in the stern and steered.

Impatiently, Barb waited, for she needed to commandeer an unoccupied sampan. If the kidnapper had sent a lookout, he would be looking for a *gwailo*. She prayed that her disguise would put him off.

The sky grew darker. An air of foreboding

gripped her. There appeared to be no letup in the endless parade of tourists. Never was a sampan free. The minute diners or tourists stepped from a returning sampan, the pilot would take on more passengers.

A *walla walla* pulled up, and the pilot called out, "Taxi, taxi?"

"Mm yew," she said, shaking her head. She couldn't risk a taxi. A taxi was far too obvious. Peasant girls did not ride in *walla wallas*. Desperately, she scanned the small boats. Would she ever find one in which she would be the only passenger? A sampan bearing baskets of fruits and vegetables that were evidently sold to boat people in the floating village drew alongside the dock.

Barb pulled out the page of Cantonese phrases she'd torn from the back of her guide book. "Please, I wish to go to a boat in the floating village."

The woman looked at her as if she'd sprouted horns, and with a vehement shake of her head, she flapped her hands from side to side and cackled a stream of words that left no doubt that she meant, "No way."

After countless agonizing minutes, another sampan laden with household items and clothes for sale tied up near the spot where she was standing. Her spirits rose. If anyone on the kidnapper's boat was watching for trouble, a sampan hawking merchandise wouldn't arouse suspicion.

The sampan pilot, a leathery-skinned woman, her gray hair streaked with white combed back from her face, her lined brow drawn in a permanent frown, looked like a tough old bird, more savvy than her sampan sisters.

Barb raised a hand, beckoning the woman near. She guided the sampan close to the dock, then grabbed a white tee shirt bearing a picture of Aberdeen Harbour and held it up. "You buy?"

"Okay," Barb said. "I wish to go to boat in floating village," she added, pointing and jabbing the air with an index finger.

The woman nodded and motioned Barb on board. Barb stepped down into the sampan and, again consulting her page of phrases, pointed out the words she needed.

"Find friend on boat."

She dug in a pocket and brought out a handful of Hong Kong dollars. She paid for the tee shirt, then handed the woman a hundred-dollar bill. Holding on to a second one, she said, "For you, when we return."

The woman grabbed the bill and stuffed it in her jacket pocket, then gunned the motor, and the sampan churned across the shiny black waters. If she thought it was strange to see a round-eye woman in the garb of a poor peasant girl, she showed no sign of it.

Barb sat stiffly on the rough wooden seat on the side of the sampan, watching the pilot and glancing nervously from side to side. A gust of wind caught at her straw coolie hat, and she reached up a hand to hold it onto her head. She could feel the long, thick braid flapping between her shoulder blades. The sun lurked behind smoky clouds. If darkness fell too quickly, all would be lost. She would never find the boat in the darkness. Worse, even if she found it, she wouldn't know where to look for Lily, and would be unable to surprise whoever might be guarding her. Barb clenched and unclenched her fists. A feeble ray of sunlight gleamed through a jagged tear in the dark, menacing clouds.

After what seemed like hours, but was in fact less than ten minutes, the sampan neared the settlement. Hundreds of fishing boats, flat-bottomed, high-sterned vessels with square bow and lugsails, were anchored in rows, separated by narrow waterways.

The woman cut back the engine speed. Slowly the sampan trolled up one waterway and down the next. Barb scanned every boat from prow to stern. Many owners had built wooden sides on their boats and hung them with old tires to serve as bumpers. Roofs sprouted a forest of TV antennas interspersed with poles. Between the poles stretched lines strung with laundry.

Suddenly, someone screamed, a shriek filled with such terror it sliced through Barb like a cleaver.

"Lily!" Barb shouted, leaping to her feet, peering over the bow of the sampan.

Ahead, she saw a small, open skiff in which sat a child of perhaps four or five years wielding a long pole with a blue fishing net. In the middle of the skiff a young mother carrying a baby in a sling on her back stood shouting and waving her arms.

"Thank God," Barb murmured. "Nobody hurt."

Now she saw that the ends of a line from a nearby boat that had been tied to the skiff were floating on the water. The sampan had severed the line and had narrowly missed striking the skiff. A stream of high-pitched, excited words that sounded like a full-blown cat fight rent the air as the frightened mother and the angry sampan pilot hurled what were obviously accusations and insults at each other.

Behind them, the driver of a *walla walla* tooted a horn impatiently. The sampan shot forward, skimmed past the skiff and putted on down the waterway, up and down the long lanes between the rows of boats moored side by side.

During the phone call from the kidnapper, Lily had managed to gasp one word that had given Barb a clue as to where she was. Desperately, Barb hoped it would be all she would need. She scanned every fishing boat minutely, looking for a dog, a small black dog. She sent up a fervent prayer that the animal would be on deck watching, guarding the boat. That it would bark its head off at a strange sampan pulling alongside. Though the dog barking a warning was a calculated risk, she hoped the floating market sampan with its crusty pilot would be a familiar sight to whoever was manning the boat.

Barb saw it before her pilot did. In the gathering darkness she almost missed it.

There, she thought elated. *There it is!* A small black dog with a bushy tail and white spots on its face that resembled a dog Barb once owned. A dog Lily had known. A dog named Freckles. It stood with its feet braced on the stern, head down, ears pricked, eyeing them with suspicion.

Frantically, she motioned to the pilot to stop.

A low growl rose in the dog's throat. It gave a short, sharp bark. The pilot said a few words in

Cantonese, and the dog sat back on its haunches,
as though reassured.

Barb's gaze swept quickly over the boat. Around
the entrance to the cabin lucky scrolls and posters
fluttered in the breeze that had sprung up. Next to
the door stood two potted rubber plants, clearly
thirsting for water. A crate full of scrawny chickens
was flanked by two orange plastic buckets and a
stack of rattan baskets. No one was in sight.

She raised a hand, motioning for the woman to
wait.

The woman nodded.

Barb climbed aboard. Immediately the dog ran toward her. Softly she repeated the words the pilot had
spoken and held out her hand, palm up. The dog
sniffed her hand, then apparently detecting nothing
of interest, backed off. She tiptoed across the deck
past a line of drying fish, whose smell stuck in her
throat. Keeping to the right of the doorway, she
peered inside. In the dusky light she made out a low-
ceilinged main cabin. The floor was covered with
blue and white floral squares of vinyl tile. From the
ceiling hung a circular lantern with beaded fringe
trim.

As her eyes adjusted to the gloom, she saw a
man in undershirt and shorts sitting cross-legged
on a box, his back to her. On a table before him
stood several big metal bowls that held coils of
white nylon. He was fixing new hooks onto a nylon
fishing line. On his left sat the black cellular phone
he must have used to call her after he had abducted
Lily.

Quietly she crept across the cabin and in a stern,

no-nonsense voice said, "I have come for my friend."

"Eiee!" the man shouted and, leaping to his feet, spun to face her. His hair seemed to stand on end as he glared at her.

Barb did a double take. She was staring into the hot bullet eyes of the old fortune-teller's assistant, Woo Chow.

"You!" she blurted. "Y. K. Poon's nephew!"

A crafty, greedy light came into his eyes. "You have the horse?"

In loud, forceful tones she said, "You won't see the horse until I see my friend. And she had better be in good health, or the horse will go overboard."

A tremor of shock crossed Chow's round, shiny face.

Barb's gaze shifted to an opening at the back of the cabin that she guessed led to sleeping compartments. "Where is she?"

"Wait here," Chow snarled.

"I will wait on the deck," she said firmly. No way would she be trapped inside this boat.

He threw her a dark, nasty look and disappeared into the compartment beyond the cabin.

She strode onto the deck. The wind had risen, and dark, bruised clouds mounted, billowing, threatening. Nervously, she peered over the side of the boat. She could hear the low throbbing of the motor running. She felt reassured that the woman would not leave without the money she'd been promised.

Barb frowned. The *walla walla* that had tooted impatiently behind them earlier had stopped behind the sampan. Wasn't there enough space for the driver to pass on through? she wondered. Had the winds made the water too choppy to circle around the sampan? Her thoughts were distracted by Lily, who stood swaying in the doorway of the cabin, pale-faced, hair straggling. Dark circles ringed her eyes.

Rushing toward her, Barb cried out, "Lily, are you okay?"

Never one to admit defeat, Lily murmured, "Right as rain."

Barb reached for her arm, then realized that her hands were tied behind her back. Barb felt hot anger surge through her.

"Not so fast," snapped Woo Chow, who stood directly behind Lily. His hand shot out, gripping Lily's upper arm. With an abrupt movement, Lily jerked her head to one side, and Barb saw that Chow held a knife, the point pressed firmly against the back of Lily's neck.

"The horse," he said in a soft, menacing voice that chilled her blood.

"Cut the ropes off her wrists," Barb ordered.

"No," shouted Chow. "First, the horse."

Slowly she pulled the horse from her pocket and walked toward him, holding it on the open palm of her left hand. When he reached for it, she would grab his right arm in a viselike grip, yank him off balance, then press the nerve in the back of his neck that she knew would knock him out.

Lily cried out, "Don't mess with him, Barb. He murdered his uncle and he won't stop at murdering us, too."

There was a sudden clap of thunder, and a high,

smooth voice that seemed to come from the clouds overhead said, "Wrong."

Clutching the horse tightly in her hand, Barb spun around. The hair on the back of her neck prickled. A black-clad man, his straight, black hair cut like a bowl around his head, hollow cheeked, under dark, deep-set eyes, stood before her. On his right hand gleamed a diamond ring.

In low, furious tones she asked, "Who are you?"

Coldly, he said, "I am Ho Kar Wei."

Just as coldly, Barb said, "You watched me in Man Mo Temple. You trailed me to the Poor Man's Nightclub, followed me through the jade market and the bird market, and you stole my purse on Victoria Peak. Now you've followed me here! Why?"

In a voice as taut as a stretched wire he said, "I follow you on night you fly into Hong Kong. My seat by you on plane. I see jade horse. I wish to have it." He smiled his Genghis Khan smile. "I still wish to have it. I tell you to go to Dong Po. You should take Mr. MacGregor's offer—keep away trouble. He sell horse for many dollars and give me cut."

"MacGregor! MacGregor!" Barb exclaimed. "That leech has been in on this from the start!"

To Barb's astonishment, Chow yelled, "You kill my Uncle Poon."

Ho Kar Wei's eyes narrowed to slits. "Y. K. Poon cause own death." He shot a venomous look at Chow. "You tell MacGregor you have horse. Poon refuse to tell where you hide it, so Poon—fall—into pool."

A cold, stinging rain began pelting down on them,

but it did nothing to assuage Woo Chow. His face contorted with rage; his eyes narrowed to slits. Scarcely able to speak, he sputtered, "Poon knew nothing—nothing!" His voice rose to a high-pitched shout. "You kill my uncle for no reason. Murderer. Murderer!"

Woo Chow's arm shot up over his head. Knife raised, he lunged toward Ho Kar Wei and plunged it into his chest. Swiftly he withdrew the knife, raised his hand and struck again. Ho Kar Wei's left hand shot out, shoving Chow backward. At the same time, his free hand slid inside his jacket. He whipped out a gun and fired point-blank at Chow. Lily screamed. The dog barked, dancing around the deck in a frenzy. Barb stood momentarily mesmerized, unable to believe the evidence of her own eyes. The next instant, Ho wrenched the horse from her hand.

Without thinking, faster than she would have believed she could move, Barb clutched the barrel of the gun. Gripping the horse in his left hand, the man jerked his right arm, wresting the gun away from her. She grabbed his wrist with both hands and twisted, hanging on with all her strength.

In the cold, pelting rain, they writhed as though welded together in a macabre dance around the deck. The potted rubber plants overturned strewing dirt on the deck that quickly turned into a slick film of mud. The orange plastic buckets slid crossways, colliding with three rattan baskets that bumped into the chicken coop. Chickens squawked. Blood spurted from Ho's wound as he and Barb struggled across the slippery surface. The jade figure slid from his rain-slick fingers onto the deck.

Darkness had fallen. The only light came from the glow of kerosene lanterns and battery-powered lamps on neighboring boats down the line.

Still Barb clung to Ho's wrist, wrestling for the gun. In the midst of the scuffle, the irrational thought struck her that she had not pulled countless calves from birthing cows without developing the strength to hang on.

With a sudden burst of power, Ho dragged Barb across the deck and shoved her back against the rail of the boat. Clamping his free hand on her shoulder, he tried to push her over the side. Abruptly, she released her hold on his wrist and slid sideways, down the side of the boat onto the deck. Carried forward by his momentum, weakened by the loss of blood from his wound, Ho Kar Wei toppled over the rail. Barb jumped to her feet and leaned over the side of the boat. Ho Kar Wei had disappeared into the dark, choppy waters below.

She wheeled around and looked at Chow. He lay facedown on the deck, one arm outflung, still clutching the knife. Blood oozed from beneath his slack body. She knelt down and grabbed hold of his wrist, feeling for a pulse. Shaking her head, she looked up at Lily. "Gone."

Lightning crackled across the turbulent skies. Barb's gaze swept the deck, momentarily brighter than day. Her breath caught in her throat. In the doorway appeared an apparition that looked like Hamlet's ghost. Black-garbed, white-faced, staring, stood the little amah she had met at the zoo.

Barb turned to Lily. "Tell her to get help. There's a cellular phone in the cabin."

Lily spoke to the amah in rapid Cantonese, and without a word, the old woman hurried inside.

Barb picked up Chow's blood-stained knife and cut the ropes that bound Lily's wrists.

"Very clever, my friend, to clue me in with Freckles, but you're still damn lucky I found you."

Lily smiled. "I never, for one minute, doubted my luck."

Cold, shivering in the murky, wet darkness, they searched the deck for the jade horse. After several minutes, Barb found it behind the chicken coop and stuffed it inside her pocket.

Lily shook her head. "Thank God nephrite is harder than diamonds."

"Lily, don't talk, move! I think—I hope—there's a sampan waiting for us below. Let's get the hell out of here."

With Lily following close on her heels, Barb scrambled over the side of the fishing boat and jumped into the waiting sampan. The pilot pulled full throttle, and the small boat putted off through the driving rain.

Twenty-three

The next morning, riding through the city in a taxi, Barb smiled to herself. Another photo-op day. The sun shone brilliantly, highlighting the technicolor scenery whirling past. She had the exhilarating feeling that she was acting out a role on a movie set and at any moment a director would call out, "Lights! Camera! Action!"

Barb told no one what she was going to do. Not on the phone to Steve, not Lily. She was determined to carry out her decision, and they would only argue with her. And not Mei Ling, or Peter Chang, or Andre Durand, all of whom would probably tell her she was crazy. And especially not Duncan MacGregor or Professor Fais, who could possibly enter into a bidding war over the jade horse and make her an offer she couldn't refuse.

Her smile widened. Despite the opinions of her friends and countrymen, which she knew without asking, there wasn't a doubt in her mind that she was doing the right thing. Last night, before falling into an exhausted sleep, she followed a well-tried and true routine. One she had followed many times in the past when faced with a puzzling diagnosis of a patient or unraveling some knotty problem.

In her mind, she had mulled over every side of the situation, logging it into her subconscious. During the night, her subconscious had kicked it around, and in the morning she knew what to do. Besides, she thought wryly, all the signs were right. The moon was new. The sun was shining. Even old Tsao Kwan, the kitchen god, had seemed to smile at her over breakfast this morning.

A few minutes past ten the taxi rolled smoothly through the tall, wrought-iron gates and drew to a stop before the heavy teakwood doors of Asia House. Barb paid the driver, walked to the door and gave several sharp raps with the bronze dragon head knocker. As she stood waiting, she felt the sun warming her back, and a brisk morning breeze ruffled her hair. She smoothed the wayward strands into place and buttoned the jacket of her forest green suit. The door swung open.

John Law, garbed in a black robe and pince-nez, stood in the doorway. At the sight of her, his eyes lighted with recognition.

"Ah, the young lady who seeks Sung jades." He took two steps backward and made a sweeping gesture with his arm. "Enter, please."

As Barb stepped inside, she inhaled the tangy scent of sandalwood tingeing the air.

John Law said, "You perhaps wish to study our jades further?"

Smiling, Barb said, "Yes, I'd like to very much. But first I wonder if we could speak privately in your office?"

For a moment he regarded her questioningly, but then nodded and led the way through the foyer to a small room in the rear of the mansion that must once have served as an amah's room. A library table awash with letters, catalogs, photographs of porcelains and furniture dominated the room. A Queen Anne tea table stood before a multipaned window overlooking a formal garden ablaze with golden chrysanthemums, scarlet salvia and orange marigolds.

The director motioned her to a chair that resembled the clean, simple lines of today's Scandinavian designs. Instead of sitting in the straight-backed chair behind his desk, he pulled it around to the far side of the tea table and sat down.

For several minutes they chatted amiably about the fine fall weather and artifacts and jade, until Barb finally realized that it was not the Oriental way to ask, "What's on your mind?" He was politely waiting, confident that when she was ready she would tell him why she was here.

Feeling as though she were about to take a high dive into a bottomless pool, she took a deep breath and plunged.

"I wonder if you're still interested in acquiring the jade horse which we discussed when I was last here."

He gave a sorrowful shake of his head. "No. I regret to say it is impossible for us to raise so many dollars. It is indeed a misfortune, for the horse would enhance our collection considerably. I fear someone else will buy it, and the opportunity will be lost forever."

She had thought it would be terribly hard, but the

words slipped out with astonishing ease. "I would like to donate the horse to Asia House."

He stared at her in disbelief. He fumbled for his pince-nez, clipped it on the bridge of his nose and peered at her through the glass. His voice was soft, incredulous

"*You* will *give* Asia House the jade horse?"

Barb nodded.

"But how can this be?" His expression was grave, his eyes filled with doubt. "Have you the horse in your possession?"

Softly she said, "I do."

His face grew stern. He looked at her as if he suspected she had stolen the horse, but was too polite to say so. After a long, thoughtful silence he said, "My colleague has told me that the horse belongs to an American physician. A Doctor McKee. I have no reason to doubt his word."

"That it does," said Barb, savoring this moment of anticipation.

As though choosing his words with great delicacy, he said, "If you have purchased the horse from Doctor McKee, why would you wish to part with it?"

"I feel that it belongs in the country of its origin, here on this island soon to be part of China. Here it will be cared for properly, and will be in a safe place, where many people will enjoy its beauty rather than only a few."

He regarded her for a long moment, as though assessing her statement. "Have you a bill of sale, proof of ownership?"

In reply, Barb reached in her shoulder bag, pulled

out a small, gold card case and extracted a card. Holding it by the corners with thumbs and forefingers of both hands, as she had seen Chinese businessmen do, she extended it to John Law.

He took the card, and as he read it, his brows rose to what Barb assumed were unprecedented heights. He glanced up at her, his dark eyes sparkling. *"You* are Doctor McKee."

Clearly, he enjoyed having unmasked his visitor. Barb gave a solemn nod.

"That I am."

"You can provide provenance?"

Slowly, Barb shook her head. "Only by word of mouth."

She told him the story of Hal's great grandfather's tour of China in the early thirties, of buying the jade horse from a dealer who had combed through the rubble left by the railroad builders, and how the horse had been handed down through generations of his family.

John Law stroked his goatee as though contemplating his reply. Finally, with obvious reluctance, he said, "In China, family and their possessions give continuity to our lives. The horse would be a symbol. I fear you and your family will lose something of your great grandfather if you part with the horse."

Barb shook her head. "We have no children. Hal's brothers care nothing for the horse. They do tell stories about their great grandfather which will pass down from generation to generation. They have many photographs and also a family history written by one of Hal's brothers. Their great grandfather will always be in their hearts."

For long moments he gazed at her without speaking. It was obvious that this Western way of thinking was totally incomprehensible to him.

Slowly, he said, "Are you positive it is true jade?"

"I have had it appraised. It was said to be true jade and valued at twenty-five thousand American dollars, two hundred thousand Hong Kong."

He appeared stunned. Finally, he blurted, "But that is one half the price Professor Fais quoted."

Barb smiled. "I'm afraid Professor Fais was . . . ," she paused, "mistaken."

His dazed expression was replaced by one of shock. His eyes grew hard. She could almost see the wheels turning inside John Law's head as the truth bore in upon him.

At last he said, "I will have to examine the horse before I can say whether or not we will accept it."

"Naturally."

Again Barb reached inside her bag and brought out the horse enfolded in tissues. She shook the little horse free and handed it across the table to John Law.

He clasped it gently, turning it over in his hands as if it were the most precious and fragile of jewels. He looked up at her, his eyes glistening with moisture. In reverent tones, he said, "This is the most exquisite piece I have ever beheld."

Slowly he rose from his chair and made a slight bow. "If you will permit me to take the stone to my workroom, there are ways to test the authenticity . . ."

"Naturally."

In less than half an hour he returned, a wide smile on his face, his eyes alight with joy. There was no need for him to speak as he sat down beside her.

John Law was so intent upon admiring the horse that Barb was the first to realize that someone was standing in the doorway. She glanced up, and her eyes met those of Professor Fais. For what seemed forever, her steady gaze held his until at last he looked away. His normally ruddy face had turned ashen. For a moment Barb thought he was going into shock. How long had he been standing there? Had he heard the director say the horse was valued at only half the amount Fais had quoted?

John Law tore his gaze from the horse and looked up at the professor. When he spoke his tone was as cold as marble.

"Ah, Fais. Enter. You will be pleased to hear that Doctor McKee has offered to give Asia House the jade horse."

To Barb's surprise, without waiting for the professor to comment, John Law continued, "Which is valued at two hundred thousand Hong Kong dollars."

She might have known, Barb thought, that the director would let Fais know he knew the value of the horse to allow Fais to save face.

Law stopped abruptly, clearly awaiting the professor's reaction. Fais stood stiff and still, as though rooted to the floor. When he said nothing, Law went on smoothly. "A great stroke of fortune, is it not?"

Color crept into the professor's face. He stared out the window and appeared to be studying the marigolds intently. Barb could sense his mind churning, like a rat in a maze frantically searching for a way out, desperate for a way to save himself.

At last, with a pained smile, Professor Fais said, "A great stroke of fortune indeed, to acquire the horse at no cost, after having been quoted twice the original price."

Oh, now hear this, Barb thought furiously, *quoted twice the original price, my foot—old Fais making me the fall guy.*

John Law's eyes narrowed. Quietly, too quietly, he said, "Two hundred thousand dollars *was* the original price. You will now excuse us. We will speak further of this later."

Without another word, the professor backed from the room and disappeared from sight.

"Thank you," Barb said softly.

They spoke no more of the professor's perfidy, but concluded the details of the acquisition of the jade horse.

John Law gazed at Barb with eyes full of wonder. "And you ask nothing in return for this generous and unique gift?"

With sudden insight, it came to her. There was something she would like in return. Softly, she said, "When you display the horse, I would like you to place a small gold plaque below it which would read, Gift of Hal Halstead in memory of his friend Y. K. Poon."

John Law nodded. "It will be done."

Barb left Asia House with a receipt for the horse valued at two hundred thousand Hong Kong dollars.

But much greater was her sense of satisfaction that the small jade horse had come home.

As soon as Barb opened the door to Lily's flat, she knew someone was there. The cluster of brass bells Lily had hung over the doorway at the *feng shui* master's bidding were heaped on the parquet floor. The magazines on the table were disarranged, and Lily's lotus flower arrangement was shoved to one side. A shiver of fear tingled down her spine. Gooseflesh prickled her arms.

Had Ho Kar Wei survived his knife wounds and somehow been rescued from the choppy waters of Aberdeen Harbour? Had he come here to steal the jade horse? If so, how could she defend herself? Clearly the man was mad as a hatter. He would never believe she no longer had the horse. A shiver went through her at the memory of the man standing on the junk, pulling out his gun, and without a moment's hesitation, shooting Woo Chow through the heart. The man played for keeps.

There you go, she told herself. *Jumping at conclusions again. Ho Kar Wei couldn't possibly have survived those two stabs to the heart.* Nevertheless, she knew with a certainty born of some primal instinct that someone was here in Lily's flat. Quietly, she backed out of the foyer and stood in the doorway, one hand on the knob ready to slam the door shut and run.

"Who's here?" she called in a loud, demanding voice.

Footsteps sounded along the parquet hallway between the living room and dining room, heavy footsteps, proceeding rapidly into the foyer. A tall, robust figure appeared, and a warm, gravelly voice asked, "Who do you think? Dog's best friend."

"Steve!"

Barb rushed toward him and, flinging herself against his chest, entwined her arms about his neck. She breathed in the warm, comfortable, leathery Lagerfeld scent of him and for a moment wanted never to let him go. Oddly, she felt as if she had come home.

Nuzzling his ear, she murmured, "How did you get in?"

"The old credit card trick."

Barb rolled her eyes heavenward.

"And those damn bells scared the hell out of me."

She drew back and gazed up into his face. "What in the world are you doing here?"

His eyes twinkled. He made a fist and brushed her chin lightly with his knuckles. "I came to save you from yourself."

Barb grinned up at him. "Been there, done that."

He reached in his jacket pocket and pulled out a plain white envelope. "I found this stuck in the door."

"For me?"

"It has your name on it."

As she took the envelope from him, she saw her name scrawled on the front. She slit it open and extracted a note. Aware of Steve standing there watching, she read it hastily:

Dear Barb,

By the time you read this I will be aboard a flight to London, where I will settle down as a proper British citizen. You are the most exciting woman I have ever met. May we some day meet again.

With much love, Pete

She could feel hot color staining her cheeks.

"Good news?" Steve asked pleasantly.

"Very," she said, vehemently.

"Care to share?" Clearly he was consumed with curiosity.

"Just a goodbye note from a—a friend."

His eyes narrowed. "A male friend?"

Barb grinned. "From the t'ai chi coach. We just never could get together."

Steve laughed, a jubilant laugh, as if exulting over vanquishing a rival. "That is good news. Feel sorry for the poor guy, losing out. Truth to tell, I couldn't get along without you. And, obviously, you can't get along without me, because, obviously, my love, you do not have enough sense to come in out of the rain, nor does your best buddy Lily."

"And what's the source of this astonishing bit of information?"

"The view of the terrace. Fascinating."

Puzzled, she walked into the living room, Steve at her side. Through the sliding glass doors she saw a line on which hung a row of wet clothes, clothes she and Lily had stripped off when they had come dripping into the flat.

"I take it that last night the two of you took your showers outdoors?"

Barb pulled Steve down beside her on the white leather couch. Smiling up at him, she said, "Just let me tell you about my day."

When she had finished, he could only shake his head.

"Unbelievable. Have you by any chance thought of reporting this abduction, robbery, two murders and a drowning to the police?"

"We thought of it, and decided against it."

"You mean you're going to let poor Y. K. Poon's murderer go scot-free?"

"Woo Chow has already avenged his uncle's murder. There's no way Ho Kar Wei could have survived two stab wounds straight to the heart. Trust me. I know these things."

"I still think you should report it."

"I think Poon's amah can handle it."

"What about the horse? Everyone and his brother will think it's still up for grabs."

"That was yesterday. This is now."

"Now?"

Barb said, "Have you ever heard of locking the barn door after the horse is stolen?"

"One or two thousand times."

"I've locked it up before it's stolen. Now the horse lives in Asia House, along with other ancient artifacts."

Steve grabbed Barb's hands. His eyes sparkled with happiness. His voice was jubilant. "You've sold the beast. Thank God! Now you can pay off your loan and—"

Slowly, she shook her head. "Not now. Later, maybe. I donated the carving to Asia House."

Steve's dark brows rose. "Donated!" he shouted. "Donated!"

"Poon said I had a priceless treasure and to guard it carefully. That's what I've done."

Steve clapped a hand to his brow. "My God, the woman *gave* it away!" He closed his eyes and threw back his head. "Listen, my love, I, too, can tell fortunes. Despite your impulsive, altruistic, generous action, I see a big tax deduction. And in your future I see a new small business loan, and a new free-standing, red-brick clinic, with white trim."

Barb watched him intently. "Is that all you see?"

Like an evangelist beholding a vision of paradise, he kept his hand pressed to his brow. "I see—" he paused dramatically—"that you have another priceless treasure."

Startled, Barb said, "Oh? And what may that be?"

In ringing tones, he announced, "Me!"

With the force of a blow, she was struck by a revelation. Softly she spoke the thought aloud. "Maybe it wasn't the jade horse at all. Maybe you are the treasure Poon foretold."

Steve bent his head to hers. His lips met her own in a long, lingering kiss. His mouth was warm and loving. She returned his kiss with all the pent-up ardor so long denied. She felt dizzy and weak in the knees, as if she were floating fourteen floors above the ground on Lily's terrace.

Gently, he broke away and looked deeply into her eyes. "Barb, was the horse true jade?"

She met his gaze head-on. Solemnly, she said, "The horse was true jade."

He enfolded her in his arms and held her close to his heart. "My love is true love."

"Mine, too," she murmured.

"Forever?"

"Forever and always."

GREAT WHO-DUNITS!

BURIED LIES   (1-57566-033-4, $18.95)
by Conor Daly

It looks like lawyer-turned-golf pro Kieran Lenahan finally has a shot at the PGA tour, but a week before he is supposed to play at Winged Foot in Westchester County, his pro shop goes up in flames. The fire marshal is calling it arson. When Kieran's caddie falls in front of an oncoming train and his former girlfriend insists he was pushed, can Kieran find a connection between his caddie's death and the fire?

DEAD IN THE DIRT:
AN AMANDA HAZARD MYSTERY (1-57566-046-6, $4.99)
by Connie Feddersen

Amanda arrives too late to talk taxes with her near-destitute client, Wilbur Bloom, who turns up dead in a bullpen surrounded by livestock. A search of the Bloom's dilapidated farm soon uncovers a wealth of luxuries and a small fortune in antiques. It seems the odd duck was living high on the hog. Convinced that Bloom's death was no accident, Amanda—with the help of sexy cop Nick Thorn—has to rustle up a suspect, a motive . . . and the dirty little secret Bloom took with him to his grave.

ROYAL CAT:
A BIG MIKE MYSTERY   (1-57566-045-8, $4.99)
by Garrison Allen

More than mischief is afoot when the less-than-popular retired teacher playing The Virgin Queen in the annual Elizabethan Spring Faire is executed in the dark of night. Her crown passes to Penelope Warren, bookstore owner and amateur sleuth extraordinaire. Then the murderer takes an encore, and it's up to Penelope and her awesome Abyssinian cat, "Big Mike," to take their sleuthing behind the scenes . . . where death treads the boards and a cunning killer refuses to be upstaged.

Available wherever paperbacks are sold, or order direct from the Publisher. Send cover price plus 50¢ per copy for mailing and handling to Penguin USA, P.O. Box 999, c/o Dept. 17109, Bergenfield, NJ 07621. Residents of New York and Tennessee must include sales tax. DO NOT SEND CASH.